Something to Write Home About

Books by Rachel Ingalls

Something to Write Home About

Rachel Ingalls

HARVARD COMMON PRESS

HARVARD AND BOSTON

MASSACHUSETTS

1988

The Harvard Common Press
535 Albany Street
Boston, Massachusetts 02118

Printed in the United States of America

Library of Congress Cataloging in Publication Data

Ingalls, Rachel.
Something to write home about.

Contents: Early morning sightseer—St. George
and the nightclub—Something to write home about—
[etc.]
I. Title.
PS3559.N38S66 1988   813'.15   88-3029
ISBN 0-916782-98-0

Contents

Theft

"Look out, Jake," I said, "there's a big stone in the middle of the road."

"Where?"

"Straight ahead, right in front of you. Hold on. Over to the left a little ways. Mind you don't bump into it."

"Can't bump into it. Can't even see it."

"Right up there." I pointed at it in the dark. "A big goddam boulder, right in the middle of the road. Who'd want to put a thing like that there?"

"Where?"

"Right there, right in front of you," I said, and fell over it.

"Where are you?" he started to call. "Hey, where did you go?"

"I'm down here. By this big boulder."

"What boulder?" he muttered. And he fell on top of me.

"Jake, I think maybe I'm drunk," I said.

"Who, me? I'm not drunk."

"Me. Do you think I'm drunk?"

"I don't know. Do you think so?"

"I believe maybe I just might be. Just a little."

"Let's have another," he said. "Where did it go?"

"I think you're sitting on it."

We had another, and then another. And one more. And

he said for about the tenth time that night, "Well, how's it feel to be a father?"

"Fine. Feels good. Feels grand. God almighty, I'm glad it's over."

"Nothing to it. I told you it was going to be all right, didn't I?"

"Sure. It's all right now. But wait till it happens to you. Man, I been scared before. Not like that."

"Why scared? Happens every day. That's nature. Annie says she'll be aiming for eight. Eight, she says. At least."

"Eight. Holy God."

"What she says. And I want to be there when it happens."

"You're crazy."

"Why not? That's life. That's important I'd want to be there."

"Let me tell you," I said, and I thought I was going to start crying, but it came out laughing, "let me tell you, it was almost death. They said she almost died. I'm so glad it's over, I'm just so damn glad it's over."

"Have another," Jake said.

I took some and held on to it.

"Listen. You want to be there when it happens? Look, I wasn't even there and I felt like you can't imagine what. All week I been all cramped up and sick with it, like I was the one having the child. You just don't know. Here, have another."

I passed it to him and he dropped it and we had to hunt around.

"Got it," Jake said after a while. "What you doing going dropping it right on the ground like that? I thought you was handing it over."

"You dropped it."

"Who, me? It's all right. Plenty left."

"Have another."

"Don't mind if I do."

I leaned my back against the rock. It was still so dark you couldn't see much.

"Well?" Jake said.

"Well what?"

"You said have another. Let's have it."

"You're holding on to it."

"Who, me?" he said. After a little he began to laugh. I didn't know what was so funny but I started to laugh too.

"You're right," he said. "I had a hold of it all the time. Do you think maybe I'm drunk?"

"Who, me?" I said.

"Here, have another. How's it feel to be a father?"

We both got laughing. When we stopped it was at the same time, so it sounded very still afterwards. I felt quiet and better.

"I'll tell you, Jake," I said. "It's quite something. It makes you feel strange. I expect you get used to it, but it makes you feel like—makes you feel real awestruck. When you think about it, it's a big thing."

"Sure. Sure is. I'll drink to that. What are you going to name him?"

"I think we'll have to name him after Uncle Ben."

"You ain't going to name him after me?"

"I wanted to, but Maddie said how it would mean so much to him and Annie says she thinks it's right, seeing how he practically brought us up."

"I was only fooling."

"No, I meant it. I did want to. We'll name the next one after you."

"Right. And we'll name one after you, too."

"One of the eight."

"I'll drink to that," he said. We both drank some more and sat quiet for a while. I got to thinking how good it was to have the worry over but how funny we should be sitting in the middle of the dark, in the middle of the road, up against a big boulder that shouldn't be there.

"Hey Jake, I don't know about this rock. Who'd want to go and do a thing like that?"

"Like what?"

"Go and put a big rock in the middle of the road like that, where somebody can come along and get hurt. I think we should push it out of the way."

I gave it a shove but it was too heavy to move. I tried again and my hand slipped.

"Leave it be." he told me. "Wait till daylight and I'll help you move it."

"All right. All right, we'll leave it. Let's have another."

"Funny it should make such a difference—names. You remember when I used to tell you the names of the stars?"

"Sure," I said. "I remember."

"Funny it should make such a difference. Why people remember a name a long time after they'll remember anything else, after they forget what went with it. Did you ever think: names are very old things. Old as the stars. Pass them down from way back, and then people give them to children when they're born. Funny way to start out."

"I've forgotten most of them," I said.

"Which?"

"Names of the stars. A long while back. I was ashamed to say, because of all the trouble you took and then me going and forgetting."

"That's all right. Everybody does. Remember some things and forget some things. I'll teach you again sometime. Not tonight. No stars tonight. It's going to rain."

"We'll name the second one after you," I said.

"Right. And we'll name one after you. The first boy. Unless Annie's got some name she won't give up."

"You mean it?"

"Sure," he said. "Promise."

He fell asleep first. During the night it rained and when daybreak came we saw that we weren't in the middle of the road; there wasn't any road at all. We were lying in some-body's field, miles from home and feeling like nothing on God's earth. I've only been drunk twice in my life and that was the first time. Almost eight years ago.

"You," the foreman calls, "you there, boy, you dream-ing?"

"No, sir," I say.

I'm not dreaming, I'm just trying to stay on my feet. If I could dream it through I would, right on through the day. What I do is more like just thinking or remembering, any-thing to take my mind off being hungry. I didn't start on it till after the fire and now I have to do it every day.

It's best if you can do it to singing or to counting, out loud. The new man gets nervous if there's too much of the singing, he thinks every song he doesn't know might be a protest song. Up he walks in his Godalmighty way like he's saving to himself: here I come, boys, here I come. And tells us not so much of the singing, it slows down the work.

I can do it in my head now and I expect it's what happens to soldiers; they say soldiers can be sound asleep and still keep on marching once they've got the rhythm. That's the way it happens. Sometimes I begin by saying over words to myself. Or names, or following the line of a song without sounding it. Then I can imagine pictures of things, people, or places, and go on from there. Just remembering back a week will often take you into a string of things you haven't thought about for a long while, and they can keep you going.

I think about my mother's voice sometimes. She could sing. And I think about my father, though only a couple of memories and they're like the ones of her, blurred and hard to get at. I remember looking into his face but not what the face looked like. I remember being held in his arms and being small enough to be held like that. Clearest of all, I have a picture of being out walking with him. He lifted me up and carried me on his shoulders—that's all I remember of it, like a picture I can stand away from and look at: me riding on his shoulders and looking up ahead, seeing the sky. But it's very strong and always when I think of him it leads me into other thoughts, I think how I did the same thing with Ben when he was smaller.

They say he was a great man, at least that's what everyone said till after Aunt Mary died. Then Uncle Ben started saying, "Yes, he was a great man all right, such a fine character, such high principles. He was such a great man and had such strong principles your Mama died of work." A long time later I said to him, "I don't know what he was like, I was too young. Aunt Mary saw him one way, you saw him another way—leave it like that. I only saw him like a child, I only remember him lifting me up on his shoulders and looking at the sky."

"Yes, that's what he was like," says Uncle Ben in a bitter voice. "He'd lift you up and show you the sky. Some it cured and some was killed by it."

I don't know if he was such a high-principled character. Maybe he was just wild, like Jake. And a man people would always be talking about, with a kind of public reputation. Like Jake; I've seen him walk down the street and have people come up and follow him, follow him around like dogs, just to be near him. And I've seen it the other way around, name-calling when he walks by, and the kids rushing out to throw a stone after him as soon as he's out of range.

After the fire Jake asked me, "You haven't been joining any of those freedom organizations, have you?"

"No, I thought that was your field. You still fighting for our racial equality?"

He didn't answer one way or the other, just said again, "You sure about that?"

It might have been. They asked me to, all right, kept hanging around, trying to sound me out and talking: injustice, freedom, exploitation of labor, all those things. I didn't let on what my political views were, just told them the truth: that I didn't have the time to join anything no matter how good the cause. I know those boys—sit around talk, talk, talk, and when they're through double-talking each other, out they go and beat up some poor fool who's just trying to make an honest living and never did nobody harm. I don't spell freedom like that.

They went away and a couple of weeks later came back a second time. Then they tried to bribe me. Dragged in Maddie and the kids and said what a better life they'd lead and so on. So I told them: Look, I had all those milk and honey lies from the competition and I'm not buying, thanks all the same. And I told them to beat it.

I don't think it was that, but you can't tell about these things any more.

"Just asking," he says. "It don't seem like it could have been accidental."

And I said, "Look, Jake, strange as it may seem, working your guts out from the age of sixteen on don't leave a man much time for long discussions on what we're all going to do when we rule the world. What do you think, now?"

He said it looked to him like a pretty unprofessional job but he'd ask around. Maybe it was a freak thing, a mistake, or what Annie said: "Maybe just somebody wanting to put you out of action so they could get their hands on that famous job of yours." I can believe that. She laughed when I took her seriously, but I don't think it's at all unlikely. Anyway, it couldn't have come from very high up otherwise Jake would have found out, working with one foot on each side of the line like he does.

"What's that you're doing there, dreaming?" says the foreman.

"No, sir."

"We don't pay you to just stand around with your mouth open catching flies."

He's got a neck like a bull, a thick bulge at the back under his hair. Not muscle; that's fat. Fat from forty years of overeating.

"Hustle it on up there," he says.

"Yessir."

The second time I got drunk was with a stranger, an old man they called Little Josh. It was the year of the big riot when they first started calling the army in and I first heard what martial law meant, that if you show yourself you're a dead man and they say you were looting. I'd lost my job and went to work with the fruitpickers. I walked all night to get there so I wouldn't lose a day's work and worked on through as soon as I arrived. I've never seen people work like that, sometimes through half the night, because we were paid by the basketload, and falling asleep under the trees whenever it hit them. There were some women there and children too. A lot of knifings in the night, a lot of drinking, and one night a man hung himself from a tree and nobody noticed, they worked all around him till daylight. That was the first time I'd seen a hanged man: mouth open, tongue out, swollen, suffocated.

We were allowed to eat all the fruit we wanted and I couldn't believe it to begin with because we can't afford to buy it at home. It tasted so sweet, the way you imagine flowers would taste, but if you try to live off it you get sick. Some of the women there set up stands where they sold bread and fish fried in oil, and now whenever there's fish being fried it reminds me of that time, being bone-tired, sleeping on the ground, and the smell of the fruit and trees everywhere, even in your clothes.

The second week I was there an old man joined the group; he was short and had a squashed-in face and walked leaned-over a little, which made his arms look longer than they should be. He stood looking at the trees, ready to choose his workplace, and somebody made a remark. A few others joined in and soon there was about seven of them poking fun at him. "That's all right, Grandaddy," I said to him. "Don't pay them no mind. You work along with me." I pointed out my place, we walked over to it, and started in. Little Josh he was called, and I couldn't believe he only had two hands—he was picking nearly twice as much as anybody else.

The night we got drunk everyone was eating and drinking in an abandoned place up on a rise in the land. There were still some walls standing, a few stone steps up the hill, and a lot of roots growing through it all. I remember they had fires going, cooking, and I was being eaten alive by the bugs. When we left five men came and leaned over the edge of the wall to see if I'd fall down the steps. I turned around and said, "You think I'm going to fall down, don't you?" One of them said yes, the others said they just wanted to see we were all right. "Well, I'm not going to," I said, turned back around, and nearly fell down the steps. Little Josh had the same amount and he was still sober long after everybody else was blind. There was a full moon out. And stars. He told me next day that before I passed out I'd pointed out the stars to him, naming them in a very loud voice as if they were being given names for the first time.

I only started thinking this last week about being drunk. Because it's the same feeling; not the happy lifted-up feeling while you're drinking. Like what you feel when you wake up afterwards: shaky, tired, and your head hurts. That's what going hungry is like.

That morning I left before Maddie could ask me what I'd eat. I had the feeling if I didn't get up on my feet quick and start walking, I'd fall down. I got to work early, which they never notice, only if you come late. And it was so bad I couldn't even work the trick with thinking and remembering.

It was a Thursday. They got us both on the same day, two hours apart between the two arrests.

Naturally, if I'd known about Jake I'd never have tried it on my own. But there were all those weeks behind me, of Maddie asking, "What did you eat at midday?" and me telling her lies. The first few days it was easy to make up a pretend meal. Later I'd begin to repeat.

"You had that yesterday," she says.

"So?"

"Are you sure you're eating all right? You can't stint yourself with the work you're doing. You'll get sick. Then where will we be?"

"You quit fussing. I'm eating fine," I say, and it was a lie again. I hardly ever ate lunch since the fire, when we lost the livestock.

Then I'd ask her what she and the kids had had. She'd say they'd had the leftovers from the night before. One evening that week I say, "Isn't this what we had last night?"

"Yes. You don't like it?"

"I thought you said you finished it off at lunch."

"There was a lot left over," she said.

Sure. Believe it every time. The children aren't getting any fatter, either, and that means she goes without hers altogether. I saw them from the field one day, off in the distance a lot of kids scrabbling around the ditches over by the spring. But I recognized my two. And the foreman, seeing me look, said, "What some folks will allow, letting it get so the children got to go digging in the ditches, eating the weeds out of the creek. Their folks should be ashamed. Letting them run loose on private property like that."

"Yessir," I said, and knew for certain then that Maddie was lying too.

"That's theft. That's what those children will grow up to," he says. "It's the parents' fault. That's what's wrong with all the young people nowadays—their parents don't set them an example. I'd give those kids a good hiding, you can bet, if I was their father."

"Yessir," I said. And I can believe it. Because nobody ever burned you out and taxed you into the ground. I can see you beating your own kids for being hungry. Bet you're real thick with the tax men. Never had to say "Yes, sir" while you were hungry right down to your bones and saw your children starve.

I used to walk through the market at midday. It's amazing how the bare smell of food can keep you going. Even watching somebody else eat sometimes helps, though you wouldn't think it. And even more curious is the way a real meal in the evening, if you take it slow, can be invested with the taste of the best things you could wish for.

Sometimes at the end of the day I'd beg scraps off the tradespeople in the square. They were good about it, they knew how it was. But at noon you couldn't ask since they had to make their living too, and sell as much as they could before the end of the day. The soldiers had plenty of food of course, and kids used to hang around them, pick up whatever they threw away. That might have been a good idea for me to try. Yet I never did know a soldier who'd dish out so much as a crust to a grown man, though he'd give anything to a child. Part of it may be natural sentiment, but I believe they also consider it actually unlucky to refuse a child. Say no to a man and the only bad luck is his own that you refused.

That afternoon in the market I couldn't stand it any longer. The weeks seemed like months, and while I thought that, began to seem like years. All the way through in my chest

and legs and belly I could feel all of that time I'd gone
without food.

It was bread set out to cool. And I smelled it from a long
way off. From beyond the fruit and vegetable stands and
the basketware it led me, pulled me, right through the
crowd. Sweet and warm, giving off fragrance like a tree in
bloom.

If Jake had been along he'd have known how to handle
the situation. He says just never give your right name and
you'll be all right. With the political atmosphere like it is
they'll never bother to pick you up on the street again unless
they recognize you. And that's unlikely, because they think
we all look alike. Or if it's one of ours working for them,
chances are he'll let it go unless it's for something so big
that he'd get a recommendation out of it.

Jake was very relaxed when he toted things off. He knew
all the right lies to tell, and the right names to say, and he'd
state with great confidence that so-and-so had sent him to
collect the article because he had an account there. "Oh,
aren't you Mr. so-and-so and isn't this such-and-such a
street?" he'd ask. And then he had a charming manner of
apologizing while he handed the thing back, and a self-
assured way of asking directions as to how to get to the
mythical place he'd mentioned.

I'd never done it before myself.

I walked blind, straight to it. I saw it sitting there, fresh
and new as a baby, and just put my hand on it like it
belonged to me, and walked off with it.

I hadn't taken but ten steps before there was a hand on
my shoulder and the law and the military were standing all
around.

"Where'd you get that?" one of them said.

I started to eat the bread because I was goddamned if I
was going to go to prison and be punished and all the rest
for something I hadn't even enjoyed.

"What are you doing there?" said a second one.

I kept cramming the bread into my mouth, all new and sweet and soft, and thought: whatever comes now, whatever else happens, it's been worth it.

"Cut that out, you. That's stolen property you've got there," said the first one.

I kept on eating.

"Leave go, I said," the first one told me.

They began to push. I got my face into the bread and had my elbows working, but in the end it was more of a fight than I could manage without my fists and anyway they kicked the remainder out of my hands. About half the bread was left; during the scuffling they stepped all over it till it flattened out into the ground.

They punched me in the head just as routine procedure and kicked me a couple of times the way I've seen them do to other people, and took me off. Theft, resisting arrest, and striking an officer in the pursuit of his duty. They told me the charge on the way. The younger one seemed very impressed by the sound of it. He kept jerking my arm up behind me while they dragged me along, and saying, "Oh, you're in trouble. Are you in trouble. Are you ever."

They took me all the way into the center of town. First they made me wait while they talked over what they were going to do with me. I think that lasted about an hour but I'm not sure, because it was like I gave up time as soon as I knew it was all really happening and jail at the end of it. Then one of them said, "All right, that's it," and they took me outside again and to the prison.

It was one of the old-fashioned kind, going all the way down into the ground below floor-level. Some of the building consisted of the original solid rock. And they put me down, under ground, into a room where the cells were hewn right out of the stone. No windows, only a view through bars into the center of the place where the jailer and a friend sat at a table and threw dice.

The first person I noticed when they brought me in was Jake. He didn't say anything, so I gave no sign and was glad I'd told them a false name.

There were six cells in all. Two big high-ceilinged ones on either side of the entrance, then two on each of the side walls. It was really a triangle-shaped place; the side walls came together in a point of rock and the roof sloped down at the join. The ceiling was also stone and gave you the feeling that at one time the whole thing had been a big natural cave with hollows. Jake was in one of the small end cells and they stuck me in the other one, so we were next to each other but almost close enough to touch, and because of being at the triangle-point where the side walls met, we could see each other's faces.

It wasn't too bad. High enough so the top just cleared my head when I stood up straight, though it was smaller and lower near the far wall, with hardly room for your head if you were sitting down.

The jailer went back to the entrance where he stood around talking to the soldiers. His friend followed after, lingered for a time, and then went out. I had a feeling he was supposed to be on duty someplace else and was making a retreat while the jailer kept the others busy. They were all in uniform, the jailer and his friend, too.

"Did you give your right name?" Jake said.

"No."

"That's the style."

"What did they get you for?"

"Stole a horse."

"A whole horse? What for?"

"Not to eat, you fool. To plow. One of the horses they were using for crowd control. I had a buyer lined up and everything. Had it walking behind me quiet as you please when the fake beggar on the corner—you know, by the fruit juice stand—"

"I know him. Paid informer."

"Oh, I know that. I been paying him too. But it looks like yesterday the military priced him out of my range, because he was the one pointed me out."

It sounded like small-time stuff, not the kind of thing Jake would let happen. But I know he still picks things up now and then just to keep his hand in, he says, and for fun.

"Bad luck," I said.

"He'll think so if I get out."

"What do you mean if?"

He tapped his foot against the wall.

"This place feels damn solid. Looks like some kind of security prison. Four armed men standing behind the jailer when he opens up to give you your provisions. Not so easy. Not so easy at all. I never been in one like this before."

"But they'll have to take us out to be tried."

"Tie us hand and foot, like as not."

"Do they usually do that? I thought you said these boys were pretty easygoing."

"Not any more." He kicked the wall again.

"Hell, all I did was steal a little bit of bread."

"Bread? Caught out for lifting a hunk of bread? Oh, Seth, goddamn. You fool, you."

"All right, all right. They got you too, didn't they?"

"Why didn't you wait till I was with you? A beginner's trick like that. I don't suppose you even thought of going up to it with your coat over your arm."

"No, I never thought of that," I said. "I'll remember."

"You do that. And you can remember never try it alone, too. Not till you got somebody to show you how. Lord, whatever possessed you?"

"I was just hungry as hell."

"Why didn't you ask me for a loan?"

"Cut it out."

"Why not? We've got plenty."

I didn't want to go into all that again. We've borrowed enough off him already. Sure, he's got plenty till they catch him for getting it. And the more he gives away, the more he's got to go against the law.

I said, "Listen, Jake, what with the last time I paid any taxes and what you gave us after the fire, that's more than any man should be asked to lend."

"I'm not any man. I'm kin. You should have asked me."

Sure. The way things stood I wouldn't be able to pay back what he'd already given us. Not for years. Maybe never.

"Let's stop talking about it. It makes me sick to think about it."

"And what about Maddie? And the kids? Maddie says —"

"What?"

His face changed and he shut his mouth. So she'd asked him. She never told me.

"Well," I said, "how much is it now?"

"She didn't want you to know. Don't tell her I said anything. I'm glad to give it, Seth. Honest. I worry about you."

"I'm all right."

"No you are not."

"You're right, I'm not."

"A long time ago somebody told you honesty's the best policy. And you been sticking to it a long time after you figured out honesty's the fastest way to starvation."

"And dishonesty lands you in jail."

"Only if you get caught."

"Well?" I said. "Well?"

I grabbed hold of the bars and gave them a shake. Built for keeps. They were solid as a mountain wall.

One of the soldiers out beyond the entrance laughed. I

could just see them around the corner. They were drinking together and the jailer appeared to be telling them a tall tale of some sort, acting out the different voices as the story went on. One of the men wiped his mouth with the back of his hand and said something that made the rest of them laugh too. They weren't looking in our direction.

"Do they beat you up or anything?"

"Not yet. I don't think it's likely. The jailer's all right. He's a good man."

"He looks like some kind of a clown."

"He is," Jake said, "but he's all right."

I began to wonder what would happen to Maddie whether she'd have enough to live on, whether she'd guess what had happened to me, or think I'd been killed, or maybe think I'd left her. She couldn't be thinking that.

"Listen, Jake. If I try to get word to Maddie, they'll find out my name, won't they?"

"That's all right. You just leave it. Sam, you know Sam, he saw me when the law came on the scene. He'll tell Annie. She'll come over here and she'll see you, then she'll tell Maddie."

"You think she'll be all right?"

"Sure, Annie will see she's all right. She'll look after them."

"I just wish I could see her, right now. They'll let her come see me?"

"Sure. It'll take a while for the word to go around."

I thought of her sitting at home in the evening, waiting for me to come back from work. I imagined the kids asking questions when it began to get later and later and still I didn't come. And what her face would look like when Annie told her, what she'd say: not this on top of everything else. And when she finally came to visit me, looking through the bars, any other woman would say: How could you, how could you be so foolish or so selfish or so cruel to us, as if we didn't have enough trouble already. But she would ask me if I was all right, if I was well.

"I don't know if I can face her," I said.

"Well, what do you want? First you're scared she won't be able to come, then you don't think you can face it."

He told me I never should have taken up crime in my old age, you had to start young while you still had a sense of humor. He was smiling, the way I'd seen him look at Annie when she sulked, but harder.

"I bet the job's gone," I said. "Bet somebody else is doing my work right now."

"Most likely."

"I never missed a day in nine years. Not even when I was sick."

"That was your trouble."

Outside the entrance it sounded as though the group of men was beginning to break up. Two of them went down the hall and the jailer leaned around the corner and gave Jake a friendly kind of look. Jake nodded to him and started to talk again, but he dropped his voice.

"Tell you the truth, Seth, most of these jailhouse shacks you can bust through the wall with your thumbnail, but this one is over my head. I tell you, I never seen one like this before, not even the military cells. And I don't like it. I think something's going on. You been listening to the news lately?"

"Politics, you mean?"

"We got them on the run, looks like. Arrests going on in batches, in bundles. All this week they've been clamping down. All along the line. And it's started up at the top somewheres. Scared stiff. I don't believe there's one empty jail in town."

"You think they put us in here just because they don't have room anyplace else?"

"Could be. I hope that's why. Hope it ain't because they

think we're special. You haven't been joining any of those freedom organizations, have you?"

"You asked me that once before already."

"I wonder maybe did somebody burn you out because you joined something or other. I wondered at the time."

"Because I didn't join, maybe. They asked me."

"Oh, my Lord. And you refused. So that's it. What did you tell them?"

"Just told them to go to hell."

"I see. Did you ever hear from them again?"

"Nope. They had somebody follow me a while back, about five months ago, but he never spoke to me and at least nobody was hanging around the kids or Maddie, which really would've had me scared. He just used to dog me around the place, him and a friend. They didn't even stick very close except in crowds, so they wouldn't lose me. And then they quit all of a sudden, about five months back, like I say."

"Sounds all right. Makes sense."

"You don't think there's a connection, do you? That they were just waiting to arrest me?"

"No, not any more. Not if that's all there was to it. I was just thinking about the time element. No, you're in the clear there. They've got better things on their minds by now, I expect."

Worse things, I'd say. I've seen some of those men around town. In the crowds. All last week and the week before, when there's that feeling in the crowd, sort of agitated but just waiting, like kindling about to go up, I've spotted them.

He said, "Something's happening for sure. I mean something more than what I know already. A lot of people are keeping their mouths shut that never used to."

From the entrance I heard steps and the sound of something being inoved, maybe a table. The jailer came in and walked over to us. He was a stumpy gingery man, going bald at the front; large in the shoulder and walked with a bit of a limp and a funny rolling, like he might have been a navy man. He rubbed his hands together and gave me a big smile through the bars.

"Hungry?" he shouted. "Food!"

I couldn't believe it. I thought it might be the beginning of one of those mental tortures you hear about.

"You no want? No hungry today?"

"Yes, sure. I'm hungry."

"Good-good-fine."

He said it all in one breath and he had a funny way of talking, like he was putting on an accent or something. He smiled again and thumped his chest.

"Homer, that's me. Foreigner. My mother she is Greek, but I been citizen a long time now—fully qualified reliable citizen, keep the law. But I know, you know—before. Before I'm so respectable, I been on the other side of the bars, your friend Adam can tell you."

"Adam?"

"Oh, so sorry, I think you friends already." He jerked his thumb at Jake. "Adam," he said, and then nodded his head at me and said, "Abe."

"How do," Jake muttered, and glared at me.

"I hear you talking and I think you know each other already."

"Just passing the time of day," Jake said.

"Yes, is good. So I put you next door. Is sad, it make you worry behind bars when you get nobody to talk to. Is true, yes? Me, I talk all the time."

"It's the poet in him," Jake said. "Tells me he's got poetic ancestors, ain't that right?"

"My name," said the jailer. "Is name of greatest poet of Greece. Homer. You know Homer?"

"Can't say as I do," I said, "but I never been out of the country. This Homer a big man over there in Greece?"

"Biggest. Biggest poet we got. But he is dead a long time. He lived hundreds of years before now, centuries before now. We got other poets, but Homer he is the best. You got poets too?"

"I expect. Fraid I don't know much about it."

"Sure," Jake said. "Everybody's got poets. But it's always the same story—the good ones died a long time ago and the ones we got now aren't any good. Five hundred years from now people will say somebody was the poet of his time today and it'll be some poor fool you never heard of. Must be a hard life living five hundred years faster than everybody else. I'd just as soon leave it alone."

"Ah but the glory!" says Homer.

"Sure. You figure it out. These poets and people don't begin to live till they're dead. So think about it: who's got all this glory? Dead men. Right? You can keep that. Besides, all the best poets are anonymous anyhow."

"Anonymous," says Homer, like he was trying out the sound of it.

"Seems to me if you're going to be a great man, be one in the world, where it counts. If you're looking for glory. Life after death ain't the kind of glory I'd be interested in."

"Your friend Adam, he is a philosopher, isn't it?"

"No," I said, "he's just got a good line and likes a fight."

"Is what I mean. Same thing. Got a good line, like a fight, it's what I call philosophy."

He turned and walked back to the entrance and yelled at someone outside. A voice answered back and he called again. This time it was probably an order, since nobody said anything but there was a lot of moving around.

"Adam?" I said. "What the hell?"

"Damn, you fool. See to it you don't mess up on it again."

"What kind of a joker is that anyway?"

"I told you, he's all right."

"I just hope he wasn't joking about the food."

"No, that's for real. They fed me once already."

"When did they pick you up?"

"An hour before noon, about then. They brought me straight here, even gave me a drink. It's all right. When did they get you?"

"About two hours after. But they dragged me around first, took me to about three different places inside this big building and made me wait."

"Did they ask you a lot of questions—I mean specific questions about people you know or business you might be involved in?"

"Just name, age, and where I lived. Most of the time I think they were arguing about who was responsible for me and whether I should be charged according to where I said I lived or where they made the arrest or what. Then I believe there was some complication about the charge being under the civil administration or the military authority—is that right? I wasn't paying much attention, I was all beat out. Does that have something to do with the trial, whether we'll be tried under some kind of martial law? I always thought martial law just meant they killed on sight."

"Did you find out which one they charged you under?" Jake said.

"I don't rightly know."

What I remembered most about the waiting was the young soldier who'd been set to keep an eye on me. He was the one who hadn't dared to beat me up too openly, but while we waited he went stiff as a plank with the strain, hoping I'd make a move so he could watch the others come kick my guts out. I kept wondering what sort of a man he'd be in five years' time, whether he had a girl or a mother, whether he wouldn't want her to see what his face looked like looking at me. Or if there was some person, anybody, for him who he wouldn't ever want to find out exactly how he was wishing the hurt on me, not out of hate but just to see it happen.

I smelled food.

It came around the entranceway and filled the place like a rain-bearing wind. The jailer came in, with four others and the food. Jake told me quickly not to try for a break.

"The one on the left is mean as hell. I think I've seen him around before, he's probably a retired professional fighter. And Homer's a lot stronger than he looks—got me in the neck when I made a move last time. Don't try it."

They opened the door, made me stand back so I had to crouch down against the wall, and they set it all down on the floor. Then they closed up again.

The smell was so good and so strong it made me dizzy. I sat down with my back to the bars and took the bowl on my knees, telling myself all the time to take it slow or it would make me sick. I don't think I'd seen so much food together in one meal for two years. It almost made me feel like crying. And when I took the first mouthful it felt all surprised, as though I'd just eaten it ten times over in my thoughts and the taste of it should be different. They'd given us something to drink, too, like Jake said they would. With every swallow I kept reminding myself to go slow, and hoping I wouldn't get so drunk I'd forget to call him Adam or that I was supposed to be Abe.

"How you doing, Abe?"

I turned my face around to him.

"Fine."

"If you could see what you look like. My, like you just been through some kind of mystical experience."

"If I'd known—if I'd known I was going to eat like this, I'd have *tried* to get in."

"It's just good luck," he said. "We're lucky to have Homer. All the jails I been in, nobody ever gave me food like this. See, the jailers get this allowance from the state for feeding prisoners. Most of them just pocket it. And some of them work it double, take the money and claim they get in more prisoners in a week than they've seen in a month. As busy making up names as we are. The officers are in on it too most times, or they know about it and let it go till they need a favor. I told you, Homer is all right. He don't even hold it against me for trying to break."

It took a long time and I was full before the bowl was empty, but I hung on to it and kept chewing real slow and washing it down between mouthfuls. Then I wondered about what to do afterwards. The only thing in the cell besides me and the walls was a straw mat at the back. And there was a funny, close smell about the place that I hadn't noticed so much while I'd been standing.

"Jake," I said, "you know, it isn't all that strong, but this place smells like they been keeping wild animals in it."

"That's us, society's wild animals."

"What do I—"

"Adam, Adam," he added. "Lord, will you remember it? You may be in the clear politically, but I'm not so sure they'd like it if they knew a few things I'd been up to lately. It's all right this time, he didn't hear. Just remember."

For a moment I thought the food would come up. I began to sweat and as soon as I felt it coming out I knew I'd been sweating in waves ever since they closed the cell door the first time.

"Sure," I said. "I'm sorry. I'm just not used to—"

"Take it easy. Don't get all panicked. What were you saying?"

"Oh, about what you do when you've got to relieve yourself in this place, just do it against the wall or where?"

"Ask Homer, he'll hand you a pot for it. I figure it's his own idea—I've got a mark on the wall over here and drawings by about five ex-prisoners. They never had it so good in this place till they hired Homer."

The whole bunch came back and we went through the unlocking again so they could take away the bowl and all, and I asked Homer.

"When he gives it to you," Jake says, "take it in the hand you aren't going to use to eat with, and then don't put that hand near your mouth again till you can wash it. Wipe it on your clothes if you have to. Be on the safe side."

"What do you mean?"

"What I say. And another thing, I haven't exactly seen anything moving yet, but I'd stay away from that straw job if you can help it. If you want to sleep, curl up on the floor near the bars."

"Not exactly the comforts of home."

"It's pretty good compared to the others. In that respect, at least."

He didn't say anything about the walls or even look at them, but he was thinking about them. I didn't mind for the moment. It went in patches, thinking about what was going to happen to us, and sweating, and then putting it out of my mind. Right then I was thinking about Maddie again.

Later on Homer came in. He gave me the pot and some water and came back again a spell later and stayed to talk. He told us all kinds of stories from all over the world and had us both laughing. It was going fine between us and I was feeling good, almost proud about saying Adam or just leaving out the name every time I wanted to say something to Jake. Once when Homer stepped away to speak to a man at the entrance Jake said his stomach turned over every time he thought I was about to come out with his name, but I was pretty sure I could handle it now. There was just one time where I suddenly felt bad, when Homer was in the middle of a story and I wondered if they were all his or whether he'd collected some of them from the men he'd been in charge of and if maybe some of those men had been put to death.

Jake started in then, and he was in good form. Nobody can tell a tall tale like Jake, specially the ones where you have to keep a straight face till the end, and he had Homer wheezing and coughing and practically dancing over the floor with laughing.

I once said to Maddie I wished I was made like that, always joking and laughing and not taking the world seriously. And she said it only looked that way with Jake because he was so energetic and he'd always had that joking way and the gift to make other people laugh when he wanted them to. But really it was all put on like an actor, and underneath Jake was very serious. "A lot more than you," she said. But I never could see it, unless she meant political things. "Aren't I serious?" I said, and she'd said, "No, you're just worried," which was true enough.

I asked Homer finally, "Are you a navy man?"

"Who, me? No, not for anything would I go near the navy. Never."

"I just thought, no offense, the way you walk."

"Oh," he said, "oh, I break my ankle, is nothing. No, I get the choice a long time ago. You see, me and some others, they catch us for taking things. Oh, we were very young but we do it for years, all together working like a team. And the law says well you can choose how to be now, in a hole for life or you go into the forces. So what do I do? My mother is in the country illegal and I know so many boys die in the navy living so close like they do, freeze in the winter and burn up in the summer, wet all the time and no sleep—nothing. Three man I know kill themselves there. No, I don't touch the navy, is slavery. I say, I go into the army and serve the country, become a respectable

citizen, earn money, travel maybe. And is what I do. Is
not bad life, the army. And people have respect. Is no
matter where you come from, how poor, if you're a good
soldier you can put that behind. And other people also
forget. Is democratic."

"Sure," said Jake. "Don't you think that's a damning
indictment of a country, that the only way a man can become a first-class citizen or anything approaching it is to
join the military? Though of course your case ain't quite
the same as ours."

"You can join," Homer said. "Why not?"

"Why not? Oh, I know the army. But do they call it by
its right name? Exploit a place here, free a place there—
everybody's still at peace but meanwhile everyplace is being
occupied and there are a lot of corpses lying around wherever the army's been. And if you look at the ordinary soldier, why, under normal conditions he'd be in the place of
these people he's supposed to be guarding or freeing or
occupying or whatever they call it from day to day. People
with no rights. He comes from someplace where he's got
no rights and the army knows he'll join it to get hold of
them. Then they make him take away the rights of other
people just like him. I don't see how anybody can be such
a—"

Suddenly he began to cover up. It sounded all right if
you didn't know him and hadn't been looking for the pause
before he started to unsay everything. I didn't think Homer
would care in any case.

"Politics," Jake said. "I expect you've got politics in Greece,
too."

"Don't speak of politics, she drive me crazy. All Greeks
talk about politics, always. Always. Since beginning of time.
We invent politics, I tell you."

He asked me if I held such strong views as my friend
Adam.

"Not exactly," I said. "I sort of agree, but not for the same reasons. I got no grudge against the military, or the law either. Not really, when you think about it. I mean, somebody's got to keep order. But I don't know. I almost did join up with the forces, it sounded pretty good. Food and pay and travel maybe, all that. But I've seen too many folks go that way. They say it's such a wonderful life; follow the rules and work hard, and on your free time there's no responsibility and you're your own man. You get drunk and get into fights, have all the women you want, and nobody holds it against you. It's expected you're going to cut loose and go wild when the discipline lets up. Wherever you go there are always girls around and drink and everybody thinks you're so big because the army's big. Well, that's all right when you're eighteen or twenty or for a couple of years more. Get's the wildness out of you. But I've seen men, forty or fifty years old, and they're still leading that life and doing all those things, the things you do when you're eighteen or twenty, and still thinking that way: how good it is to be independent and tough and not to be tied down. Those men, it's as if they never grew somehow. And they're the ones that feel very strong about the army, get tears in their eyes when they remember how good it's been to them. Just because they've made the army into what they should have had if they were grown men. Work, get married, have a family and work for them— that's what a man should do."

"Lots of men in the army has families," Homer said.

"Sure, I know. The army'd rather have them single, though. And I was talking about career soldiers, that's what I'd have to be. Otherwise you get in there and get married, say, and then you can't get out because you need the pay twice as much, and what else are you fit for except soldiering if you've been in there for four or five years? You'd have to start right at the beginning and you can't do that because you got a family to support. And you're only half a family man besides, because you see more of the men you work with than you do of them. And when you get your time off, most of these men will try and talk you into going with them to hit the town, and they'll keep picking at you if you say no, tell you you're going soft, and make you think you're not a real man any more if you just want to have a quiet evening alone with your family. They're wrong. They're the ones don't know what it is to be a man. But it's hard to stand up to that kind of thing, especially if they're your friends, challenging your manhood like that. In the end you're only half a soldier and half married and you can't give your best to either side."

"You don't have to give the best," says Homer. "You act sensible and do not worry about the pride, it works out all right. Lots of soldiers have their families to live with them."

"And a lot of them only think it's going to work out easy that way and then find out it's harder than they imagine. The way things are, it's easy for army families to break up."

"But lots of men has their family come along and no trouble," says Homer.

"Sure, I know. The family ain't too happy about it, though. It takes a real solid marriage for it to work. Even then, I know of cases where they split up. It's just that you can only have the one or the other all the way. Sometimes it works out. That's mostly when the boys go in there for the money and save it up, send it home, and don't get married till they're out. But that's dangerous, of course. I could have done that, I suppose. Go in to fight, right into the front-liners—that's where the money is. But we were too poor to take the chance. Even allowing for me being scared to die, I couldn't afford to—no honest, it ain't so funny. Say I lasted two years and get killed, well what happens to my family in five or ten years? That means they're one worker short for the rest of their lives. And now I got a family of my own. I could have joined the military yesterday. Sometimes I got so desperate I thought I'd maybe do that. But the way the political situation is now, you know they'd never send me out of the country. I'd have more value to them here. They'd stick me right here in the middle of the city, keep me on home ground, so the next time there's a big riot I'd be out there doing crowd control. And who'd be in the crowd? Some day I might come face to face with my best friend or my wife or even my kids. So you see I can't, the choice isn't really there. It doesn't make sense to say I could join. I couldn't, not the way it's set up."

"You married?"

"Yes, married young. Are you?"

"Oh yes," Homer said. "But I'm not so young when I marry. She's back home. Across the water. I save to bring her over."

"A Greek girl?" Jake said.

"Girl?" Homer laughed. "I tell her, she like that." He drew a picture in the air with his hands, showing us his wife's shape. "A woman!" he said loudly. "A big woman, built big."

"Big as that?" said Jake. "That's something you can hang on to in a storm, all right."

"You bet," said Homer, and winked. We all laughed.

"Plenty storms in marriage, I guess. She is not beautiful. But I miss. She has a pretty voice, soft. And she is funny—no, is fun. Fun to talk with, not stupid. She make you feel good. Is most important of all, isn't it?"

"Yes," I said.

Jake shrugged and said he'd never thought about what was the most important thing of all.

"I got the one I wanted, anyway, that's important. Only I like them a little smaller."

He put his hands through the bars and shaped a curve out and in and out, and looked at me.

"What do you say, Abe?" he said.

I wondered what would he do if I came out with it and told him: I say that's my sister you're talking about so freely. He was enjoying himself, putting me on the spot when he knew there was a doubt about how far he could push me, and whether I'd remember his name right. It's strange to have a friend like that, so close you know each other like your one hand knows the other, but you don't understand, like I still don't understand how Jake doesn't worry or how it is he's got to walk right on the edge, always, and thinks it's fun.

He said, "I always found those big girls give you a lot of working space, but in the long run most of them are kind of low on activity. Make you do the whole job yourself. I like something with more action."

Homer leaned his hand up against the wall just far enough away so Jake couldn't grab him if he wanted, and said, "Is lots of men play the trumpet, but not all of them can make her sing."

"There's one on you, Adam."

Jake was smiling, and said "That's pretty good. I'll have to remember that one."

"You married too?" Homer asked him.

"That's right."

"Children?"

"No."

"You?" he asked me.

"Two. A boy and a girl. One of each."

"Is good. Me too. My boy Alexander, twelve year old, and the little girl is ten, Cora. We disagree about the name, so we just call her Cora which means girl. My wife has a beautiful name, is Phyllis, which means a green bough."

"The which?"

"A green bough. How you name your children?"

"Ben, he's seven, going on eight. And Mary. She's, oh almost six now. Every time somebody asks me I have to think. They grow so fast. And my wife's name is Maddie, Madeleine."

"Madeleine, is nice. But you are young to have a boy eight year old."

"Twenty-five," I said. "I told you, I married young."

"You ever regret?"

"Not about that, no."

"Is very young," he said.

That's what they said when we got married. And afterwards somebody always says don't you have second thoughts about it now. I don't see it, like asking a man does he regret being a man, does he have second thoughts about his own family. Everything else could go, and does, and that's the bitterness. But if that went, that's your life, the people you love. Jake says it's freedom and ideas that move the world, but the men who keep pushing freedom and ideas know that's a lie, and if instead of just buming us out they'd tried to do something to Maddie and the kids, they could have had me doing what they said, for a while anyway, till I figured out how to stop it. They know that. They just must have thought I wasn't worth their time.

"It's been hard sometimes. It would have been harder alone."

"Twenty-five," said Homer. "If I was twenty-five again, oh, that is young. Me, I am forty-seven. Forty-seven."

"Old enough to be my old man."

"No," he said. "I was not here then."

He turned to Jake, who was laughing at what he'd said.

"You are older a little?"

I thought how funny it was that out of the two of us Homer liked Jake better, but I was the one that trusted

Homer. I forget just when it was I began to trust him, but now I'd have told him anything about me and I didn't believe he'd carry it to anybody else. But Jake didn't trust him. He never trusted anybody unless he'd known them nearly all his life and even then you could count the ones he really trusted on your fingers. And there were things he wouldn't let people know just because he said it wouldn't be good for them to know.

"Oh, I'm bowed down with age compared to him."

"How old?" asked Homer, and Jake decided to tell him. "Twenty-nine."

"Old? That is young. Very."

"Young for some, old for others. I'm no spring chicken any more."

"What's that?"

"Just a phrase. Means not in the first flush of youth, not green, not younger than most. Old Abe there is what you call green."

"Green?"

"Lacking in experience."

Homer thought about that and I thought: that's why he likes Jake better, because of being experienced, which is true, though Maddie always said not to mind. That day after I lost my temper she said not to mind, she'd rather have a fool with a good heart any day than a worldly man who said bitter things. "He's what you call cynical," she said. "And you don't know what he's thinking. I know, when you get mad you just roar and break things and lash out, and when you think something you say it. But what it is he thinks, Jake never shows, not anything. It makes me nervous. I wonder it don't make Annie nervous. Maybe he shows it to her. I'd rather know where I stand." And I told her, "Annie knows where she stands, all right." That was early, when we were first married, and I was ashamed to lose my temper, I didn't believe it could happen where you were contented. Some little thing it was, and all my life I been careful not to get mad like that, because being stronger than most through the chest and arms and shoulders, you have to be careful or your own strength can turn against you and break you. Like I never like to get into fights or even be in crowds that might be about to demonstrate or something, I always try to avoid it, because I get that feeling once I was in I'd kill somebody. Or hurt somebody by mistake. And you can get so you like it, I've seen that happen too. Once when we were kids, I remember hitting Jake harder than I'd thought, turning around and seeing the blood on his face, and it made me want to die. He didn't say a thing. It's as though you can't hurt him. And he still loves a fight, but not for anger. For fun. I know when he's angry: he gets very calm, his voice goes gentle, and it's worse than if he hit you or shouted or smashed something. Like that day he came in the door and he'd heard the rumor the neighbors started, saying the Lord had put a judgment on him for his way of life and that was why he and Annie didn't have any children and wouldn't ever. He put down something he was carrying and said very quiet, it only took one spiteful tongue to take away the good name of a thousand people and what did it matter to him, what the hell. Annie tried to run out of the room but he caught her by the elbow going around the doorway and just said, "Let's have my dinner, it's been a long day."

We talked a little more and Homer left us for a while. He said there was a friend he had to see. As he walked off through the entranceway he called out, "Don't run away."

"A lot of speechifying you been doing," Jake said. "You don't usually talk so much."

"It's the worry."

I thought how all the time, even when I was talking, I kept thinking about things that happened a long time ago. And thinking about Maddie and Jake and Annie and my

life, like I was far away someplace or like maybe inside I
knew I was never going to see any of it again.

"Quit that. Nobody knows, we may need all the energy
we've got in a while. You just quit worrying and sit tight.
Keep your eyes on me and if there's ever a chance for a
break, I'll give you the sign."

"I just can't stop wondering."

"Well, try."

"I thought you said we couldn't break out of this one."

"Not yet. Later, when they take us out."

I thought: I should have tried to get away before they
brought me here. At the time I never even thought of it, I
couldn't think of anything except I'd been caught. Not till
they closed the door.

Homer came back in with a friend, the same one I'd seen
him with when they first brought me in. They sat down
at the table in the center of the room and played dice again.
They were talking in a language I didn't know the sound
of, so I guessed it must be Greek. The friend spoke it slowly
and let Homer correct him every now and then. In the
middle of the game Homer turned around and said, "You
gamble?" Jake told him yes but he didn't always play it
straight.

"Nobody else I gamble with does either, so it works out
the same."

"I used to play," Homer said, "here, with men in the
cells, but just pretend, no real money. One day a man's
widow come to me and she swears her husband dying words
was I owe him twenty-five thousand and she is to collect.
You see, we play very high because is pretend. So now I
don't do that no more."

The friend didn't do much talking. Just once he looked
us both over and said to me, "You fight?"

I didn't understand.

"Fight. You fight ever, for money?"

"No," I said. I don't like it. With the money or without. I figure why hurt people you don't even know."

"You got the build."

"Not me," I said, and pointed to Jake. "He's the one fights. He's been a boxer."

"I mean wrestling, that's the game. Too short in the legs to box. You'd be all right as a wrestler."

Jake was giving me a long, dirty look. The man said to him, "Where you box?"

"Oh, just here and there."

"Professional?"

"No, just amateur stuff."

"With the army?"

"Against the army."

"You know Big Quint? Old One-Punch Joe and the Sicilian Lion and Cassius what's-his-name?"

"I did," Jake said. "But a long time ago."

"And Killerboy Dexter? What a slugger that one was—and a fine left he had too, that fooled a lot of fighters. I suppose that was before your time. Best of the young ones coming up is that boy Rufus, comes from somewhere up North, someplace outside Syracuse, around there. Rufus —I forget his other name. I hear they're keeping him hid on a farm down in the country somewheres, training him with some of the old-timers. Rumor is they're grooming him for the Olympics, but nobody admits to seeing him fight yet. Everybody just says he's the best coming up. A lot of money's started changing hands on that boy. I'd bet myself if I could be sure. You hear anything on that score?"

"I wouldn't know anything about it," said Jake. "I haven't been around to the gym for a couple of years now."

"Wrestling's the game," the man said, and he went back to the dice.

It was hot. And it was getting darker. All the light came in from the entranceway and now that the sun was beginning to move, the place was almost in total darkness. Homer had brought a light in and put it on the table, and there were two more lamps up on the walls in front of the middle cells. But from where we were the light came dim and uneven and the place seemed cruder than before as the sun went. I began to long for air and the light that was still shining outside.

Another man came in suddenly and said something to Homer. The game broke up and all three went out.

"Listen," Jake whispered to me. "You're so nice and friendly today, but we all know already what a pal you are, so let's just have a little less of this exchanging birthday dates and how old people were when they got married and what's your great-grandmother's name and where you were when and what's your favorite color, right? And if you can't shut up about your own life story, just at least leave mine out of it. What are you looking so pleased about?"

"I was just thinking about Homer and his wife. Shaped like a whale, with a name that means a green bough. That's nice."

"You goddamn fool," he said.

There was some shuffling around outside and a loud, firm voice I hadn't heard before. Homer's friend mumbled something and Homer began to talk, too. The big voice went on, lower and impossible to tell what it was saying. When he came back in Homer told us there'd been a big riot about two hours ago.

"Lots of arrest. Then there was two small riots in a different part of the town. Everybody say it look like she was plan like that, to take away attention and let the leaders escape. That's what they look for now because there are so many and you can't arrest allbody. Is bad, riots. Lots of people they don't even know there's riot going on, they just standing there doing nothing. Then the law bring them in to me, saying this is a dangerous criminal, and sometimes it's just girls and boys, so young and all beat up. Once I have a mother and child in the cells, very dangerous, they tell me. What they call—agitators, is it? Very dangerous agitators, this mother and child."

"How long do you keep them?" said Jake.

"Oh, that one, I mark it down and let them go, and lose the record later. That was on the other side of town, bigger jail and always full. Also I work with my friend, you see him? The one just leave. We have arrangements, you know."

"How'd we stand for an arrangement here?"

Homer looked over at the entranceway, rubbed his chin, and moved over to Jake's cell, right up near the bars.

"Here is different. I don't take the names, so I can't fix."

"But you got lots of friends in that department," Jake said. "Ain't that right?"

"Some, yes."

"I got friends too. What do you say to combining?"

"Not for theft," Homer says, and he pointed at Jake. "You, you do something. You know what the law is, but you do that anyway. I only fix it if people are here by mistake."

"It was a mistake. Mistaken identity. They mixed me up with somebody else. Some fool yelled stop that man, and I looked around, saw him going around the corner, and the law grabbed me instead. I tried to tell them at the time, but they were so all-fired happy to get their hands on anybody at all, they wouldn't listen."

"No?" said Homer. He didn't believe it.

"Truth," Jake said. "What do you say?"

He shook his head.

"No bad feeling, I do it if I believe is just. But is not so bad, you get out soon."

"Not soon enough. Look, Homer, you know how it is."

"Enough. Don't say no more, you make me angry. Sure,

I know how it is. I always take what is coming to me. You do the same now. Is not so hard. I know how it is, so I know also what stories people tell the jailer and how you try to make sympathy and so on. See, I used to do it too, she's the first trick after telling the story to the law. All the things you say, I say them a long time ago."

"No harm trying," said Jake.

"Understand, I have sympathy, yes. What do I care? So they catch you, they take away what you try to take, so you don't profit. I think people should be charge money as punishment for theft. Charge them more money than the value of what they try to steal and give it to people they steal the thing from. You can't pay the charge, you can work it off. Then for small things, why make a thief stay in jail? Is not sensible. Because nobody is really hurt by it, not like hurting somebody's health or murder or other things. But that is personal opinion of mine, I don't let that change my mind. Is a question of law, you know. I know what is law. You know what is, and you know before you come to my jail. And also, here it is more difficult than any other place I been. Very difficult. Other people are working here that I don't know. This place here, even if I think you are bad-treated when they bring you in, when they take you out, I cannot change it. Is my job, is my job to see you stay here till they have a trial. What else happen is not my job. Beside, I could help at the beginning if you get arrested by the regular authority, but it was soldiers bring you in, isn't it? I got no friends high up there, up at the top where you need. Only with the local force I got friends high up. All I can do with the army is fix food and transportation and transfer, not take the name off the record."

I remembered what Jake said about how rickety the other jails were and how the best time to try for a break was when they took you out into the street.

"Could you get us transferred to a different place?" I said.

"Not now. All the jails is full now. But later, if they keep you here a long time, maybe."

"Thanks."

"No, no thanks. I only say maybe and if. It depends maybe on how many arrest they make with the riots and how they do the trial. Sometimes after riots they try all together in a block, get the jails clear quick, but sometime they wait and wonder who they got, specially if they think this riot was plan careful, not just a lot of people standing around. I see later if there's another place. But is too difficult, then I don't push. You understand is difficult for me without giving reasons why I change you. It use to be easy. I could do something even here, four, five month ago. Not now."

Jake asked him how long he expected they would keep us here.

"Hard to say. Maybe they keep you a long time here to wait for the trial. I hope is what they do."

"Like our company, do you?"

"Sure, sure, you and me we get along, right? I understand, you joke. Is not that. I mean, if they decide fast, give you a quick trial, it is with military trial and you get a harder sentence."

"But I was under civil arrest. I only met up with the military when they handed me over."

One of Homer's friends looked in at the doorway and said something. Homer turned around to answer him from where he stood.

Jake said, "Listen, Homer, if you would, there's something we'd both appreciate."

"Unlock. Yes, I bet."

"No, just if you could find out exactly how they've charged us, civil or martial law, and when they plan to try the cases."

"Sure, I do that anyhow. I always do that for my prisoner to save the worry."

"But don't lean too hard on the questions if it looks like some official's going to let it slide. I mean, if there's a holdup maybe I could get someone to change things from the outside, if you see what I mean."

"Sure," Homer said. "Is fair enough. Good luck to it. I cannot say exactly till the end of the day, maybe till tomorrow when they have gone over the day record. But I ask around, I find out what happen to your record, who got it, what they think happens to you. Meantime, I think you have company tonight—I hear there is some arrest to be transferred here, and maybe more people from riots, we see. Hope it don't mean you must double up. I keep saying to them it looks big but is small, only big walls is all."

"You're right there," said Jake.

He sat down on the floor. I'd been sitting on mine for some time, even though Jake had told me not to stay on the floor too long and not to sit totally still there because you'd lose the strength in your legs, and we might need it for a break later on. He kept moving back and forth and doing a knee bend up and down every once in a while. But I didn't believe any more it was going to be a question of getting out. Now I believed in the trial and didn't think it was going to be as bad as I'd imagined. I was feeling generally better about the future, except for what was going to happen to Maddie and the kids, and how she'd take it. If I was away for a long time, Annie could look after them. Jake always had plenty of money put by for when he was up against the law. But it couldn't turn out to be such a long time, not for just a piece of bread I didn't think. I wasn't sure about the horse.

"Do you think they'll try us about the same time?" I asked him. "I wish it could be together. What's it like at the trials?"

He started to say something, but Homer came in again and sat at his table. People kept walking by and talking outside and the place seemed more open and lighter because now it was near sunset and the light was coming in on the slant. You could see it lying like patches of sand or like dust on the floor at the entranceway. Men came in, asking Homer things and going out again, talking to each other in the passageway. Then there was a commotion outside, a lot of voices and then stillness and right afterwards laughing and whistles and voices that seemed to be humming like water. Homer got up to see and went out the doorway. Jake stood up in his cell and then I did too.

"Another prisoner?" I said.

"A woman, bet you anything. Probably Annie."

Homer came back in sight. Annie was standing behind him, next to an officer who held her by the arm and grinned down at her. She said something to him, looking back into his face in a measuring sort of way, and almost smiled. He laughed and let go of her.

"I leave you to talk," Homer called, and waved his hand towards us so she could see we were at the far end. Then he turned and motioned the other man to follow him out. Annie walked forward from between them, alone, across the center of the floor. She had her head up and walked easy, keeping her eyes on the side of the room where Jake was.

It was strange to watch how she was and know she didn't know I was there, or looking at her. Stranger than seeing somebody you know walk by in a crowd. She looked hard. Full of devilment, able to take care of herself, and ready to talk back. It made me almost shy, seeing her, the way she was when she wasn't at home and wasn't a sister—a woman coming to see her husband in jail, which was a thing she'd done lots of times before.

She sauntered up near the cell, flicked her eyes past me, lazy and sneery, and then looked. She stopped in the middle of walking so she nearly tripped, and her face changed.

"You? I thought it was Jake."

"Right behind you, honey," he said. She whipped around.

"You, oh you—this is the last straw. Lord, this is the limit. It's all right for you to go taking chances, but why you have to drag my kid brother into—"

"He didn't," I told her.

"This was one he done all by his own fool self," Jake said.

She turned around again and curled her fingers closed on the bars of my cell and leaned forward like she wanted to put her head through.

"Ain't you ashamed?" she said. "And what's Maddie going to do now you landed yourself in this place? Ain't you shamed?"

"No," I said, "I am not." I started to explain, but she didn't want to listen. All the time I was talking she was giving me her own talking-to. I couldn't listen to her and talk at the same time, and I suppose she couldn't have been listening to me either, for the same reason. But it didn't seem important. At the time it only mattered that I was getting the explanation out.

"I was hungry," I said, "and I stole some bread. That's all there was to it. I was hungry enough so's I didn't bother much about who was going to be looking at me. That's all there is to it. I'm not ashamed, I'm just worried, sick with the worrying. And you don't make it any better. Do you think I like being here?"

"You should have thought. Oh my Lord, why didn't you come to me and say? You should be—"

"Cut it out, Annie," Jake said.

I said, "Listen, you'll tell Maddie, won't you? And tell her not to worry."

"Not to worry?"

"And see there's somebody can look after the kids for a while, so she can come and see me. I got to talk with her."

"I bet she'll enjoy that, walking through that line of studs out there and at night-time, too."

"How many out there?" Jake asked.

"About ten."

"Come over here, Annie."

She dropped her hands. They came away from the bars all at once as though they'd been stuck there instead of holding on. She went over to Jake and he put an arm through the bars and around her shoulders.

"They been giving you a hard time?"

"Just the usual, saying things. Asked me how much I cost."

"How much did you say?"

"Told them to ask my husband."

He put his other hand through and started to touch her face and neck. I had the feeling I shouldn't look and turned to the side, to the wall.

"Something I want you to do for me," he said. He began to tell her names of people and where to go and what to say.

"Keep your eye on the entrance, will you, Seth?"

He started whispering something to her and she answered, and after a while sighed and said all right. Then he squeezed her to him against the bars and drew his arm back so it was just lying along her shoulder. She turned around and told me not to fret, that she'd see Maddie was all right and try to keep her from worrying. She looked tired.

"Somebody coming."

I could just see Homer's head moving into view and another man's hand, waving fingers in the air as he walked. Jake looked, too.

"What were you giving him the eye for?"

"Who?" she said.

"That tall number had you by the arm when you came in. Who is he?"

"How should I know? He was standing outside. Said he'd show me where you were."

"You have to play up to him like that?"

"I didn't play up to anybody. Anyway, who's talking? I bet you missed me last night, didn't you?"

"I missed you," he said. He was looking over her head at the other man and his face turned peaceful and set, getting angry.

"If I died," he said, "you'd get married again before the year was out, wouldn't you?"

She didn't move for a while. Then she lifted his hand, knocked his arm away, and walked back to the entrance without looking at either of us or saying good-bye. Jake leaned up against the side wall and ran his hand over the bars where she'd been.

"What are you looking at?" he said.

"Just looking."

He let go of the bars and turned his back.

I've seen it happen so many times before and every time it jars me up, because I don't understand how it can be. I've lost my temper with Maddie, hit her because I couldn't help it. But I never wanted to hurt her. And afterwards, knowing I'd hurt her, I felt as scared and miserable as if I'd killed her, so in the end she was the one who had to comfort me, though she was the one got hurt. With Jake and Annie it's different, they set out to hurt each other. That's what I can't understand about it, that they love as much as we do, and still they can plan out a hurt the way you would prepare a pleasure.

He's treated her so bad sometimes, not beating her around, but just saying something mean. She does the same. Both of them wild with the notion that the other one could be

fooling around with somebody else. And all of it is uncalled
for. I don't believe either one of them has stepped over the
line since they got married. But they talk about it all the
time, and threaten each other with it, and hint it might be
so. At first I used to think it happened because they didn't
have any kids, that they needed an extra thing to be in their
marriage. But then I met up with other married people who
were jealous that way, with two or three kids, and that just
meant two or three more weapons in the battle as far as
they were concerned.

Jake said to me once I was lucky I wasn't jealous. "I got
no cause," I told him. "You don't either. So why be jealous,"
and he answered, "There don't have to be cause. You're
born that way or born without it. Jealous means jealous
from the start—possessive." Maybe that's what it is, that
people just have different ideas about what belongs where.
So if you are jealous that way, you imagine it should be
possible that a body is yours when you have possessed it,
and everything inside the body. I know he thinks that way
about other things, like a horse or something like that belongs to the man that can take it, and if you can't hold on
to what you've got you don't deserve to have it. I don't hold
with that—I don't approve. When I stole, I knew it belonged to somebody else. I knew it perfectly but I took it
anyway. But for Jake, the horse was his as soon as he began
to lead it away. Finders keepers is what he thinks about
things, about objects.

But about people, how can you say that? I told him, the
people you belong to, it's in your mind, in your soul. They
could be a hundred miles away and living with somebody
else but it would be the same inside you, wouldn't it? And
you could belong to somebody who never belonged to you,
who didn't give you a second thought, not even if you were
married. "I'm not talking about love," he said, "just who
she sees in the afternoons." I'd only be worried if Maddie

didn't love me any more. As for anything else, I don't think it would happen, but if it did it wouldn't be the end. "You don't even have any cause, Jake," I told him. "And even if you did, you know where her heart is, so can't you stop treating each other like that?" He said, "A change of bed can cause a change of heart."

I couldn't get anywhere talking about it with him. Maddie used to talk to Annie too, after a quarrel, till we got dragged into it that time and I had to tell them. I told them both it was all right for them to get into these fights and come ask us to take sides, but in a week they'd be together again and meanwhile they'd have broke up our home so in the future they would have to settle it alone. Mostly it was just all the talk that went on, that's what I couldn't stand. Both of them, it's as if you could almost see them sewing or weaving with the words, as if they are ornamenting—a jab here, a stitch there, and it's obvious they enjoy it, but it makes my head ache. I figure if you think something, then say it and don't take all day over it, but if you aren't sure what you think, shut up till you've made up your mind.

Jake can talk. Like anything. I think he used to make up his mind while he was talking. It's not so much like that now, he's quieter now. But at the wedding when he came with Annie, Maddie's mother said, "Can he talk? That boy could steal the brains right out of your head with his talk." Now he keeps a lot to himself because of politics, and you don't know all he's thinking.

"Will you quit looking at me like that?" he said.

"Just looking."

"She'll get over it. It don't mean a thing. Just keep her so mad she won't have time to think about anybody else till I get out."

I said, "You know if anything happened to you she'd kill herself."

"Maybe."

"You know she would. Maddie's the one would get married again."

"You think so?"

I'd never thought about it before but now it seemed like I'd known all the time.

"Sure, and I'd want her to. If anything happened to her, I'd get married to somebody else again too. Not right away, but I would. I couldn't live alone like that. And neither could she. It would be worse for her—I'd want her to get married again. How'd she live with two kids and no man in the house? It's bad enough you'd have the grief, why should she be unhappy too?"

"You wouldn't be jealous?"

"What do you mean, jealous? I'd be dead. But I'd like to know she's all right. I'd like her to get married again to somebody would make her happy."

"You mean you'd want her to love some other man? Really, like she loves you now?"

"Yes, I would. After I'm dead." I wouldn't want to leave somebody and have the world turn black and be dead to them whenever they think of me not being there. Much better if they think of me kindly and know I want them to be happy. For the children, too. Isn't that love?

Jake said, "Well, you don't know what it is. My, I feel like I'd be jealous even after I was dead."

"That's why she wouldn't be able to go on afterwards," I told him. "You wouldn't either. Think about it. What would you do if anything happened to Annie?"

"I don't want to think about it. I don't know."

Homer came in with his keys and began to unlock one of the middle cells.

"She is pretty, very," he said. "Lots of what you call it? Temperament. We got girls like that at home."

You got everything back there," Jake said.

"Sure. I have a cousin like that a long time ago. You say something and her eyes flash and she tell you to go to hell. Then she wait till everybody leave her alone and she cries, cry like she will die. Is pride, is wonderful in a woman."

"You know all about that too?" Jake said.

"Two years ago, three years ago—well. Now I am feeling old. Is the job, maybe." He went over to the other middle cell and unlocked that one too so the doors stood open.

Jake said, "Is there anything you don't have over there in Greece? By my count you invented poetry, politics, philosophy, women. What else is there you don't have?"

"Money," Homer said.

"How about religion, did you start that too?"

"You very religious?"

Jake laughed. I heard shouts out in the passage and stamping feet and a roar of people coming closer. And then an armed guard burst through the entranceway, about seven of them, and they were dragging eight or nine people with them.

"Five in here," Homer said, and stood back. "Rest over there."

The soldiers began to cram them into the cells. They were young kids, looking not more than nineteen or twenty and two of them girls. All of them were kicking and hitting at the military and calling them paid tools of the government and hired butchers of imperialist tyranny and things like that. Then they started shouting names and dirty words, the girls too. But they must have come from good families; they were rich, you could see that. Most of the boys, about five of them, were dressed like me, dressed to look like a poor man, a fieldworker. But if you looked you could see their poor man's clothes were made out of real quality stuff.

The doors shut and they quieted down just for a moment. That's the bad time, when the door closes and you know there's no choice any more. But then they decided to put up a good front, and they yelled even louder than before, calling Homer names and jeering at him. I could see five of them, four boys and a girl. And if I got down into the corner I could see the other four on my side of the wall. But I didn't like the feeling of having those five all able to look straight into my cell with nothing I could do about it except turn my back. I got into the other corner and stood sideways so I could turn around whenever I wanted to, and watched them.

Homer waited for them to get quieter and then he and the friend he'd been playing dice with, the one who liked wrestling matches, started to hand in water and pots and things. One of the boys got his arm through the bars and poked the wrestling man hard in the eye. He grabbed the arm and twisted it and I heard a snap. "You've broken my arm," the boy yelled, "my God, he's broken my arm!"

The girl in the cell started to scream: "You dirty bastard, you filthy motherfucking son of a bitch." The ones in the other cell were shouting, "Police brutality, imperialist pig," and then all of them smashed the pots against the bars and the walls and threw the water out over the floor and began to throw the broken pieces into the center at Homer and his friend. There was water and smashed pieces everywhere, and they began to sing. One of the freedom songs, one of ours.

Homer stood by the table and put his hand to his friend's face, looking at the eye. Then he took him by the arm and they both walked out, leaving everything on the floor. The singing went on.

When they'd finished there was a silence. The reaction's coming, I thought. "Hey, how's your arm?" one of them said from the other side. I moved over and looked out to the side and could see him with his face against the bars. I thought he must be the leader; he'd started the song. He had a little beard and a sunburn. I imagined he must have worked hard for both of them. The others were all very white from sitting up late at night talking about politics. Jake says I should be aware of what's going on but he didn't appear to be too set on them either. I looked over and saw him yawn and do another knee bend.

Back in the cell I could see, one of the boys said, "What a filthy place. I've got to pee." "Go ahead," one of the others told him, "give them some work to do for all the money they're getting beating people up." The girl and some of the others began to giggle. "Me too," said another boy and then they both did it against the wall while the rest cheered. After that they were quiet for a while. I could smell it coming through the place, a hot vegetable smell, going sour. There seemed to be less air than before.

A couple of them sighed and mumbled to each other. One of the boys said, "Well, what are we going to do to fill in the time?" and put his arm around the girl. I supposed she was his girl because she let him and they began to kiss up against the bars. One of the boys looked embarrassed and turned away, but the others looked on while they kissed. Then they began to do more, he started to undo her clothes, and I thought: Lord, they're going to, right where everybody can see. But the girl appeared to be bored and pushed him away. "I'm not in the mood," she said. He nuzzled up to her again and said, "Come on, you're always in the mood, aren't you?" She took his arms away and said, "Cut it out," and moved away from him, one elbow out with her hand on her waist and holding onto the bars with the other hand. She tossed her hair back from over her eyes and stayed like that. I saw her face; she was still trying to look bored. And I thought: that one's just lost her forever, and it's a good thing. That's what they come to jail for, to get right down to real life, to the truth, and if you're looking for it there, that's where you'll find it.

Someone was crying outside in the passage. Everybody

looked. "Beating up some poor kid," one of them said, and the crying went on. Homer and his friend came around the corner of the passage and out through the entrance, supporting a man between them. He was one of us, and he was still crying and had trouble standing. But he wasn't hurt, I didn't think. It must have been grief. Because he was crying the way people do when it's all over, and everything around you disappears so you can't even see what you're looking at and you don't care any more. They put him in one of the big cells, the one to the right of the entrance, and closed the door. Homer said something to him but the man couldn't answer. He sat down on the floor and kept on crying, running his hands over his head and face and not even bothering to turn away.

One of the kids called out, "What did you do to him? Are you proud of that? What did you do to that man?" Homer didn't look around. He went back outside with his friend and came in again alone and began to clean up the floor. The kids said things to him, trying to get his temper, but he kept on cleaning, not looking at them and his face resigned, not grim like I would be. When he finished, he stood up, holding all the broken pieces.

He said to them, "There is three men outside, your fathers or your uncles or something. They pay to get you out. They also pay for destruction of government property, for this. Men come in here and I try to make it clean as possible because it is bad enough to be in jail without the discomfort. You think I got lots of these? You think with all things going on so fast the state has time to give me supplies? No, I buy things myself and I keep the place clean myself and if I don't, there come diseases. Now you go piss on the wall and what happens if twenty more people come here and no time to clean it up? You do not think of other people who come after you, they have to live with all the things you break and make dirty."

"That's tough," one of them said. "You're making me cry." And another one said, "That's what you're paid for, isn't it?"

"I am pay by your fathers and uncles and the rest. They are rich and they treat me all right. When you have money, twenty years from now, you will pay me. But you will treat me like dirt. That is the difference," he said, and went out. The man in the front cell kept sobbing and I began to feel bad and tired from all the noise. I sat down on the floor.

"Hey," one of them called. He was in the cell on my side. I thought it was the voice of the tanned one with the beard. He was calling to Jake. "What are you in for, brother?"

"Brother, hell," Jake said. "I never seen you before in my life."

"We're on your side," the voice explained. Jake didn't answer, and the voice said again, "What are you in for?"

"Child rape," Jake said. A few of them laughed, and then it sounded like the laugh was dying out and they weren't sure, because his face hadn't changed.

"You're kidding," the voice said.

"No," Jake told him, and turned away.

"How about you?" another boy said from the cell that looked into mine. "What are you in for?" He smiled and I had that feeling that we were tied together, like when somebody you don't like smiles and it's as if you're standing at the other end of the line, his smile jerks up one on you, and you don't want it to happen, it makes you mad that it might respond all by itself, because you don't like the person. I thought against it so my face didn't move and I didn't answer him, and turned my head to the wall like Jake.

The man at the far end kept on sobbing. Some more of the kids tried to speak to us but I wasn't playing. Neither would Jake, which surprised me. He knows all their ideas and the language they use. I don't understand it and I'm damned if anybody is going to do that charity thing to me:

we are sorry for you, we sympathize, we're fighting for your betterment, stand here like a monkey and look pleased and think how good we are. Or they give you food and clothes which you're not in a position to refuse, and when they leave they've robbed you of your honesty, your smile tied to the one they have that says: aren't you grateful, don't you like us, isn't it a lucky thing for you that we think about you once a year. They get very uncomfortable and vexed and sometimes scared if they think you're laughing at them behind their backs, and then they don't come back the next year and your kids have to do without, like you.

I heard Homer's voice and a lot of steps coming in. The military was back. "They buy you out," Homer says, and began to unlock the cells. One of the kids said they hadn't asked anybody to buy them out and they were going to stay there as a protest against police brutality. The soldiers began hauling them out. The one with the hurt arm came out quiet enough, wanting to get to a doctor. Some of the others put up a fuss. The girl from the other side suddenly kicked one of the guards for no reason at all, it looked like. He swore and let go and she kicked him again. His friend who was standing next to them pulled back his fist and hit her in the breast. She screamed all the way out and was crying and saying, "You coward, you dirty coward."

Then they were out in the passage, the sound of them going, and it was quiet except for the man who was weeping.

"Did you see that?" Jake said. "Got him on the shinbone twice before they ever thought of laying a hand on her, and she'll go home and show her bruise and tell how she was roughed around by the hired imperialist thugs who've got nothing better to do all day than beat up women and kids."

"I thought you liked those kind of people, protest and rights and all."

"Not from them, it's too late for it now. It was a nice

gesture, very helpful in the beginning, but we don't need them any more, they're just in the way. Besides, it's a kind of mental slumming for most of them. We want them out in the streets when they're landowners and senators and running import-export businesses like their folks, when they've got the pull to change the laws, change everything. But I bet, I bet you anything, in twenty years when they've got the family holdings and the house and everything, they'll be taking their kids on vacations to a little villa outside Rome or someplace and voting themselves tax reductions so they can keep what they got. And once in a while they'll boast to the kids about how they went through that stage too, they were idealists and right in the middle of the violence, where the action was."

"Singing our songs," he went on. "They've got songs of their own—why don't they work on that? They take it from us and they'll drop it in a few years. Retain the sympathy, of course, a lot of good that does."

"You're always saying people should fight for their rights."

"Sure, sure. If you know what they are and know what you're doing. I'm just sick of all this idealism running around the place. It's like an epidemic, everybody's got it. Trouble with idealism is it kills people. I'm not interested in motives, I just want something that works out without too much strain on everybody. Man, you talk with some of the people I know. Fanatics. Got a lot of schemes but what's in their minds is that they want to take over the show. Just the system all over again, we'll get on top and then we'll stomp on you for a change. And the people who've really got something to cry about, can you move them? Hell no. If there's a takeover they'll still be at the bottom. And all the ones that complain and won't lift a finger, think if everything was distributed equal nobody'd ever have to work again— I'm sick of all of it."

"Well, they wouldn't. Have to work again."

"You're crazy."

"Not what I call work, not what I been doing for the last nine years every day."

"That ain't work, that's slaving."

Homer came in again and started to clean out the floor of the cell and scrub the walls.

"What about them?" he said. "Did you hear the things that girl was saying? If that' my daughter I throw her out of the house and never come back, you bet."

The weeping man calmed down a little and started to moan. Every once in a while he'd break into sobbing again, but it was quieter. He had his head down on his knees and his arms around them.

"What's his trouble?" Jake asked.

Homer came over and said in a low voice that the man had stabbed his wife.

"Dead?"

"Instant, just like that. The neighbors say they quarrel all the time, shout. He never beat her, maybe he should. This time they shout at each other across the table and there's a knife there on top. He says he don't mean to hurt, all he mean was to shut up the shouting so she would listen. He is heartbreaking, he loves her very much. The neighbors say is true what he says, no other man, no other woman, just being angry. Very sad. They will try it as accidental I hope. He says he wants the trial right now, wants to die."

"Poor bastard, poor fool," Jake said.

Homer went back to scrubbing down the cells. I had to use the pot and then I thought I'd sleep. All day I usually move around, I never knew how tired you get if you stay shut in. And I was feeling the bruises and beginning to stiffen up from when they pushed me around making the arrest. They can tell who's rich and who isn't and who's got friends. They never roughed Jake around unless he got in first. He looks too smart and too important.

I stretched. Homer began to whistle and to hum. I lay down on the floor and put my head on the stone, cold and hard. Then I changed around and put my arm under my head and closed my eyes.

I must have gone right under. When I woke up a man I'd never seen before was talking in whispers to Jake, saying good-bye. I sat up and watched him leave and saw Annie at the entrance, going out with him into the dark hallway.

"How long was I out?" I said.

"Not very long. She says Maddie's coming later. Uncle Ben will walk her here, and Annie's going to look after the kids."

"She still mad at you?"

"No," he said, "no, we made it up," and smiled.

"Good."

The man who'd killed his wife was still sobbing quietly.

"Has he been at it all this time?"

"No, he let up for a time. He only started again a little while back. Homer says they're moving him on later."

"I hope we don't get any more rioters."

"So does Homer. It cuts down on the food."

"That's funny, you know, I thought it would make me feel sick. I did feel sort of unsettled, but not sick. And I'm hungry again. Already."

"It's the idea. Watch out for that. You know in your mind you'd like to keep on eating all day long. But your stomach can't take it. So take it slow."

"Is there any news?"

"Not much. Not good. I got Joe to hunt out my army friends."

"Virgil?"

"Him and others. They don't know anything, don't know

where to begin. I never knew such a total breakdown of grapevines. We'll just have to sit it out till something comes through."

Homer came in and unlocked the other cell by the entrance, the big one on the left.

"Another noisy one," he said. "I put him far away as possible." While he was speaking four guards came in with the prisoner, squirming and writhing in his clothes like an animal in a sack, and muttering to himself. He was the strangest-looking thing: all gawky, skinny as a reed and dressed in rags that were covered in dirt. His hair fell all over his eyes and below his shoulders and even from a distance I thought I could see things hopping off him. He stuck out one long bony leg while they tried to move him along, and you could see the toenails on his bare feet, longer than I imagined nails could grow, like the nails on his hands, black with dirt. And there were sores on his legs, which were the color he was all over, a kind of livery yellow.

"Blasphemers," he blared out in a voice like a trumpet call, but it made you want to laugh. Then it broke, and he trilled what he was saying in a high quavering voice that sounded as if it was coming from a completely different person.

"Repent, the day is at hand. Oh ye ungodly, ye of little faith." He screwed his head around and I stepped back farther into the cell. His face gave me the kind of sinking feeling you get when you see blood, but that kind of fascination, too. I'd never seen anybody like that, so that you felt revolted but you couldn't take your eyes off him. They say snakes do it to birds.

"Goddamn, we've got the whole works now," Jake said. "A week in this jail and you could write a history of the world."

"Unrighteous and ungodly," said the stranger. "Pharisees, Pharisees!"

He had great blazing eyes and inside his beard a loose mouth full of rotten teeth. When he called out "Pharisees" the eyes rolled up and his face went all meek and mock-pious, so for a moment I was sure he was putting on an act for some reason.

They shut him in the cell and Homer turned the key and stood back, brushing off his clothes. The stranger rattled the bars and sang out, "Eaters of offal, ye that persist in the ways of the ungodly, Pharisees!" He went on like that, his eyes roaming over the rest of the cells for a while, but none of us gave him a reaction, so he turned around and sat down with his back leaning against the bars, and scratched his head and muttered to himself.

"What kind of a thing is that?"

"Some religious nut," Jake said. "Some kind of faith-healer probably."

"Why's he in here? He looks sick."

"Maybe he was preaching to the multitudes or something when the riots broke out. Start screaming and kicking enough and they pull you in. Some of them do it for the food and a place to sleep for the night."

Homer came up to Jake, who said to him, "I got a complaint to register about the way the tone of this place is going down. It's turning into a regular sideshow. What's the world coming to when a man can't find any peace and quiet even in jail?"

"You tell me?" Homer said. "You tell me. Food is soon."

"And drink?"

"Sure, drink too. Coming soon," he said, and went out.

"I could do with a drink," Jake said.

Lots of things I could do with, I thought. The air was still heavy and thick and the place had the sense of something wild having passed through and gone, time coming back and sitting there slow. I was thinking I hoped they'd put me out to do hard labor because I couldn't take a lot of this, being shut in. Maybe you got used to it, though. I planned the first thing I'd do when I found out how long the sentence was going to be. It would be to do what all the others do, so they tell you: find someplace where I could mark off the days one by one.

"Goes by slow when you got to wait it out," I said. "I wish we knew one way or the other right now without a trial, what the sentence is."

"I know right now. I know they aren't going to keep me in for long. Not if I can help it. I been sentenced three times and never yet served one. Don't let yourself slide back that way. Do you want to be cut off from the world for the next ten years?"

"Ten years for a piece of bread?"

"Lord, Seth. Don't you know anything?"

That's what he always said when we were kids. Nobody would believe he was older because he was so small, it took a long while before he got his growth. Maybe that's why he likes to fight, because he's never forgotten how he used to have to. "Don't you know anything?" he'd say, and pretty soon they weren't laughing any more, everybody was taking orders from him.

"Don't you know anything? You don't imagine they're going to go easy on you because you give them some hard luck story, do you?"

"For taking a piece of bread? What do you think they're going to do, cut my hand off or something? They couldn't give me more than six months, could they? I never stole anything before."

"So you say. But wait till you hear what they say. Wait till some man stands up and says, yes that's the one that burned down my business last year, and some woman says she's positive you're the one raped her grand-daughter just a week ago, she remembers your shifty eyes, and swearing up and down on oath and a dozen witnesses to prove it.

Asking you where you were on such-and-such a night three years ago and looking triumphant when you say you can't remember. Don't you know that? If every man was just charged with the crime he's done, everybody there is would be in jail for something. Hell no, you get arrested and you're a representative for all the ones who never got caught out."

I thought it couldn't be like he said, he was trying to scare me about it. Maybe he figured if I got too relaxed I'd drop some hint about his political doings. I wasn't all that relaxed; my hands were sweating again.

Homer and the four-man guard came in with the food. First they went to the cell on the right, where the man was moaning to himself about his dead wife. He didn't raise his head from his knees or move in any other way. Homer gave his keys to one of the others, went into the cell himself, and laid the provisions down on the floor while the ex-fighter stood behind him. He locked up again and the man still didn't move. Then they went over to the left-hand cell and started to open up. The religious nut jumped to his feet and began chuckling to himself. "Stand back, there," one of the guards said and he moved a little way back, but he kept pacing back and forth, making noises to himself like he was agreeing with something someone was saying to him, and holding his arms out with the fingers bent like claws.

Homer went into the cell and was about to set the food down when the religious nut made a dash at him, knocking everything out of his hands and sending it way up into the air. The food and drink and water splashed all over the inside of the cell and on the walls and over Homer and the guard by the door. The nut shrieked out, "Get thee behind me, get thee behind me, spawn of the devil," and began to dance around the cell. The ex-professional stepped forward and cracked him across the mouth. And he let out a yelp, not sounding like pain, sounding like some kind of a love-sound a woman might make. They closed the doors on him and Homer went out into the entranceway with the fighter, leaving the other three men behind. The religious nut capered around his cell and began to harangue them, saying, "Man shall not live by bread alone but by every word that proceedeth out of the mouth of God." His voice kept changing, sometimes loud and strong as a whip cracking and then going all quavery and high and his face would turn back to that mealy-mouthed humble look. When he said "mouth of God" he lifted his right hand and pointed his finger up at the ceiling, throwing his eyes up dramatically.

He went on parading in front of them, stalking back and forth and shouting out a long string of stuff at them. He said, "I am the living bread, the living bread which came down from heaven, and if any man eat of this bread he shall live, he shall live, live forever. And the bread that I will give, the bread, the bread that I will give is my flesh. My flesh which I give, my flesh which I give, give for the life of the world."

"I know what's wrong with him, all right," one of them said. "Is that your trouble, sweetheart?" He laughed.

A second one said, "God, it makes you sick, look at him."

The religious nut was panting with excitement and his mouth was wet.

"I knew a nut like that once," the second one said, "went around hammering nails into his hands. It's a sex thing, gives them some kind of a kick. They run around shouting at people till somebody beats them up—that's what they want. Did you hear him squeal just then? Loves it."

The third guard, a good-looking boy and younger than the others, said, "You shouldn't laugh at crazy people."

"What's eating you?" the first one said. "You got religion all of a sudden?"

"I just don't think it's funny, that's all. They can't help it. Some of the things they say aren't so crazy—they're just like everybody else, only it comes out scrambled. He's not hurting anybody, is he? Everybody's a little crazy, every religion's a little crazy."

"Not everybody," the second one said. "And not every religion. Is that what you meant to say, *every* religion is crazy?"

The younger one shrugged, and said he just didn't think it was funny and besides it was unlucky to laugh at crazy people.

"Crazy? Why, he's a goddamn raving pervert," the first one said.

The religious nut kept muttering all the time they were talking about him. As soon as they stopped he got their attention again and said, "The hour is coming, the hour is coming when the dead shall hear the voice of the son of God. I am the son and he that honoreth not the son honoreth not the father that sent him. The hour is coming. I am the son of God, I am the son of God. As soon as they hear of me they shall obey me, the strangers shall submit themselves unto me."

"What did I tell you?" said the first guard.

"It is God that avengeth me and subdueth the people under me. He beat them small as the dust before the wind, he cast them out like the dirt in the streets."

"Who are you calling dirt, you bastard?" the second guard said to him, and started to put his arm through the bars.

Homer came back in with the other one and said sharply, "What you doing making him shout like that? Come on, this is time for working. What you think, you can stand there all day? The food is getting cold." He shooed them into the passageway and came over to us, not looking at the religious nut who was still mumbling and shouting and hopping up and down. He shouted, "I receive not honor from men. Blessed are they that hear the word of God, but I know you, that ye have not the love of God in you. I am come in my father's name and ye receive me not."

"I'd like to receive him," I said. "Right in the teeth, I'd like to."

Homer said, "This day is the longest day in my life, I bet. First one thing, then another. Why they get him started like that? And I got to clean that up too. And now the other one start to cry again, no wonder. Oh, I am feeling old as one hundred today. And there is more people coming to-night. When I sleep I don't know."

"Who is he anyway?" Jake said. "What's he in for? Exposing himself to little girls, or what?"

"Is a mistake, all a mistake. I don't know why they send him here. He is sick and crazy. This is a jail, not a place for sick peoples. I ask his name to put it on the record and he just keep saying: I am the son of God. Like that, in a big echo voice and turn his eyes up. What he is arrest for I don't know because nobody send the charge record and he is transferred from someplace else. What a mess in my jail all day."

"Try a little of that Greek philosophy," Jake said.

"My philosophy for today is this," Homer says, and made a gesture with his hand.

Jake laughed. "Is that Greek, too?"

"Is international, yes?"

The food came in with the four guards, first to Jake's cell, next to mine, and then they all went out. I had some of the drink first and felt better. That man was crying again but the other one had stopped, and I began to eat.

Suddenly he started up again in that high, quivery cooing voice.

"I know you, that ye have not the love of God in you," he said. "I am come in my father's name and ye receive me not. My God, my God, why hast thou forsaken me, why art thou so far from helping me and from the words of my roaring? Oh my God, I cry in the daytime but thou hearest not, and in the night season, and am not silent. But thou art holy, oh thou that inhabitest the praises of Israel. Our fathers trusted in thee, they trusted, and thou didst deliver them. They cried unto thee and were delivered, they trusted in thee and were not confounded."

I began to feel let down and sad again. The noise kept going on, sometimes soft and sweet and sometimes bleating out strong and showing off. The soft voice was the worst, it made you feel crawly inside.

"But I am a worm and no man," he went on. "A reproach of men and despised of the people. All they that see me laugh me to scorn, they shoot out the lip, they shake the head, saying: he trusted on the Lord that he would deliver him—let him deliver him, seeing he delighted in him. But thou art he that took me out of the womb, thou didst make me hope when I was upon my mother's breasts. I was cast upon thee from the womb, thou art my God from my mother's belly. Be not far from me, for trouble is near, for there is none to help."

I turned around in the cell and put my back to the bars, feeling terrible all of a sudden and wanting to cry. I thought: if that man who killed his wife starts up again I won't be able to hold it back.

The voice went on: "Many bulls have compassed me, strong bulls of Bashan have beset me round, they gaped upon me with their mouths as a ravening and roaring lion. I am poured out like water and all my bones are out of joint. My heart is like wax, it is melted in the midst of my bowels, my strength is dried up like a potsherd. And my tongue cleaveth to my jaws, and thou hast brought me into the dust of death. For dogs have compassed me, the assembly of the wicked have inclosed me, they pierced my hands and my feet. I may tell all my bones, they look and stare upon me. They part my garments among them and cast lots upon my vesture. But be not thou far from me, oh Lord, oh my strength. Haste thee to help me."

"Seth?" Jake said, and I turned around. "Not hungry?"

"It's that goddamn nut. That awful mealy-mouth voice and the words so beautiful. What is all that stuff he's been spouting?"

"That? That one's a psalm. He's praying. The rest of it he's grabbed from all over the place, quoting from lots of different parts of the scriptures and getting them all mixed up."

"It's that voice, that awful voice. Can't they shut him up?"

"He'll stop it if you leave him alone. He wants an audience, is all."

"I can't stand him," I said. "I hate him."

"Shouldn't hate."

"Why not? I'm beginning to think there's lots of things I hate. Never had time to think about them before."

"It's bad for the digestion," he said. "Besides, you hate somebody, that means they got a hold over you. They got you right in their hand."

"I don't see it. What is that, religious morality? All they tell you about in religion, it's full of hate. Hating all the ones that don't agree with you."

He began to tell me a story about a boy that lived next door before his family moved near us and we got to know each other. This boy took a dislike to Jake, a real hatred. One day the boy was making fun of him and Jake turned around and told him he wished he'd die. Next week the boy hung himself. I didn't believe it.

"It's true," he said.

"I mean I don't believe he would do it just because you said that."

"Lots of things people do. Specially when they build up hate like that and don't know how to get rid of it. If you're going to hate you should know why and what it is and how to keep it in control. Otherwise it can turn around and fall back on you. Why do you think you hate him?"

The voice had stopped now and I felt easier.

"I just can't abide his sicky-sweet psalm-singing voice. I don't mind so much that he's a nut."

"What's wrong with the voice?"

"Gives me the cold shakes," I said. I began to eat, to feel filled with the taste of it, and it was much better and I thought about seeing Maddie soon.

Jake sighed. He said, "A brother-in-law that's got the cold shakes, a weepy homicide case, a religious maniac who thinks he's the Messiah, and a jailer who's a Greek philosopher—Lord, do I pick them."

"Do you remember when you were religious?" I said.

"A long time ago, that was."

I remembered. I remembered he even thought he had a calling and would go into it for life. Some of them are like that. They say a reformed sinner makes the best man of God because he can know and understand other people's weaknesses and help them to peace the way he found it. And it works the other way, too—the ones who brood about religion suddenly throwing it over and going wild, like Jake, and they never go back to it. When they change like that it's lifelong. Not like me. All my life I could never make up my mind about those things and in the end I realized I never would. I remember Jake would say, "There's got to be something more, there must be. Sometimes I feel like it's all a reflection or like a shadow of the real thing," and to listen to him talk about the mystery of things, you'd get all calm and serene and inside you were buming with the knowledge that everything was completely mysterious and large and full of unthought-of marvels. But I never felt that way by myself. It took Jake talking about religion to make it happen.

Then he changed. Once he said maybe God was just the way things happened, that everything that took place, all put together, made God. He said how he'd always wanted to experience what the scriptures spoke about: that God would talk to you. But that would mean God was a person and acted like a person, and if he was perfect and all-powerful he wouldn't be a person, because people—are so small. Not just that they die, they're all-over small. All the believers who tell you you're doing something wrong or a thing or an action of yours is immoral because God wants this and God wants that; Jake said this God that's talking to them, that's themselves. That's their idea of what their good selves are like and what they'd wish to have happening in the world.

Then he got stuck on ideas. And he said religion was ideas but he wanted ideas that could handle people in this world, not deal with some world after death, which he'd never really taken to heart anyway. He began to get interested in politics. And he told me, like telling me I was lucky not to be jealous, "You're lucky you've got that instinctive certainty of what's right and what's wrong. I never had it." And by that he meant that I wasn't as smart, since I'd never gone into the question deep enough to find out that there's no such thing as right or wrong. Just how you happen to look at it, which was another thing he told me. I knew he was smarter, but some things he didn't see, for instance that I'd know when he said I was lucky to be this or that, that it was a way of telling me I had a place and it was just a notch below his. Some of the mistakes he makes with people—that's why, because he could misjudge those instinctive certainties. Not so much with strangers, there he was always all right.

And he made friends in the army and got them to give him information about where certain troops were stationed and what maneuvers they were carrying out, how long they'd be staying, how the communication lines were set up, and so on. Passing it on to freedom fighters and the protesters, I suppose, and I'm sure, I know, there's a name for that and a very special law that covers it, overthrowing the state and all. They've got his name in one place and his description in another, and nobody's put the two together so far, but Maddie says she wouldn't be in Annie's place for anything in this world.

One day he says to me, "Maybe you're right about it all being in the mind, who you belong to. That's the thing, to possess minds, to be able to influence people, make them change their minds and change their lives. That's the real power, to get other men's minds under your control." So that's what he does now, and I still don't understand and maybe never will. What on earth would you want with somebody else's mind? Bad enough you're stuck with your own.

"Thou didst make me hope when I was upon my mother's breasts," Jake said, "that just tears my insides out. I think that's what I liked most about it, just the words."

"You called me Seth," I said.

"Nobody to hear. Don't you start doing it or you'll trip up."

They came back and opened up to take the things away. I was feeling a little drunk, though it was hard to tell, sitting down. They'd given us more this time. When they went to the religious nut's cell and cleaned it up he began jabbering again, and after they'd locked up he made a grab at one of them through the bars. Homer wasn't with them this time, he'd given the keys to his wrestling friend and you could see his eye was already swelled out a lot from where the protester had hit him. At the cell on the other side they took out the food but left everything else. And then they went out again.

Homer came back with a new set of guards, the night shift, I guessed. They had about six people in tow and put them into the side cells where the kids had been. They were all working men, most of them looking pretty much like me, and very beat up, looking tired and dazed and not talking or trying to push back. The religious nut quoted a lot to them but they took no notice. Two of them lay down on the floor. Homer and the guards handed in water and something to drink and pots, and came back later with food but not as much as they'd given us.

While they were eating, the religious nut's speech dribbled off into muttering, then he quit entirely and sat down with his back to the bars. Homer came across the center of the floor, around the table, and said to me, "Is Maddie, yes?"

"Yes," I said and stood up. My heart started going all the way up through me and I hung onto the bars. He walked her across the room from the entranceway towards my cell and then went out, leaving us to talk. She looked shy and scared coming across the floor with all the men in the place.

When she got to the cell she put her arms through and up around my shoulders. All the hard work she does, and her hands so small. I put my arms through and held her close up to the bars and wanted to get my head through.

"Are you all right?" she said. "Are they feeding you all right?"

"I'm fine. Don't worry about me. I'm sorry, I'm sorry about all of it, Maddie. But you get Annie to stay with you and don't worry about me. It's you I'm worrying over, everything else is all right."

"Ben and Mary asked about you," she said. "Annie told them you'd gone to visit her cousin Liza, so I had to back her up. I didn't know you had a cousin Liza."

I had to laugh because cousin Liza was a family joke and a name to use for excuses when you wanted to get out of something. I was never sure we really had any cousin by that name; Annie knew more about those far-off cousins than I ever did. I remembered she once told me cousin Liza had been a notorious old woman who disgraced the family at some point and died about forty years ago.

I told Maddie and she relaxed a little and didn't look so strange. She gets that pinched-up look sometimes like she's a very old woman, and when she looks that way she also appears to be about four years old, all the ages come into her face.

Jake said hello, and she said hello to him and turned back to me. I wished there weren't any other people around, so I could really talk. It felt shaming to be overlooked by so many people and not able to speak really. I thought: this must be the worst part of being in jail for a long time— standing near the people you love but not quite able to touch them and not quite able to talk to them and sweating with the constraint; counting, all the time they are there, how much more time there is until they've got to go. So much to say, and unable to.

"Well," Maddie said. "Well, I'll look in tomorrow."

Just then the religious nut threw himself against the bars of his cell and pointed his finger at us, and bellowed out, "Daughter of Sodom, Jezebel, beware the sins of the flesh, beware!"

Maddie looked behind her and I looked, over her head, seeing him writhing himself up against the bars, moving in a jerky rhythm and roaring, "Beware the unclean lusts of the flesh, beware the guile of painted women that leadeth unto temptation! My judgment is just because I seek not mine own will but the will of the father which hath sent me."

I tasted the food coming back up my throat and felt Maddie in trembles between my hands, like from cold, and I couldn't take it any longer.

"Shut up," I yelled, "shut that goddamn bastard up, shut him up, Homer, make him quit!" And then it happened again like I always try to avoid, like a curtain of blazing light coming down over my forehead, getting mad and not knowing or caring any more, not hearing what anybody else was saying, just yelling that I was going to kill him when I got my hands on him.

Then I heard Jake, quiet, saying, "Easy, take it easy. You're making it worse."

I looked up and saw his face and felt the hotness begin to go and the shaking come on.

"That's just what he wants," he said. "Take a look. It's you he's interested in, not Maddie."

I looked and saw the nut with one foot through the bars now, weaving his body back and forth, and looking straight at me. His eyes were nasty and pleased, his mouth wide open and blood down the side of his face from where he'd been hit. Seeing me look, he started up again, started whipping himself into a frenzy, running his hands all over his body. But Jake got in first.

"Just don't listen," he said. "Now he knows he can get a rise out of you, he'll try it again."

I turned my head away and began to cry. Maddie smoothed her hand over my neck and said, "Oh Seth, oh Seth."

Homer came in then and said what was the trouble, what had happened.

"That crazy son of a bitch, insulting my wife."

Homer went over to his cell and the nut pulled his foot in and gave him a short lecture in his trumpet voice. Homer stood there without saying anything, and the nut slouched off into one of the far corners and sat down.

Maddie said, "Oh Seth, putting you in with horrible people like that."

I told her again not to worry, and touched her face and took her hand in through the bars and kissed that. She did

the same with mine and Homer made a sign from the entranceway that it was time for her to go. She looked back
as she went, and I thought: if that other one makes a remark
or does anything at all, even coughs when she gets up
close—But he didn't look at her and she went out with
Homer.

Later in the night the guards came and took the homicide
out of his cell. He'd stopped crying but he went with them
blank-faced. I wondered if they were taking him to trial.
Homer had quit work for the night. Before he went he'd
promised us to remember about looking up the day records.
The man who took over was one I hadn't seen before, very
thin and grey-haired and sullen. All night long they were
changing men in the middle cells, taking out the ones who
were there and replacing them with others. I didn't think
they could be rioters, only a few of them looked like they'd
been in a fight. The rest were all ordinary-looking men,
some young and some older. They tried to sleep when they
came in, but hardly had time because the guards were moving them so fast. I guessed finally that they were all being
held for questioning about something. Jake said he was
going to sleep. Over by the entrance the religious nut was
rolled up in a ball in a corner of his cell. I was tired, but
it had been so dark in the place for so long that I didn't
think I could sleep. I lay down and kept watching the people
going in and out.

Finally I thought I would sleep after all and make myself
a dream. Maddie said once she didn't dream, she said she
supposed that meant she didn't have any imagination, and
looked embarrassed. I told her all it means is that she forgets
them when she wakes up. I'm always talking about them
since it means a lot to me. Some people don't care about it
or don't like the thought of dreaming, or are scared by it,
by the thought that they go someplace away from the body.
Jake says you don't, it only seems that way, like being able

to remember a face, you can close your eyes and call it up by thinking, and you don't truly leave. Maybe Maddie has dreams she doesn't want to remember; I'd want to remember even the bad ones.

When we were kids we used to compare. Annie dreams in black and white and repeats dreams and remembers what people say in them. Jake's are in color, like mine, and people in them talk but you don't remember what they've said, only maybe a word once in a while. Same with mine. But he dreams about people he knows and I don't usually unless they are far away. My little girl Mary is the strangest one —she's dreamed some things that have happened afterwards. She dreamed about the fire before it happened, and about Maddie's grandfather dying. Last week she said she had a dream about me, she dreamed I was in a big parade or some kind of celebration and we were all going somewhere to do something important. She said it scared her but afterwards she thought it must be all right because though she didn't see the end, the dream finished halfway, when I was in it I was looking happy.

I closed my eyes and tried for a good dream. I like planning them out just before you go under. Then they take over and change, of course, and the real dreaming begins.

When I woke up I didn't know where I was and then remembered and knew the dream had been a bad one. I'd had a feeling in the dream that I was all bent down and weak and couldn't move very well, and people I'd met a long time ago kept asking me what had happened to me. And the trouble was I was old, about a hundred years old with a long white beard. But I'd felt it in my body, withered up and broken and too feeble even to say what was wrong with me.

Jake looked like he was still asleep. The cell where the weeping man had been now had about six men in it, all asleep on the floor. The grey-haired man was also asleep, at the table, and the middle cells as far as I could see were empty with the doors closed. I thought I remembered Homer unlocking the empty cells earlier in the day and I wondered if that was a safety precaution, to add time in case somebody got hold of the keys and tried to lock the jailer in. Or maybe I'd misremembered and he hadn't really used the keys. I had that feeling you sometimes get after a bad dream, that you don't want to go to sleep again right away.

I lay there and waited and tried not to think about anything particular. Things from the past started to go through my head, like before at the beginning of the afternoon, making me go back to when we were all kids, as though I had to say good-bye to it.

I saw Homer come through the entranceway. He didn't make enough noise to wake the other man or the other prisoners, but Jake was suddenly up on his feet. I stayed where I was and half-closed my eyes.

"It's like I am afraid," he said. "They try you together."

"When?" Jake said.

"Now."

"In our absence?"

"Yes. It is going on now, is what I hear. Rumors everywhere, but that is mainly what I hear, and I think is reliable. Also I hear out of all arrest made yesterday only one or two come on any list at all. There was no time. Nobody is going to bother, it's either let them go or try them quick and the charge the same for all, sedition, incitement to violence, treason. You know."

"Both of us together?"

Homer flashed his hand out and said, "All of you, all in here right now. Seven, eight, nine, ten, they do it by the block."

"But we must all be in for different things."

"That's all I know, what I hear."

"Listen," Jake said. "You know we didn't exactly give our right names. I think they've got us mixed up with somebody else."

"Oh, I suspect that, is not that, is not because of any names."

"But the charge is straight theft, isn't it?"

"They don't say. I will tell you soon as I hear more."

He left and Jake sat down. He stayed like that, waiting, and I kept the way I was.

I slept again. Some dreams I have places I go to with fields and mountains, sometimes the sea. And in some dreams I have cities that I've never been to before. But the dream I had this time was just countryside, nothing particular, and I was walking in it and don't remember anything happening,

Jake was sitting the way he'd been before.

"Any idea what time it is?" I said.

"Sunup, I imagine. It's hard to tell in here."

The other jailer was gone, and the other prisoners still asleep. I felt ghostly and cramped. Jake stretched and did knee bends and told me to do the same, but I couldn't face it. We waited. It began to get lighter and some of the men in the big cell by the entrance stood up and stretched, sat up or lay down again. The light grew, and time dragged.

Then there was some noise outside and people moving around, it sounded like a lot of them, talking and walking through the passageways outside. Once I caught sight of some lumber being carried by some of the military and jailhouse guards, down the corridor and past the entranceway.

"Barricades for another riot, I suppose," I said.

Jake held onto the bars and looked at me. Sometimes I've seen him go like that, looking steady as if he's looking straight through the world and out the other side, and it seems to be a face I've never met before but would never forget.

"What?" I said.

"Start doing those bends, Seth. And remember to make the break when I give you the sign."

"I don't see the use—"

"Just do what I say."

Homer came back while I was holding onto the bars and swinging my feet around. Seeing him from the side and then the back when he turned, he looked old and tired, like a different person, not like a man who would enjoy clowning around and laughing. He went over to Jake's cell.

"They decide," he said. Jake nodded.

I stood still to listen and it was so silent I could hear my eyelids creak when I blinked.

"Death," said Homer.

Over his shoulder I saw Jake's face looking as though he'd known.

"The whole bunch of us?"

"Yes. It is martial law, for all of you."

"How's it going to be?" Jake asked. And Homer told us.

"I send for your families already," he said, and went out again. He hadn't looked at me.

I shut my eyes and swallowed, and heard it loud in my throat and in my ears.

"What martial law?" I said. "They couldn't have proclaimed it or anything till the riots started, that was hours after they caught us. I can't believe—"

"Hush. It's like he says. You remember what I told you, we'll make the break when they get us in the streets."

Out in the passage somebody started hammering. Soldiers came in and stood around the doorway. Homer came back in once more and talked to the others, the seven men on the right, and the religious nut. The men got up on their feet but the nut didn't seem to have taken anything in. He stood leaning against the bars, looking mopey. The other men began to talk, low and scared. One of them shouted out something just once and afterwards they went back to the same uneasy mutterings.

Guards came in and some of the soldiers were called away. The hammering went on and a sound of chopping, and then a group of people, women, came in and rushed for the right-hand cell. All hell broke loose then: screaming and crying. But I still couldn't believe it.

Two more guards came in, and Maddie and Annie with them. Maddie was running.

She reached me, saying, "They can't do it, Seth, they can't do it," and beat her head against the bars. That was when I believed it; when I held her face up, I saw it there in her eyes and believed it for the first time.

The place was loud as a storm now, it was hard to hear anyone. I said, "Listen, Maddie, we're going to try for a break in the street. But I don't want you there, you hear? You stay away. I specially don't want you there if it won't work. Promise me. It's important. Promise me you'll stay away." I've seen it, mouth open, body twisted out of shape, swollen, suffocated.

"If it happens," I said, "come for the body after."

"Oh no, oh no, no, no," she said, "they can't do it to you, you didn't do anything."

"Promise, Maddie. Nothing's certain, it can go either way whether we get away or not. You stay away, please, I ask it."

"I promise," she said, and cried. A guard came to take her away but she wouldn't go. He lifted her away like a child and she looked back at me all the way. They were taking the other women out, too. One of the guards came for Annie, she was the last, and she hadn't made a sound yet, but when they touched her on the shoulder she crumpled to the floor, sobbing, and put her hands through the bars, holding onto Jake's legs. They carried her out. She was crying like the man who'd killed his wife, and didn't see me when her face was turned in my direction and looking at me.

"How's it going?" Jake said.

"I don't know. My throat's all tight. I got the jitters. I don't know if I'll be much use when it comes time."

"That's all right. Wait for me. Take it easy all the way till I give the sign. Then give it everything you've got for as long as you can. If it don't work out make sure they have to beat the life out of you to stop you getting away. It's better than letting them get us there."

Homer came back and asked Jake if there was anything he wanted done for Annie.

"I say it just in case, because I am married and father and so on. You try to break, yes? There's ten of you, is a chance."

"Don't miss much, do you?"

"Just in case, I keep an eye on her if you want."

"Don't he have any kin?" Jake said, looking over at the religious nut. "Nobody say good-bye to him?"

"I ask him but he keep saying he is the son of God and nobody else."

"Lord, not even a friend. What happened to the man that killed his wife?"

"They take him out in the night."

"Is he being tried quick, like he wanted?" I said.

"No, he is transferred."

"He was arrested after us, wasn't he?"

Homer said yes. "They don't need a trial for that one, he has another knife on him."

"You let him keep a knife on him?" Jake said.

"I see he does not get too close, to me or to the others. He wants the knife, he can keep it."

Jake looked over his head and saw the last of the guards go out the door. The hammering outside had stopped and it was quiet.

"Homer," he said, suddenly, softly, "unlock it. Now."

He looked into Jake's face for a long while. I felt the sweat coming down in floods and thought it must be possible to hear my breathing clear across the floor to the street outside. Homer walked to the table and got his keys and started back to Jake's cell.

He had the key out in his hand when four soldiers and two of the guards walked in through the entranceway. The guards sat down at the table and one of the soldiers called Homer by name.

"Coming," he said. More came in and stood up against the bars of the empty cells.

"Is too late," he said, and whispered to Jake. Then he said, "I get you fresh water," and went to say something to the soldier, going out afterwards.

"What's happening?" I asked.

Jake said, "Shut up."

We waited. The numbers kept changing in the room. It began to get hot. Finally more were leaving than were coming in, and when Homer came back there were only three left, leaning up against the entranceway, and all the rest were out in the passage, talking.

He came over to us and handed Jake some water through the bars. Then he did the same for me, and I saw he was handing me something else, too: a knife. Then he reached inside his clothes and pulled out a fistful of what looked like leaves.

"No chains, no tying up, I don't think," he said. "But maybe you can't get your hands free. Take these, is for the pain, in case."

"What is that?" Jake said.

"I know a friend get it for me," Homer said, and left, to stop one of the guards who was about to walk over to us and say a word to him. Homer edged him back to the entrance and they talked there.

"What is that?"

"Looks like just leaves." I began to chew them up. All the time I'd thought: don't ever take that stuff, that's the poor man's grave, pretty soon you just live on dope and aren't even hungry any more. Besides, they say it does things to your head, even when you stop and get over the craving for it, you're never right in the head again. I always thought it wasn't worth the chance you took.

"What are you doing? Holy God, Seth, it's them African weeds. Don't take it. How much did he give you? It'll knock you right out."

"For the pain," I said, and kept chewing, and wiped the juice off my mouth.

"Are you crazy? Are you out of your mind? Don't take it, it'll kill you, all that amount." He turned around in his cell and slapped his hand against the wall.

When I'd chewed up all the leaves I expected something to happen right away.

"It's all right," I said, "I just feel sort of full and sleepy."

"You fool, you fool, you damn fool," he said. "I'll try my best. Homer says he'll help as much as he can. Hide the knife. If you get your hands free, use it. And if it looks like they've got us for keeps, use it on yourself. Remember."

"Sure," I said, "I'll remember. I feel fine, everything in working order."

He sort of laughed at me and put his hand up to his eyes.

"Oh Seth, goddamn," he said, and turned away.

"What's the matter? I'm just fine."

He turned back again and I saw the shine of where tears had been in his eye-sockets. I'd never seen him cry before in my life.

"What's wrong, Jake? I know what you're thinking. You're thinking you're going to have to leave me behind."

He didn't answer.

"Want to say good-bye now?"

"Not yet. Do you think you can fight?"

"I don't rightly know. I suppose, when time comes. But I feel fine. I'm not scared any more."

Homer came in and three of the military with him, with an officer in charge. "Those first," the officer said, and Homer unlocked the big cell on the right, opened the door, and stood back beside it. The two soldiers moved the men out of the cell and more guards came in to hustle them along. One of the men didn't want to leave and sat down on the floor, holding onto the bars. After they'd taken them all out Homer shut the door.

"Not yet," the officer said.

Two more soldiers and two guards came in. Homer told one of the guards to be ready to take over, that he was going as an escort. Then we waited. The guard Homer had spoken to went out and another one came in to take his place.

"I don't think those leaves are all they're made out to be," I said. "Hey, Jake, I said I don't think—"

"I heard you. Take it easy."

We waited some more and then Homer unlocked the cell where the religious nut was. The two guards led him out and he walked quietly enough to the entrance and out. Then he came running in again, with both men holding onto him and his feet sticking out in all directions, it looked like, as they pulled him back and out. He was shouting, "Pharisees, blasphemers!"

There was a lot of noise coming from the passageway, it sounded like there must be about thirty or forty people standing out there, and they laughed as the religious nut was taken through. Then it was our turn. Two soldiers and the officer walked in front and on the sides and Homer and another guard took up the rear. I'd forgotten what the passage looked like, I hadn't noticed much when they'd brought me in. It was lined with soldiers from end to end. As we passed through, Homer handed his keys to the guard he'd spoken to.

We came to the door and stepped out, and I stood stock still, blinded by the sun. I thought we must have been wrong about the time; it felt more like midday than morning. But I couldn't be sure, couldn't be sure about what time it was or what day. It felt like a day that wasn't spaced like others, a day that was running like a river and would always be the same wherever you were set down in it, and might go on forever. The other guard jabbed me in the back. "All right," I said, and moved forward, but I was feeling strange, very good but strange, like I was another height of myself above where my feet were going.

We walked down the street and there didn't seem to be too many people around. Some stopped when they saw us and others just looked and kept on walking. Then we came to a knot of people who were shouting things; there were soldiers standing around, and in the middle was the religious nut, bending down, and I thought: they're beating him up and he doesn't know what's happening, I feel sorry for him. But then I caught a look at his face as we passed by. He had on that secret, smug, mealy-mouth look and I realized he was enjoying whatever it was, being in the middle of a fuss.

I noticed that all the sound had blocked out of my ears. It was very strange. My feet kept walking and I could feel Jake very tense beside me. I said, "Jake, you know, the sound's just gone," and I couldn't hear myself say it but I thought it must be coming out slowly and not all formed. He touched my arm, and that was strange, too. It felt like I didn't have skin any more but something else that felt all different. I said, carefully, "I think those leaves are beginning to do something."

Up ahead the seven men and their guard branched off

down a street and started to head in the opposite direction
from us. We went around a comer. There were more people
now, filling up the side of the street and blocking the corners, looking as though they'd been expecting us. I looked
behind and saw the guards and soldiers with the religious
nut, following along behind. Then I saw somebody throw
something but still I couldn't hear. More people began to
file into the street till it was like walking between walls of
them and I could see their mouths opening and their faces
having expressions and their hands moving, shaking fists
and cupping around their mouths. Then something else
started, like I was going away and coming back again, seeing
everything far and small and taking place from below.

And then it happened, suddenly. Like a wall breaking
through, it happened far and then it happened near, as if
it was all going on inside of me, and the sound came back,
loud, people screaming and shouting and calling names and
everything near, near. Whatever that stuff was, it hit me
all at once, like nothing in this world, making me ten times
bigger, lifting me right off the ground so I knew I could do
anything, anything at all, I could jump over houses, I could
fly. And I shouted.

"Now, Seth, now!" Jake yelled. Homer fell down, taking
a soldier and the other guard with him, and I began to fight
like it says in the stories when they slew ten thousand,
hitting everything. People were yelling, "Get him," and a
woman spit in my face and I saw Jake lifted like a swimmer
coming up for air and lashing around him, and Annie hitting
the officer with a stick and a piece of his tooth fly out,
separate, into the air. I was down and being kicked and had
dirt in my mouth. Jake called out, "Run, Seth, run, run,"
and I was up again, running into the crowd. And all at once
Maddie was there. I called to her, "Maddie, Maddie," and
had my arms out and she pulled me into the crowd, her
breast coming into the crook of my arm, lovely and fright-

ening to feel, like when we danced at the wedding. "Seth!"
she shouted and they dragged at me from behind and tore
me away. I saw the knife fall and took it up quick and hit
everything, everybody, it was happening so near and so
strong inside, burning and huge, and lifted me away with
it, slashing, seeing the red come out. I fell again and I saw
Annie, and two of them hitting her, and Jake on the ground
with the others pulling him back and beating him on the
face, and saw blood from his mouth and nose, and the
religious nut screamed and screamed somewhere but I couldn't
see him. All of them came down on me all of a heap and
dragged me along, about five of them hanging on. Jake was
saying, "The hell I will, the hell, lift it yourself you bastard,
you son of a bitch." And then I thought how funny it was,
how they were going to kill us and Jake had said don't take
it, it'll kill you. I started to laugh. They punched me around
the head and l still couldn't stop. My knees went under and
I sat down in the dust and laughed and laughed. They got
me on my feet and I went down again, and then up, laughing, and they had to carry me with my arms all limp, and
laughing. Because it was coming from the center and bloom-
ing out, enormous all the way through the world making
my arms and legs all laughing too, like my face.

After that I didn't mind, about anything. I thought I had
blood on my face but I didn't feel the hurt, and we went
forward, the crowd shifting place and changing size, and
I'd stopped laughing but I was happy, happier than I knew
it was possible, and liking the noise and thinking what a
fool I was never to take that stuff before, because I didn't
know there were such things in the world and how it makes
you feel, so fiercely happy. The procession went on, seeming happy and joyous, as if we were going to some wonderful thing, and all of it more beautiful and exciting than
anything else that had ever happened or anything to come
after it in the whole history of time. The people and the

noise bright and singing and lovely, and strangely wonderful. I could see the sound, real, and I could hear the
shape of the people and what the colors did, the inside of
me out and free and the outside beautiful and changed, like
being a god, and felt good and thought I never knew what
it meant before.

Then I was standing and I saw Jake's face altered and
large, far away and then near, and the sun and the sky, and
a soldier near me.

"There," he said. A lot of people came up close and the
military pulled me down to the ground and then everything
stood still and at peace. I looked up and saw a soldier's face,
I saw the sun on his cheekbone and his eye, spoked with
light, perfect and close. I saw him take his arm against the
sky and then there was a scream, and I knew it must have
come from me though I didn't feel the hurt. But I looked
at my hand and there was blood. I heard praying, and I
thought it wouldn't be so bad after all.

The holes were there and the stones and they got the
ropes on. I started to go up.

"Clear the area," the officer called. "Clear the area."

I went up and I went up and then I fell, all at once I fell.
And it began.

You always think it can't go on, it's got to have an end.
And I thought maybe I shouldn't have taken those leaves
because they say that's what's wrong with it: it lifts you up
but it drops you down afterwards lower than you were
before. I wondered if that could be why and that was why
it was hurting so much. I thought: could it go on like this
to the end, never getting less but always more and more?
Jake was there and the religious nut, and Jake called, "Good-
bye, Seth," and I shouted, "Good-bye, Jake." Then he
called to the religious nut, saying, "Good-bye, put in a good
word for us when you get there," but he didn't answer.

They say it usually takes three hours. To me it seemed to be more like three days. I passed out and I came back again and I imagined I saw the light go and the stars come out white, very bright and pure. And I could hear my breathing, loud, reaching, as if I was trying to swallow all the cool darkness and its many stars which make you feel so strange and yearning to see, all of them so small and so many and not touching but looking as if there's a life there and a special thought in the way they are spread, specially right and like it could be no other way. It seemed to me I saw the dawn and that I was stiff as though I'd been sleeping in the dew, and that I was wet from making water in the night but hadn't known when it happened and couldn't believe I'd slept, because of the pain.

That was growing more. You hear, they always say, nobody can hurt you that much because when the pain is too sharp your body protects you and makes you numb against it so that the bad part only lasts a short while and after that you know you are over it and it can never be so bad again.

But this was more. I lost the feeling in my arms. Not numb. They had a different feeling now. A no-feeling. And the no-feeling hurt like they say of people who lose an arm or a leg: they will complain of terrible pain in the limb that is no longer there. I thought now, yes, it's happening, and this no-person is coming over me, starting at the edges, and I can feel him coming more and more, closer to the center of me where I still know who I am.

I remember the sun and what it did. Sometimes there were tears on my face, I think, and sweat all the time, and I was half blinded, trying not to look but wanting to now and then to make sure I could still see. Drying up, my eyes were drying up and no place to turn my head. Once there was a vulture moving slow in the air above me and I thought: not my eyes, not my eyes. And I shut them though it would have been no use. There is always something to lose, something that can be taken from you. Even at the end you don't think this is going on forever; nothing else does, so this has to stop too, you think, and at the end I'll be well again. Even when you know.

Three days and two nights I thought it lasted. Pulling and pulling. And a wind roaring in my ears. Not the sound of the crowd—that's my blood going by, like you can hear it jumping in your ear when you lay down your head to sleep.

I tried to moan then, but my voice was taken in my breathing, stretching for the sky with my mouth open and all dry down to my throat and beyond, drying up and burning out like grass on the hillsides in high summer when the sun stands hard above and kills the green out of them. First they go brown and then like ashes, gray. And lastly they are bone-white, skeletons that were once gardens, and the dust blows from them.

I tried to look, to see Jake, but it was like looking into a wall of brass. My eyes opening, heavy and swelled, the glare striking deep into them, and closing up again slowly and not able to shut tight. I thought: it's too late now, I can't call, and it's too hard to look, eyes turning to leather and the no-person weighing down on me, blood falling through my ears.

I thought I heard the other one, the religious maniac, screeching high and thin into the air. And then I heard him clearly. He was starting to pray again, quoting that psalm, saying, "My God, my God, why hast thou forsaken me, why art thou so far from helping me and from the words of my roaring?" And I heard Jake, from where he was, cough. And then I tried, my eyes wincing back from the light, to look, and I saw Jake heave himself and yell, all strangely misshaped like he was singing, "God almighty, why can't you pull yourself together and take it like a man?" And I blacked out again, not knowing whether he'd meant it for himself or for the other one.

When I came to, I thought it must be either dawn or sunset, the air still and calm, and I could open my eyes on it and see.

There was a terrible sound coming from somewhere. And then I placed it: the sound I was making in trying to breathe.

The things I knew now, it would almost have been worth it to find them out: how important it is to breathe. You gulp in the air, you fight for it and try to hold onto it and there is no holding.

Strong in the chest, that made me need food. But I knew now, all the things you need in life have to be stolen from somewhere, from the earth or from other people—food, water, warmth, you need them to live. But they can be taken from you. And you can live for a while and can come back to health after you have had fire and food and water taken from you. But the air—take away all the air just for a few moments and life is over. It is death to take that away, because it is free and freely there, the only thing in the world that is truly free. And you live on it as much as you live on food, but do not realize.

I thought I would look down for the last time. But something had happened to my neck and my head; I thought somebody must be holding me and pressing something against me there. I tried to move, and my face was like stone, and all the parts that could make it turn, like iron. I tried and I forced. And I tried it until it worked, stone coming into motion, iron bending, my head sideways, and I could look down.

I saw the hills and the trees and the city beyond, and below me some of the crowd still huddled behind the guards and some looking up, I thought. A shine came off something, a weapon or a helmet, and as I looked to see what it was, a breeze lifted the corner of a soldier's cloak and threw it back over his shoulder, showing the scarlet suddenly like a bird turning wing. I thought: quickly, turn your head back, quickly, or it will stay like this and you won't be able to look up again.

This time it was harder and took much longer. When I had my head up again my eyes were on the religious nut. He was dead by the look of him, and he looked at peace and beyond the moving of any pain. He looked somehow better that way, stretched out, better than he'd looked when he was alive. Being all skin and bones, he seemed to look right there, as though he'd meant to be there all the time and his body had fulfilled itself in the shape it took when he died.

Then I looked at Jake, and a smarting came into my eyes, needing tears. He was dead, you could tell, but not like the other one. You saw the agony of it on him, all of him, the strong body and the open-mouthed face, swollen, wrenched, disfigured with pain. And looking desecrated, shameful to look at, like butchers' meat if they did that to men. I wanted to cry aloud to him, and saw him like it was my own soul I was looking at but more than my soul. And wanted to call to him though he could not hear, hanging as he was bloody-armed from the cross and dead as the other one against the other cross that stood between us on the hill.

I was the last. And this is the last thing, I thought, the last I'll ever see.

I was looking at the sky. I saw it and I knew it as no man ever saw it before, looking into the heart of it, as no other man will ever know it.

I'd never noticed before just how it is, how it is a face that looks back and looks with love, and is arms that open for you. How sweet and calm it is. How blue. How it is lovely beyond belief and goes flying away into farther than can be known. And it goes on like that, on and on. Forever and ever. Without end.

The Man Who Was
Left Behind

Mr. Mackenzie sat in the park and dreamed of Mexico.
There were four green-painted wooden benches set in a
semicircle around a patch of scrubby grass. Beyond the
grass rose a high brick wall, the boundary of a squeezing
outcrop of tenement houses that swelled forth into the air
as though they had either taken their unplanned mushroom
growth from the steadiness of the wall or possibly come like
a tide from far away in search of a wall and might some
day break over it. He imagined that the wall, brown in color
and made of fine, small bricks, had been there before the
rest of the surroundings. Perhaps it might have been the
last upright of a mansion burned by its owners or by north-
ern troops a hundred years before when that part of the
world was countryside.

The green paint was bubbled and flaking off the benches.
During the months he had known about the park he had
never seen anyone official around the area, no repainting,
no planting or weeding had taken place, nor was there a
waste bin to fill or be emptied. The spot lay in one of the
poor districts of town. Possibly no authority knew that it
still existed.

Occasionally a cat or dog would stray into the cramped
space to sit in the sun which except for the direct downward
focus of the noon hour fell unpredictably, making its way

from uneven rooftop landscapes and deviously notched streets
to light now here, now there over the bunchy, long-bearded
grass. One day, presumably during a school vacation, a
group of four small boys tried to make the park a play-
ground. They lasted a day and a half and then gave up.
Without a word even among themselves they came to the
conclusion that it was impossible to claim possession in the
face of the owners.

For the park belonged to the three colored hobos who sat
on the other three benches. On his first visit he realized
that they were in permanent occupation. If they were to
leave the place for a month, when they came back it would
still be theirs as though they had never gone.

That first day when he came back to look and found it
and stepped through the entrance he had felt something go
through them slowly like a water level rising and then holding there as he sat down on the remaining bench. He felt,
but forgot. They made no move to show him what they
thought. What was happening among the three of them was
so strong and obvious that it needed no expression. They
simply looked at him without looking, waiting for him to
go, knowing that sooner or later he would be submerged
by the wish and feel that he was out of place. But at the
time he had not noticed. At the time he merely thought of
them as "the other people" coincidentally stationed in the
park to which he had been drawn. Only afterwards, after
a few days, he remembered them and guessed what had
gone on in their minds and what strategy they had used
towards him as, so he later discovered, they used towards
other intruders.

He had seen the entrance around a street corner and
thought: if I can find my way back to it tomorrow I'll go
in and sit down.

Places you see in a town when you are walking without
aim have a way of disappearing. Sometimes it strikes you

that a certain arrangement of steps and balconies is Renaissance Italy, that a segment of gallery railing seen through
leaves is part of a French colonial villa. But when you look
for those times and nations the next day, there is only the
jumble of today's buildings with the washing hung out and
a full-rigged harbor of television mastheads unsailed and
stiff against the moving sky. The more you look, the more
familiar and reasonable appear the obstacles against what
you are searching for. Soon you believe it was a trick of
the light as you turned your head.

He had walked by the entrance and seen part of the wall,
clung to by creepers and brambles, and against them a tangle
of bushes and a few small trees, one taller than the rest, a
kind of palm. It was this tree with its awkward windmill
leaves that suggested the thought of the tropics and of Mexico. And when he had sat down on the bench, he set himself
the task of bringing back the full flavor of that first look by
concentrating on the object which had given the hint.

He screwed up his eyes and looked directly at the tree.
Then he found out that it was not necessary to contort the
expression. The best effect was achieved by staring with
the eyes wide open, looking and not looking, a trick of mind
as much as of the vision. It seemed a wonderful discovery
in the beginning, and he felt the way a child feels when he
discovers that by wanting to, you can look at something
close and blur the background, and then wish your eye to
change its focus to the background, blotting out what is
near. The eye by itself has always been able to do this trick,
but the marvel is in first knowing that you can wish it into
happening. Not two years before, Mr. Mackenzie had heard
a friend's grandchild declaring to his mother that he could
see atoms with the naked eye. "You look right up into the
sky and you can see them moving around," he explained.
"I bet I'm the only person in the world can see them without
a microscope." The parents had told him that he must have

been seeing the reflection of cells on the retina, it was not
an uncommon phenomenon. It seemed a shame. He remembered the confidential tone and the awe in the boy's
voice as he had said it: I can see atoms. Mr. Mackenzie felt
like that the first time.

He could see Mexico all at once emerging beyond the
sorry bushes and weeds and spatulate, hangdog leaves of
the tree against the wall. It seemed wonderful and extraordinary in the beginning, to have the knack of doing it,
making a breakthrough that no one else had ever imagined.
Later it became natural. He would sit there looking and not
looking and go out to the tree, the bushes, the wall, and
through it into Mexico.

They had taken the trip to celebrate his retirement. He
and his wife. Margie and her fiancé had come too, and Jim
on his own without his wife or the adopted children. They
visited the ruins: solid, heavy triangles and trapezoids and
steps. There was sun on their heads. And he remembered
the jungle. Even when not in sight you could tell it was
there and recalled it afterwards like a scent bound to a
certain part of your life or a special kind of weather or a
town you have lived in for a year and never returned to.
They used to sit in the square two streets down from the
hotel; a band played, and he remembered the flowers and
the trees in the square and the peace of sitting near a green
place, like sitting near water.

Margie and her young man—what was his name? Harvey,
something like that. They bought ponchos, the man behind
the counter telling them about the quality of the material
and how it was made, how it was like no other. They tried
them on right there in the street and laughed, and bought
several. But Mr. Mackenzie did not think the shape of the
thing went with their faces. You ought to have been an
Indian to wear them. And you had to be an old man to
know why wearing Indian clothes didn't make you an In-

dian. One day he stood with Betty in a tourist office and there was a loud sound of cars braking outside, like a squeal of pigs. "Look at that," said the man behind the counter, who was also American. They looked through the glass wall and saw an Indian wearing a poncho and walking across the stalled street. "They're a terrible problem. The don't understand any of the traffic rules. And they have this inborn fatalism—they figure you die when your number comes up, so they never take any trouble to avoid accidents. Just step right off the sidewalk into the street anywhere, any time when they feel like getting to the other side."

He liked the Indians. And the weather; sunlight as strong as iron, and then for a few hours in the day, every day, it would rain. Really rain, coming down so fast and close that it had no quality of rage, so much of it and so intensely that it had to be accepted as natural, coming down as though something had broken up in the sky. That was one of the strange things about Mexico—you accepted it as natural, knowing that behind all the extremeness of life there, the colors, the weather, the temperature, the people, was something absolutely objective, impassive.

He remembered the beautiful fruit and cooking in the streets, but they all decided from the start never to eat anywhere except in a restaurant. Not healthy. Then Margie and her fiancé came down with stomach cramps. He felt fine. He wondered whether they had stayed behind in order to be alone in the hotel, and the thought pleased him. But later in the week his wife caught whatever it was, and after her Jim had it. He, the old man, retired, was the only one not to catch it. He had not even felt the altitude.

There was a man who made guitars, a delicate business involving mathematical calculations as to the spacing of the fret-bars. He had no tools for measuring, perhaps knew no higher calculations than counting from one to ten. He spaced the instrument by eye.

"Will you look at that," Jim said. "I'd say that's pretty damn smart. What do you think, do you think Billy could stick with it and learn to play it?"

Betty said she was afraid Billy might be too young. Margie thought he'd probably be old enough, but wouldn't the noise drive Alice crazy? Jim supposed so, and they went on with their stroll but he turned back twice to watch the man at work. Mr. Mackenzie thought: I was the same buying the electric train set for him at Christmas how many years ago. Fathers and their children. Even when the children are not really his. You could see he wanted the guitar for himself as he used to be when he was a boy.

"Buy it anyway. He'll grow into it in a few years."

"I think maybe I will. There's only one trouble with it, that's the wood. Best guitar wood comes from Spain, I hear. But to begin with—what do you think?"

"Go ahead, buy it."

Jim had a camera with him that hung on a strap from his shoulder. He took a picture of the hotel, of the square, of the woman selling tortillas at her stand by the red flower bed, and of the man who sat on the pavement and made his guitars while Margie and her young man watched him, wearing their ponchos just that once because otherwise it was too hot. And he took pictures of his father and mother standing in the court where the Mayans used to play basketball. Over to the left, Daddy, no not that far.

Betty said, "Honey, if you want to take it in the sun like this, I'm going to have to put on my glasses. Hold this for me, Charlie."

"All right," he said, and took the packages she handed to him. "And now if you'll hold this for me, I can get mine out, too."

"But if I'm holding all these things, how can I—oh Jimmy, you didn't take it then, did you?"

They laughed, and there were more photographs. He

hated having his picture taken, but that day it was all right except for a moment, when Jim was saying no Mother over there and you Daddy that's right now Daddy no a little to the right there Daddy, and he felt a sadness, knowing that Jim was not his favorite son.

They had come through everything and out the other side into holiday and reunion, to being a family together in a strange land. Margie would be married soon and have children, not children to carry the name, but that no longer mattered. Just that they were real grandchildren. Before they left for the vacation his wife had said, "This house, it gets bigger every day." But what was the sense of moving? Especially since Margie had told her mother she wanted to have children right away. That would fill the house again. It was good to have come through and have a sense of the future there for them. Just for that one instant he had thought about Ben who was dead. And about Jim's first wife.

They walked around the square in the morning and his wife called to him, "Oh Charlie, come look at this."

"Ee, what awful things," Margie said, and clung tighter to her fiancé's arm.

"Can you beat it?"

"What are they?" he asked.

"Spiders on cards. They wear them like a brooch. I saw one the other night when we were in that restaurant with the fountain, and wondered what it was. Boy, wouldn't Alice love one?"

"Like a hole in the head. Look at your mother, look at Margie. They don't like it either."

"But it's too much. I'm going to buy one anyway. I wonder how long they live."

The man who sold the spiders explained to Jim how long the lifespan was likely to be and how to take care of it. They walked on. Jim pushed the card under Margie's nose.

"You aren't afraid of a little old spider, are you?"

"Oh ugg, Jimmy. Oh barf. Get that horrible thing away from me. For heaven's sake, Daddy make him stop."

She let go of her young man and came to him, crouching up against his shoulder while Jim darted the card at her. It was as though they were both children again. Like going back all that time to when Ben was still alive.

Later in the day he began to feel unwell.

"Let's sit down for a minute," he said.

"Don't tell me you've finally got the bug," Margie said.

"I think maybe that's just what it might be."

They sat down at one of the tables in the square. His wife sat next to him and put her hand lightly over his wrist. He looked out to where the people were walking by, and they seemed to be going past him behind a block of water.

She said, "Miserable luck. We'll just sit here for a couple of minutes and if that's what it is then you get right to bed. Remember what happened to me just because I wanted to get up? That's the way it works—you feel much better all of a sudden but you're not. It takes about forty-eight hours."

A waiter came up and stood by the table. Jim ordered a beer and the young man thought he'd have one too. "Do you want one?" he asked Margie. She said, "No, I'll just have a sip of yours," and he put his arm over the shoulder of her chair. She leaned back into it and said, "Poor Daddy." The pit of his belly clutched together with cramp.

Jim said, "I thought you couldn't be made of sterner stuff than the rest of us. They tell me it's called the Aztec Two-Step because it comes on so hefty it takes you just two steps to get to the john." The beer came and Jim lifted the glass to his mouth, tipping it into the sunlight and making the beer look larger than it was, hanging in the air and corn-colored. Sweat came out on Mr. Mackenzie's forehead. "I think I'll go on back to the hotel," he said.

"I'll come with you, honey."

"No, no, you all stay there. I'll be fine. See you later."

He went back to the hotel, undressed, and stayed in bed all afternoon. The cramps became worse, stopped, and began again. He tried to read a detective story and then tried to sleep. When his wife came in she said, "How are you feeling?"

"A little better. I've been trying to read. Where did you go?"

She told him what they had done during the day.

"I think I'd like to get up in a little while."

"Certainly not, don't you dare. You stay right here. I'll stay in tonight and read up on that place we're going to on Thursday. Darn, there goes another nail, I think it must be the climate."

"No," he said, "you go on out with the others, enjoy yourself. I tell you what, when you're all ready to set out, we'll all just go sit in the square for a few minutes and I'll have a cup of coffee or something with you."

"I told you it comes and goes."

"I'd just like to get out for a little while. Then you go on with the others. No sense in staying here. Did I stay in when you were sick? Where've you all decided to go tonight?"

"We thought we'd go back to that nightclub where we saw the bullfighters at the next table. You know, the one with the good band."

"That one. I remember."

"I'll go down and see if that man's there behind the desk and get them to send you up some soup and crackers later on."

"Last thing in the world I want."

"I know, but you must. Otherwise it takes an extra day before you feel like getting on your feet again."

"I couldn't look it in the face. Honestly."

"Just something light. Now don't make a fuss," she said, and went out.

Later, in the evening, but still light enough to see, they sat together in the square. The women were wearing silk cocktail dresses. His wife had brought a fur wrap and his daughter kept a light wool coat over her shoulders, for the nights were cooler than one would have expected. He did not talk much although the others kept up an animated conversation. They let him sit there with them without fuss, without pestering him about his health. And then they parted, he to go back to the hotel, they to continue on to the nightclub. As he walked back, he took another look into the trees. The trees in the square were like the trees and bushes in the park: if you left them they went back to jungle.

Usually the remembrance of Mexico came to an end at this point and he would leave the park or join in talk with the three tramps. His recollection seldom pushed him past that evening, and on the few times when he had gone beyond it, the pursuit of thought had not been carried out willingly; he had found himself trapped in it, immobilized. Mexico ended when he walked back to the hotel that last night.

Only sometimes, hideously quickly, he saw the rest rush past him—waking up in the morning to find that they had still not returned to the hotel. Being sick but going down to talk with the man at the desk who didn't understand. And a friend being brought in, he gesticulating and holding his stomach, saying he was not well and he imagined at first that they were just having a late night, although now it looked as though they couldn't have come back at all. Where had they gone? Some sort of nightclub that had a restaurant. The name, began with a *T* he thought, though maybe not, maybe that was another one, maybe it began with an *S*. If he heard the name again he'd know it. The friend of the man at the desk said something, was that the name? Yes, that was the one. Oh señor, you will sit down please, you are not well. And he made a telephone call, and talked into the receiver for a long time. What was it, what is it, is something wrong? Please señor, one moment please, I am trying to find out. And hung up and made another call. Señor Mackenzie, I must tell you, it is on the radio this morning . . .

And you read about that kind of thing all the time, about earthquakes, floods, fires. This one must have started in much the same way as the great Coconut Grove fire, with the curtains catching and a panic and people trampled in the push. But this one seemed to have been more complete, since hardly anyone present in the club had suffocated in the smoke. Those who got away were bruised, in some cases had bones broken; those who did not get out, burned. The catastrophe was later to cause a tremendous furore in the press, as the survivors alleged that after the initial storming of the exits, the management issued orders that the doors should be locked so that no one could get out before paying. In a matter of weeks the case was brought to court and the staff, owners, and management acquitted. A hundred and thirty-four people died.

The hospitals (the first telephone call) had no patients of the name Mackenzie on their lists.

They took him to the nightclub. It was a hot day and people walking on the street again looked as though they were moving behind water or perhaps the waves of fire. His head felt cold and he was sweating. He staggered when he got out of the car. And inside they asked him questions. Do you recognize this woman, señor? Could this be your wife? Could this be your son? Does this look like your daughter, señor? The police were there in uniform and other people like himself, and newspapermen and a crew of men in their shirtsleeves, removing bits of débris and taking the bodies away in large wicker laundry baskets. There was the smell of fire. Everywhere. He kept saying, "I don't know," and "I can't be sure." And the police asked: What jewelry did your wife wear? What make of watch did your son have on? Can you describe your daughter's engagement ring? And the young man, do you remember his watch? Yes, he had an old-fashioned pocket watch, it was his grandfather's, he told me. "It is difficult, you understand," said one of the policemen. "Some of the rings, they have melted."

But they were found at last, all four; two at first, and the other two had to be identified by sending back home for dentists' x-rays.

"Coming out, Lucky?" one of the hobos called over to him.

"Not just yet. I'll set a spell."

He watched the three of them go. From the houses behind the wall a smell of grease and vegetables came to him, now perceived and now not as the wind changed. The branches of the tree flapped, making a noise against the wall, and he stood up.

He thought he would have a drink.

Before he found the park and met the hobos he used to spend his days in the bars, going from one to another in that long street which was like a street that might reach all the way around the world, every bar the same and the neon lights going even in daylight. That was before he learned what made him feel at ease. He had tried to talk to people then and once picked up a woman. But when they got to the room, the walls jerked in front of him like the walls in the nightclub and he thought how stupid it was not to realize what it would be like: the sprung, creaky bed, sheets that hadn't been changed from the time before, and the woman herself as she undressed and the clothes came away like the store wrapping on an uncooked chicken, a large piece of meat sitting down on the bed and nothing to do with him. He got as far as removing his shirt, and he kissed her, but he did not like touching her and knew it wouldn't work, it was a mistake to have thought it would. He finally said,

"I'm sorry, I thought it would be all right. I'm too old for this kind of thing any more." And she said, "Relax, sugar. Like they say, you're as old as you feel. Come on, I'll help you along." She put her arms around his neck; he remembered a story about a girl who danced with a mechanical robot which went berserk and smashed her against the wall—this woman, made of mechanized flesh. He said no, truly, he hadn't been feeling very well lately. "Suit yourself," she said, lighting up a cigarette and looking mean, as if about to tell him, You're not getting out of this room without paying me for my wasted time, mister. He put on his shirt again, gave her something for her trouble, and said he'd buy her a meal. But that had been a mistake, too. She had wanted to talk.

Now he knew, and now he could always go to the park. Before that he had gone to places and done things without knowing why—sitting in the waiting room at the railroad station, or driving out to the airport to sit there. He knew now that he had done those things because he wanted to be where there were other people, but not to talk to any of them or to be alone with them. He liked to sit there and not have them bother him, have them go about their own business.

Dr. Hildron had seen him on the street one day, a month after the house had been sold.

"Charlie," he said, and looked concerned.

"Doctor."

"We don't see much of you nowadays, Charlie. How about coming down to the club, having a round?"

"Thanks," he said. "Everything's packed up in storage—golf clubs, books, clothes, the furniture. I didn't know what to do with it all. Thought I'd just keep it there till I decide."

"Where you living now?" the doctor asked.

"Oh, some cheap hotel. Over there." He threw out his arm in the general direction of the hotel and began to cough.

The doctor's eyes became sharp, clearer than they had been. What does a hawk's eye look like when it sees a sparrow down on the ground? The look that goes with professional interest is a special look, full, absorbed, riveted, almost like the look of love at first sight.

"Don't like the sound of that cough. Why don't you just drop in and see me about it? Wednesday? Thursday?"

"I feel fine."

"Don't leave a thing like that." He wanted to know how Mr. Mackenzie was living and what he was eating and if he was still off the cigarettes. He thought he should get himself a decent place to stay, just until he made up his mind about things, and someone to look after him—a house-keeper or a cook.

"Bessie's not earning much. She might be glad to take on the job."

"Bessie?"

"You know, *Mrs.* Rider," he said, and laughed.

"Oh, sure. I remember."

Bessie worked behind the bar at the clubhouse. She was there one day when Mackenzie came in from golf with three of his friends, and he went up to her to order drinks while the others sat at a table and went over the day's scores. "Three beers and a Coca-Cola, please—" he started, and then he forgot her name. It vanished away from him, leaving only a dark hole where it had been. All he could remember was that she was married to Spelly Rider, so he said, "Three beers and a Coca-Cola, please, Mrs. Rider." And she seemed to get taller and glow, brighter and crisper than her white apron. "Yes *sir*, Mr. Mackenzie," she said. It wasn't true that you couldn't see colored people blush. After that she always liked him, maybe she always had. She was a nice woman. And she had troubles, he had heard that.

"All right," he said. "I suppose I should see about a place. Seems such a chore. Unnecessary."

Dr. Hildron patted him on the shoulder, the hand knocking against the coat, but no warmth coming out on his body
around the touched place as there used to be when someone
touched him, even lightly. The doctor said he could take
care of it, he'd put out a word here and a word there, and
have a talk with Bessie. He looked into Mr. Mackenzie's
face, saying, "You know we haven't forgotten you, Charlie.
You shouldn't go on like this. And I want you to make an
appointment now about that—"

"Later, later. I told you, I feel all right," he said. And
he apologized for the way he was, explaining that for a little
while longer he felt the need to be alone, and added that
he was much obliged to the doctor for taking the trouble
to see about getting the room. That was back in the days
when he still said such things.

Now was different. Now was better. He learned by himself during the first four days of sitting in the park. And
after that the hobos had taught him the rest.

They let him sit there for four days before they made a
move. Then, while he was still in the middle of Mexico,
the youngest one shambled up to him and, looking at his
chest, muttered, "Cigarette, boss?" Mr. Mackenzie hadn't
heard. He was still staring at the wall. Then the man brushed
him hesitantly on the sleeve. He turned his head and found
the face looking at his face, doing exactly what he did:
looking through.

"Got a smoke?"

"Don't smoke," Mackenzie said. The man turned away
and went back to his bench.

That afternoon he had an appointment to see Bender
about making a will. It came about because of the telephone
and the messages Bessie left for him on the table. He told
her to say he was out, always. After Bender had left eight
messages, he telephoned back and told Bessie next time to

say he'd gone to Chicago or California or some other place and she didn't know when he'd be back.

When he walked into the building the receptionist threw a look to the man standing by the elevators, and he walked up, his arm out to bar the way, saying gruffly, "Can I help you?" No mention of "sir."

"Have an appointment with young Bender," he said.

"Name?" No "please."

"Mackenzie."

"Just a minute." They didn't ask him to sit down, either. The receptionist lifted the receiver on her desk and said, "Sally Ann, there's a man here who says his name is Mackenzie and he's got an appointment with Mr. Bender. Would you check that, please?" She looked over his head while she waited for the answer. Then the man came back and told him, "It's the fourth floor, turn left," which he knew already.

He stepped into the elevator and looked at the elevator boy's profile. Young, he couldn't be more than twenty, good-looking, friendly looking, and stood easily. He looked very healthy. Mr. Mackenzie thought he must be new at the job and wondered how friendly, nice-looking, and healthy he would be after five years of going up and down in his little box, never breathing the air or seeing the sun.

There was a sign up in the offices on the fourth floor. It read: *If you must have a drink on your lunch hour, kindly do not drink vodka. We would rather our clients thought you drunk than incompetent.* A boy carrying a tray of coffee cups passed, saw him standing by the sign, and said, "That's Mr. Buxted, he put that up—he's a real joker."

The secretary stiffened for a moment as he walked in, seemed nailed to her chair, and then rose, smiling uncomfortably.

"Mr. Mackenzie?"

"Hello, Jeanie."

"I hardly knew you with your beard."

"Not a beard. I've just been forgetting to shave. Maybe I'll grow one."

"I'll just tell Mr. Bender you're here."

Mr. Bender. Young Stukely Bender, who was Ben's age; very outgoing, but not smart enough to deserve the job he had. He got it through his father, who had been Mackenzie's best friend. They had been in the war together and after the funeral he thought: people say that, we've been through the wars together, and that's exactly what it means, it says everything.

The door opened and the secretary came out, showing him in with her hand. At the far end of the room Bender could be seen advancing with his hand out to be shaken, his face as the door closed still friendly but rigid. Mackenzie nodded, said, "Hello, Stuke," put his hands in his pockets, and sat down. He hoped they would dive straight into the business. But Stuke just wanted to say how sorry, fiddling with a paperweight on the desk, how very sorry he had been to hear, and Mrs. Bender too, in fact how sorry they all were, and though of course he must have gotten his letter of condolence, what can you ever say except you sympathize, which is true of course, but so difficult not to make it sound like a hollow commonplace.

Mr. Mackenzie had nothing to answer. Something evidently was needed, so he managed a sound, a grunt of assent to show he had been listening. It wasn't enough. Young Bender's round face colored up with annoyance. He had expected more in return for his sympathy. Most people did. There is only one thing pity can do, make you a better person. It cannot help the one you pity. He's old enough to know that, Mackenzie thought. Maybe if he had been in a war like his brother he would know.

"Well then, about the will. Have you thought about that?

I suppose you'll be wanting to set something aside for your daughter-in-law."

"She's no kin," said Mr. Mackenzie. It came out abruptly, even surprising himself. Then he thought: well, it's true enough, she isn't.

"Still—"

"And she's got the insurance money, anyway."

"What about your grandchildren, then?"

"They're not even related to me."

"But when they grow up, education, enough to start a business on—insurance money doesn't stretch that far."

"She'll probably be married again by that time. Besides, her folks are pretty well off. I imagine she'll get by all right."

"Well. Well, let's see now. Daddy said you had a brother, as I recall."

"He died four years ago."

"Oh. I'm sorry. Did he leave any children?"

"Two. The family's rolling in money. They don't need it."

"I see. Any cousins?"

"One or two. Too distant. I haven't seen them for years."

"What about your wife's relatives?"

"There's her Aunt Sophie. I never did like her. And I believe she's got a nest egg she's been sitting on for the past fifty years or so. When she dies she'll leave it for the care and upkeep of that orange cat she's got." Cassandra—the cat was called Cassandra, he remembered.

Young Bender laid down his pencil and swiveled his chair from side to side. Mr. Mackenzie thought: Christ, he's going to tell me that old office anecdote again.

"You know, Mr. Mackenzie, Mr. Buxted told me his uncle once had a client named Mrs. Cartwright, an old lady that owned a little piece of land over near Baton Rouge. One day he calls her in and says, 'You're getting on now, Mrs. Cartwright, don't you think you should make a will just in case? You've got this little bitty piece of land and it should go to somebody. Would you like to leave it to your cousin Sue?' 'Not on your life,' says the old lady, 'I never did like her.' 'Well, do you want to leave it to your nephew?' 'No,' she says, 'I never did like him.' Mr. Buxted's uncle went right on down the line, about twelve people she could have bequeathed something to, and at last she gets up and says, 'You know, Mr. Buxted, I don't believe I want to leave nobody nothing.' "

Young Bender began to laugh. His teeth were larger than you would have thought. When he stopped, the annoyance came over his face again. Mr. Mackenzie was not responding to treatment.

"I think she was right," he said. And then suddenly a great devil laugh burst from him and he said, "I think that old lady was pretty damn smart. And right." Young Bender looked uncomfortable now and fingered some papers on the desk. His hands were trembling slightly.

"Perhaps if you could hunt up the last addresses of your cousins. Any rate, think about it. There's always charity."

Not charity. Sixty-eight percent of what you give goes on advertising and paying the staff and what's left over is spread so thin it's never enough to get any one person out of a hole.

"It's a sizable sum," Bender said. "A very sizable sum," and the eyebrows went up in his round face, staying there astonished at the size of the sum.

"I'll think about it some more," Mr. Mackenzie said.

Out on the street again, he did think about it for the first time. It had not really crossed his mind before the interview.

He thought about Jim's first wife. When Jim went into the army, after Ben, Betty said she'd die if anything happened to him. He applied to be sent to Germany but in the end he was shipped to Hawaii instead. And he married a Japanese girl. He called her Mitsy, from her Japanese name, though she had been brought up in the western way, speaking English, and had the English name of Lily. Betty took it badly at first. "Think of the children," she said. He did not think it mattered. But there were no children, and two years later Betty told him that Jim had asked her to talk some sense into Mitsy because she refused to have tests done and they should both go together, otherwise there was no point to it. "I tried to explain, but Charlie, she just sat there and cried and cried and said no. I can't do a thing. Maybe you can. She likes you." He had a talk with Mitsy and asked her why she wouldn't agree to the tests. She told him, "Because if I find out for certain that I can't, it's the end of my life." "There could be all sorts of reasons," he said, but she was afraid to find out any of the reasons and he did not insist because he was not quite sure how occidental she really was; she might do something terrible and Japanese, unforeseen, like killing herself because her husband did not consider her the perfect wife. However, she didn't do anything terrible after all. That was Ben. Also, the matter was soon taken out of her hands, since by that time Jim had met Alice. Mr. Mackenzie thought his son was behaving shamefully. But you can't run your children's lives for them. He went to see Misty and talk to her all through the divorce proceedings. He liked her. He wished she were still his daughter-in-law. Three years after the divorce, after Jim and Alice had adopted the first grandchild and were taking steps to adopt the second, she sent him a letter. It arrived just before Christmas, a short letter telling him that she thought of him often and always with gratitude and affection and that he had been right and very wise in all the advice he had given her. A photograph was enclosed, showing her and her second husband, very tall, standing with his arm around her, and towards the camera Mitsy was holding, half as big as herself, an enormous sleeping baby wrapped up in a blanket. Jim saw the envelope lying on his desk. "From Mitsy?" he said. "Can I see it?" He said, because there was nothing he could do, "If you like." And Jim picked it up, read the letter, and looked for a long time at the photograph. Then he said, "Well, that's settled. I was worried about her—she never wrote. But she seems to be happy now. I'm glad. I hope she's forgotten now." And Mr. Mackenzie thought: it took a lot to say that, probably took more than I'll ever know, and maybe he's more like Ben than I thought.

Perhaps he would leave something in his will for Mitsy and her child. Then he reconsidered it and decided no, she was happy, there was no need.

If Ben had lived there would be no question about where to leave the money.

Ben was younger, and his favorite. Not so good-looking as Jim, almost ugly, but more attractive. Brave. It was a thing you didn't talk about and Ben never gave it a thought, but Mr. Mackenzie loved it in him. He went out to Korea with Cal Bender's son Carl, who died in his arms. And Ben was shipped back with one leg missing and the other one off at the knee. They put him in a rehabilitation hospital. He was not ready for it, but the doctors believed it good psychology to place him where he could see other boys like himself who were making the best of their amputations and preparing to begin life again. There was some trouble about getting to see him, and Betty was down with flu, so Mr. Mackenzie went alone. And the doctor took him aside beforehand, telling him that at first Ben had been so wild that none of the staff could touch him, then he went on a laughing fit; it took five interns to hold him until the sedative had been administered. And when he woke up he refused to talk. He had not talked for three days. They had had to put him in a room by himself—the effect on the other patients had to be considered. It was a major battle to get a dose of penicillin into him, he wouldn't eat, he threw things, he was in pain but it still needed more staff than could be expended to change his bandages. Naturally the wounds weren't healing so quickly as they ought to. Mr. Mackenzie entered and looked at his son's head turned away towards the window. He sat down by the bed and put his hand on the boy's head, smoothing his hair which had grown out from being so long in the field and had not been cut again because he wouldn't let anyone near him. "Ben?" he murmured. "Don't say anything," said his son. His voice was hoarse and fierce, hardly above a whisper. "Just stay like that, but don't say anything." Mr. Mackenzie began to cry. He blew his nose and continued to stroke his son's head. He wanted very much to talk, to say even if they'd shipped you home so mutilated that I didn't know you, even if all that was left was something the size of a stamp, I'd thank God, thank God you're still alive. And he wanted to say that there are lots of things to live for, on all levels, small and big. And it could be worse, he might have been paralyzed or blind. But he would walk again and there was everything in the world still there, good friends and good talk, a spring day and coffee in the morning, music, laughter, learning, and he mustn't let it go. And he mustn't also because whatever he thought or wished for himself, he could not be more than he was now and always had been, his father's heart. But Ben wouldn't let him speak. Only at the end of the time, when the doctor came in to say he might consider ending his visit, Ben turned his head and looked at him and he was surprised because Ben's eyes were blue-grey and usually looked grey, but on that day they looked blue. He stretched out his arm and pulled Mr. Mackenzie to him by the elbow. All the strength in him even then— he had always been strong even as a little boy. "Listen," he said in that strange whisper, "you know me, Dad. I can stand anything. Don't mind the pain. Don't care about hurt, I can take it all. I can face it, anything. Anything but this. I can't take this. You understand?"

"I understand," he said. "But you're wrong. You can take this, too, Ben. I know it. It's going to work out all right. It won't be easy, but we're behind you. We'll help."

Ben shook his head. "I don't want it," he whispered. "You don't understand."

"I do, Ben. Believe me. And it's going to be all right."

Ben turned his head away again. He said, "It's the shame." He let his arm fall back and rest on the blanket.

Shame? What shame? Wounded fighting for your country? Decorated how many times—they had lost count.

"Ben, I don't understand. What shame can there be?"

His son wouldn't turn his head again and the doctor stood at the door. Mr. Mackenzie said good-bye and that he'd see him again the next day.

He thought some more about the will and couldn't decide. He deliberated where to go to fill up the rest of the day and found himself walking towards the library. He had hardly ever used the ticket; Betty used to get books from the library. He had all he needed, but now they were all in storage and it seemed too much trouble to get at them.

A young girl was behind the counter, talking on the phone to her boyfriend. She looked up as he came in, gave him a cold look, and turned her back to continue talking. He held the ticket in his hand and stood there, leaning on the counter, looking at the trays of tagged cards and waiting. She let him stay there until at last she thought fit to turn, the receiver in her hand, and said, "Yes?"

"I wonder if this ticket is still good."

She put down the receiver, highly vexed, and came forward, darting a look at the clock on the wall and muttering something about her lunch hour. Only quarter to twelve, it couldn't be time for anyone's lunchtime. She snatched the ticket from him, stared at it, and told him, incredulous and angry, "This card has expired."

"How do I renew it?"

She sighed. "Just a minute," she said, and went back to her telephone conversation, at last saying into the mouthpiece that she had to go.

She produced a card from a drawer, began to write on it, slapped a rubber stamp over it twice, and said, "That'll be two dollars and thirty cents." She watched him with distaste as he got out the money; all his movements had seemed to slow down lately. Her face watching him told him how old and ugly and dirty he was and the Salvation Army should deal with people like that, not someone like her. As she put the money away in the cash drawer he looked at her—once, seeing her hair snagged up into a ball, beehive they called it, and orange makeup. You could see the seam where it stopped, as though you could take hold of the skin there and start peeling the face off. Her lipstick was a whitish orange color too, and there was something on her eyes, the eyebrows above plucked very thin and shiny, looking as though they were made out of metal.

And she thought she was beautiful. She must, or how could she do all that to herself? Her hands had long orange-painted nails that recoiled from him as he handed her the money and drummed on the counter afterwards while she waited for her lunch hour. He noticed that she was wearing a pin on her sweater, a wooden mouse with leather ears, a long leather tail, and red glass eyes.

What things people did, wearing a wooden mouse, wearing a live spider. You hardly ever saw a woman wearing flowers any more. When he was courting he brought Betty flowers and she would wear them. Wear them in her hair, which was long then and done up with combs. You hardly ever saw that any more, either. When you take out the combs how it falls down like ribbons, and braiding it up for the night, he in his nightshirt and still not liking pajamas, wondering how could they say modern youth was so immoral because if they wore those things he didn't see how they'd manage, taking them off and putting them on again all night long. He brought her flowers and chocolates and they took walks. Who took walks now? And you never thought of smoking if a lady was in the room. All the things that had changed. But it was always so, his father having to have the newspapers read to him in nineteen forty-two and saying: in my day cavalry meant just that, you were on a horse, not some new-fangled machine or other. In my day this, in my day that. The children had thought it was funny, but he understood better now.

In Mr. Mackenzie's day he had studied the classics. He thought he would reread some of the works he had forgotten, though he had always had a good memory. He remembered the time he had had to have the operation, it must have been five or six years after he'd passed the bar exams, and the surgeon told him that under the anesthetic he had quoted about two thousand lines of Virgil, and he had thought it was because of cramming for exams all that time ago and imagine remembering it for so long. But now he thought: pretty damn smart of that doctor to know it was Virgil.

He looked for a book in Greek or Latin. They were all translations. The girl at the counter was craning her neck to see what he was doing, if he was stealing the books or defacing them. Suddenly he wanted to go. Unless he was drinking he did not like being inside places for very long. He grabbed a book off the shelf and took it to the counter. He saw as she marked the inside with the stamp that the book was a copy of Marcus Aurelius combined with essays on Greek and Roman Stoicism, a textbook apparently, and that there was a printed notice pasted on the opening page which cautioned all library users not to return the book in case of scarlet fever or other contagious diseases.

In the street again, he flipped through the leaves. The book fell open to a page where the writer commented on the necessity of looking upon death with equanimity and explained the construction of the world and the process of man's return to the seminal principles of the universe after death. No later consciousness, no personality, no afterlife. Just as he had always thought, just as he hoped. A few pages later another author said that the ideal Stoic philosopher should be able to look back upon ruin, to accept the destruction of his property, his house burned down and his family all killed, without shedding a tear.

Mr. Mackenzie closed the book. He did not believe such a thing could ever have happened to that philosopher and he didn't want to read any more. He put the book in his pocket and thought he would return it as soon as possible in exchange for another one.

He started off in the direction of the park and then changed his mind. To the house. He would go look at the house just once again, just to see. He walked slowly. There was plenty of time. And when he arrived by the fence, looking over the grass and garden into the white house, it was like a face looking back at him. He had spent nearly all his life in that house, he was born in it. And his father before him. It was strange to think that he could not walk up the path and go in. What was the sense of one old man living in a large house like that, even if there hadn't been memories? He had had to sell it, naturally. But it was quite a thing to see it again; it did something to his insides like music or books or paintings, though he couldn't yet tell if the effect was good or bad, just that it was strong.

Whoever had bought it had made some changes. They had put up different curtains in the dining room and in the room he had used for a study. That used to be a library—not very sensible to keep a library in the sunniest room of the house. Good for reading, but bad for the books. After his father's death he had moved the books into another room and taken it over as a study. All those shelves, it had taken weeks. Now the owners had changed the curtains. That upset him, he liked the old curtains. He was beginning to feel cranky about the alterations. Other changes too, a blue-painted tricycle leaning up against the toolshed in the distance. And two children were playing on the lawn, two little girls throwing a ball back and forth to each other. A song went through his mind: *They play in their beautiful gardens, the children of high degree.* That was all he could remember, just the first line. One of them was standing on the exact spot where Ben had stood when he and Betty and her Aunt Sophie had looked through the windows and seen Ben, aged about five then, taking aim with his bow and arrow, being egged on by Jim and Carl and Stuke Bender, to shoot the second in the series of orange cats with literary names. And he hit it, too, although the damage was slight as the arrows were tipped with rubber suction cups; they were later taken away because Ben had shot them at the ceiling and they pulled the plaster off in two places, besides making smudge marks on the wallpaper.

He became aware of the fact that he had been standing in front of the house for a long while. The two children were edged up against the tree, peeking at him around the trunk. When he turned his head to look, they dashed out over the grass and ran into the back of the house. A few minutes later a colored girl in a starched maid's uniform came out from the back into the garden, looked over at him, and disappeared. He stayed where he was. Then the curtains twitched at his study window and he felt a small thrill like a twinge of toothache, to see the curtains move in the

room where he used to spend so much of his time, in the
house where he was born.

He turned away and shuffled off down the street, moving
slowly and looking at the flower beds as he went, not thinking anything in particular. It was summer and he remembered many summers, but for the time being no one of them
stood out and spoke to him. He was three and a half blocks
away from the house when the patrol car stopped at the
curb and a policeman got out of the front seat. Another
remained seated behind the wheel, a third sat in the back.

"Going someplace?" said the one who got out.

"Just walking."

"We've had a complaint about you from some folks down
the road. Want to tell me why you were hanging around
those kids?"

"What kids?" said Mr. Mackenzie.

"At number seventeen." He jerked his thumb backwards.
"Back there. The whole family saw you, hanging around
the kids."

"I was looking at the house."

"That's right."

"That's right."

"What for?"

"My house," Mr. Mackenzie said.

The policeman in the driver's seat leaned towards them
and said, "Give him a warning and let's go, Frank. We got
a call." He began to talk into a shortwave microphone.
Noises came out of the radio like the sound of frying fat.

The other one said, "Your house, huh?"

"Used to be."

"Oh sure, sure. Don't try it again. Not in this part of
town, you hear?"

"I heard you."

"Okay." He pulled out a notepad and said, "Let's have
your name."

"Vanderbilt," said Mr. Mackenzie. The one behind the wheel laughed. The other, in the back seat, said, "Okay, pull him in."

They put him into the back of the car and drove off. He let himself be squeezed between the two of them until it struck him how hot it was and how he didn't like being so near. He tried to stand up, and said, "Hold on a minute, I don't want to go anywhere." The one who had the notepad chopped him across the cheek and the other one, who had been sitting there all the time, thumped his fist hard into his ribs. Mr. Mackenzie began to cough.

Later in jail while they decided whether to book him with just loitering and resisting arrest or with drunk and disorderly and perhaps molestation also, somebody jokingly asked him if he wanted to call his lawyer. He said what for, he *was* a lawyer. And while they were laughing Rick Spooner, coming around a corner in the corridor, saw him, did a double take recognizing him, and said, "Charlie, what the hell?"

So then he was out, on the street again, with Rick asking him to have something to eat.

"Can't, I've got to go somewhere."

"Are you sure you're all right?"

"Fine, fine," he said.

He remembered to buy a pack of cigarettes and went into a store where it appeared you could buy most things you'd need in life: fruit, bread, vegetables, sandwiches, candy, papers, magazines, and cigarettes. As he put the change in his pocket he saw, through the window, a serviceman carrying a duffel bag on his shoulder. The bag hid his face, but the way he walked, it looked like Ben. Mr. Mackenzie ran through the doorway and onto the sidewalk to watch the boy move away into the distance, feeling his eye traveling hard among the crowd to latch onto the soldier. And then he saw the bag swing off, turning, and the back of a head, not Ben, because this one had red hair. He felt cheated, running out into the street to look at a stranger. Yet something remained, a kind of tingling all over him, like the time when the phone rang.

The call came through at four in the morning, saying nothing definite except that there had been an accident, and he just had time to answer, "I'm coming right over."

The doctor did not understand how it could have happened. It was hard to understand how anyone could want death that much, suicide so they tell you being a negative action, not a passionate proof of will. And how he must have wanted to die! He had pretended to take the sleeping pills—a child's trick, keeping them in your hand or in the pouch of your cheek like a squirrel. All during the evening he had been quite docile, had talked, said he felt much better, let them change his bandages and give him shots. The nurse on duty had been called to another ward during the night because there was one patient who suffered from screaming nightmares and wouldn't go back to sleep unless she talked to him—the other nurse would not do. He must have known that. He had taken in a lot of information that no one had suspected: where the soap and sheets and towels were kept, the razor blades, the drugs. His condition was such that it precluded movement, so everyone thought, although he was not strapped to pulleys like many of the other patients who had single rooms. As for getting out of the bed, half-healed and with only half of one leg and none of the other, the pain would cause immediate blackout, so they believed. He had done it in spite of the thought and belief and professional opinion, pulled himself along the floor all the way down the corridor to the razor blades, reaching the cabinets God knew how. He made it as sure as possible by swallowing a quantity of pills, torn from the shelves by the boxful, and washing them down with a bottle of rubbing alcohol while he dug at the veins in his wrists and throat.

Mr. Mackenzie didn't know how to tell his wife. He asked the doctor: how can I tell her? And in fact he never did tell her everything, not because she wouldn't have been able to take it, but because he could not bring himself to say it. Hemorrhage, relapse, he wasn't trying to live, he wanted it that way—that was as close as he got. She saw the body, but often people do not see what they are not looking for, and most people only really see the face of their dead, so perhaps she never knew.

After the funeral he held back for two days, all day long, all night long. Then Betty went out, shopping and probably to go back to the graveyard, and he went into the study and closed the door and wept, wept until he thought it would kill him. That was the first glimpse he had of the truth, the reason why Indians step right off the curb into the traffic: because it can happen any time and happens to everyone, since for everybody, for all, the management orders the doors to be locked to make sure nobody gets out before paying.

He remembered that he had forgotten to buy any matches for the cigarettes, and had to go back to the shop.

At the park again he found that he had the place to himself. He sat down on the bench, concentrated on the tree, and went out into Mexico. Afterwards, looking up, he saw that the three had returned. He got out the cigarettes, ripped off the cellophane, and lit one. Then he held out the pack to the one who had come up to him in the morning. The hobo came over, took the matches and cigarettes, and was followed by the other two. They all lit cigarettes and returned to their benches; the one he had given them to pocketed both cigarettes and matches. It didn't seem to matter. Mr. Mackenzie continued to smoke. It lasted a long time and the taste was heavier than he remembered, and the kick in the lungs—the reason why he'd liked to smoke and had had such a hard time giving it up—was sharper, almost like pain. He looked at the tree some more and did not leave till twilight.

The next day he bought some more cigarettes and again offered them around, though this time he held on to the pack. The hobos had brought a bottle with them and offered it to him. He took a long swig and handed it back, thinking that it must be homemade.

After that he began to know them. It was a slow process but there was plenty of time, he was in no hurry. They never introduced themselves. He only discovered their names from the way they addressed each other. The one who had first talked to him was called Spats. He was tall, younger than the others, and at the bottom of the hierarchy—that was why he had been delegated to sound out Mr. Mackenzie. He only understood that later, when he realized how they worked and how they must have regarded him at the beginning

The second in command was Elmie, a small man with a big, square face and a whispery monkey laugh that ran through all his speech and was mysteriously pleasant to hear. The third hobo, the leader, was named Jumbo: lean, white-haired, with a long lantern jaw and a peculiar shape to his head. From the side it was long, from behind you could see the part of the skull which gave the head its length, round as a billiard ball above his coat collar.

The first personal question they asked him came from Elmie, who said, "In trouble with the law?" He shook his head. Later he wondered if they had known about his being in jail that noon for looking at the house. They knew a lot of things but never gave any explanations.

A few days later he was standing on the post office steps. A lot of other men, some tramps and some just passing the time, were hanging around leaning against the wall, some sitting on the steps. Spats was in the crowd but had not seen Mr. Mackenzie, or so he imagined. Two policemen walked by and moved a couple of the men, pointing to a sign that said No Loitering. One of the police took hold of an old man whom Mackenzie recognized as being the younger brother of the man who used to work as his father's gardener. At the same time he gave Mr. Mackenzie a push, saying, "Out of the way."

"Leave him alone," he said. He said it in a terrible voice at first not comprehended as his own. Then he was taken by the arm and the voice came out of him again, saying, "Go away, leave me alone. Can't you find any expired parking meters?" He must have been drunk that day. And then a second policeman came running up the steps, looked in his face, and said, "Why, Mr. Mackenzie, what on earth?" And then he began asking him if he was all right, was he all right, and he said, "I'm fine, just leave me alone," blundering down the steps and away into the street.

He wondered afterwards how much that incident had told against him; the three might have thought he was on friendly terms with the law. But apparently Jumbo had not taken it seriously. For they accepted him and he discovered that he could tolerate being with them for hours or days at a stretch, whereas he could not bear to be long in the immediate company of anyone else.

Sometimes, in the warm weather and when it was dry, they used to sleep out in the open. They got drunk together and slept rough by the railroad sidings, cooking soup in a tin pot. One day Bessie told him that she had found a bug—a *bug*, Mr. Mackenzie—when she'd changed his sheets that morning. He went up the stairs, pulled back the covers on the bed, and looked. He thought he saw something and slapped his hand down over it, but there was nothing there when he took it away. He had begun to see spots lately.

What he liked most about them was their sense of time. He assumed that Spats had joined the group comparatively recently, say two years before, and that Elmie and Jumbo had known each other for a long while, perhaps fifteen years or more. But the assumption might have been false. It was hard to tell. They gave him patchy information about themselves when they felt like it, and he talked or did not talk about himself, just as it came to him, not feeling either curious or anxious to tell.

His hair began to grow long, and his beard. Twice he had cut the hair himself. He did not like going to the barber's because they talked so much even in the parts of town where he would not be recognized, and besides he needed to have the sense that he could get out whenever he wanted to. You wouldn't be able to feel that in the chair, with all those towels around your neck; it would make a fuss if you had to stand up and leave. In the bars they made you pay as soon as they handed you the drink. That way you could go whenever you wanted to, just run out the door without having people rush after you calling, "Where are you going?"

They took their time. It wasn't until a week after he had first talked and drunk with them that Spats said, "Thought you say you didn't smoke."

Mr. Mackenzie said, "The doctor told me to give it up."

"Doctors," said Spats. "Don't tell me about doctors. Doctors and undertakers, don't I know."

And it must have been three weeks after that that Spats explained: "Tell me about doctors, I know. Here's Spats, married man, and she going to have a child. Very unusual case say the doctor. Care and attention, difficult birth, all that. And it come time for the child to be born, doctor says congratulations Spats, I been making medical history with this very unusual operation, but sorry—mother and child is dead and you owe us nine hundred and eighty-fi' dollars. He says. Then the undertaker send his snaky friend, don't

I want the best money can buy for the dearly departed and sure, I just say I'll take that one, how do I know? I just know she dead. Deepest sympathy in your tragic hour, Spats, and you owe us thirteen hundred. My, yes—get it off my bones in twenty years. Melt them down and sell it. Wonder how much would they get."

"When was that?" said Elmie.

"What?"

"When you was married."

"Oh. That was nineteen thirty . . . one. That was."

And one day Spats asked Elmie, "You hear from Blue Siddy?"

Elmie said, "I heard he died. Last year in Louisville, but I don't know." That was the way they thought of time. Maybe in ten years Elmie would be in Louisville and then he'd find out if Blue Siddy was dead or alive.

At some time Mr. Mackenzie had heard or read that the main topics of conversation among hobos were war and politics. The main topics of conversation among these three were guided by Jumbo, who evidently did not interest himself in the subject of war. In fact the only time any war came up was when Spats said that he'd been in the quartermaster corps in the First World War and got all the way to Paris. My war, thought Mr. Mackenzie, but didn't say anything. As for current affairs, the matter of Cuba was raised only once and then dropped, nor did they tax him on the question of racial harmony except once, when it came to light that Mr. Mackenzie was or had been a lawyer, and Elmie wanted to know, "You ever defend any colored folks?"

"Some," he answered.

"For murder?"

"No, divorce, that kind of thing," he said and the subject changed. He remembered Mrs. Bean's divorce which never took place, how hard he had worked on it and how he got into trouble at the firm because he'd overspent the allowance set aside for charity cases. Then after her husband got out of jail he ran off with a fourth woman and she wanted the divorce in order to marry a different, a third, man.

They talked a lot about money, once asking him directly, "You got money?"

"Some, but the bank doesn't like giving it to me." That was true. Every time he walked in there now their faces said: now it's here it's ours, and we don't want you taking our money out—you shouldn't be trusted with it.

Once he considered giving them something. Not bequeathing anything, because they were older than he was. He asked them seriously what they would do with a lot of money, not a million dollars but, say, thirty thousand apiece. They didn't quite know. They could only really talk with deep feeling about other people's money.

But money was a secondary topic of conversation. The main topics came from the newspapers which Jumbo read out loud, holding the papers authoritatively in his great flipper hands with their delicate long fingers. He'd once played the piano in a speakeasy. Also, if he could be believed, he'd been affiliated with the Wobblies and been witness to the assassination of Huey Long.

"Listen here," he'd say, and read out the items for the day, which were all of the same nature and fell into the category termed by insurance companies "Acts of God." Earthquakes, volcanic eruptions, tornadoes, avalanches, landslides, cave-ins, and similar occurrences were Jumbo's delight. During the hurricane season he could hardly wait for the editions to come out on the streets. Then a mining disaster in West Virginia had them all in deep discussion for four days while the men were being dug out and their families listened for tappings within the rock. Mr. Mackenzie wondered if Jumbo had read about the nightclub fire in Mexico. Yes, of course he would have, naturally, opening up the paper and saying, "My, listen here, Elmie, it says here . . ." He thought Jumbo would have made an outstanding newspaper correspondent, in fact he was one, since he interpolated his comments into the text as he went along.

They fell in with each other so easily, but when he thought about it he was still surprised that they had taken to him. Jumbo entertained deep suspicions towards other people, even other tramps passing through or sleeping rough out by the railroad yards. He would not mix with them, nor with the local jobless men who could be found in the big parks or outside the post office. Once they passed a blind guitar player and Mr. Mackenzie, being reminded of the guitars in Mexico, asked, "Who's that?"

"That's Sam."

"Must be bad to be blind," Mr. Mackenzie said.

And Elmie laughed with his soft musical laugh and Jumbo with his short, deep bark said, "Oh sure enough, you know how much that Sam take in every day? Thirty bucks at least," and he went on to describe Sam's method of collecting: standing outside the big restaurants at lunchtime and outside the churches on Sundays, his fattest collecting day. "Sa'day night it's good-bye dark glasses, good-bye raggedy clothes, and there's Sam in a pinstripe suit with a rosebud, one whore on the right arm and one on the left and down to the crap game at Sally Anne's all night long, poor Sam. It's a hard life for some of these guitar players." Mr. Mackenzie couldn't decide how much of the description was true. Jumbo might have said it simply because he didn't like the man's style of working.

When talking about other people's money, Jumbo was willing to forgive a millionaire a lot if he did things with style. His own method of making money had a style of its own if you knew the principles behind it. Mr. Mackenzie had been wondering where they got the money to buy liquor and food and newspapers and sometimes cigarettes. Then one day Jumbo outlined his handout system. He had other systems, too, much more complicated and refined and involving talking to people and trying to interest them in a variety of nonexistent schemes, but that was the one for the immediate amassing of small sums of money to see you through. First rule, go for a courting couple and ask the man for money. He'll want to impress the girl and she will want to think he's kind-hearted. Second rule, don't ask the married man, because the wife won't want to see him spend what she considers is money for her use, and the husband will look at you and think at least you got your freedom and you're standing up all right so there's no reason why you can't work steady like him, and he won't feel sorry for you. Third rule, learn to spot happy families.

"What do you mean, a happy family?" Mr. Mackenzie said.

Jumbo explained, "Happy families is where the woman wants to get you away from her children fast as she can and the man don't want them to see him turn his face from a poor man. Happy families pays the best next to turtledoves."

One day a stranger came into the park while Jumbo was reading the papers. He sat down and stayed there, another white man. He fidgeted with his own newspaper for a time, lit a cigarette, and said, "Nice day," to all of them. "Half dead with loneliness" was Mr. Mackenzie's diagnosis. No one answered him. But he was drunk as well as lonely. Mr. Mackenzie looked at the caved-in hat, the hole in the shoe, the tear at the shoulder, the bloodshot eyes. But he's been to a barber, he thought, he still cares.

"Have a drink?" the man said, pulling a bottle from his coat pocket. They passed it around and Spats held onto it..

The man said, "My name's Homer Conway, bankrupt in the hardware business," and he smiled. "What's your name, friend?" he asked Mr. Mackenzie, who was counting how many errors the man had committed: making the first move, volunteering his name, telling about his past, giving information as to why he was where he was, asking names. He didn't answer.

"Oh c'mon, let's be friendly," he pleaded.

Elmie, in his light, chuckly voice, told off their names, "Elmie, Jumbo, Spats, Lucky Mackenzie." He heard it clearly for the first time. Before that he'd supposed it to be a mumbling of some other word or expression but now he knew that they'd been calling him "Lucky" for the past six weeks. He wondered why and then remembered the first day when he'd brought the cigarettes and it had been a pack of Lucky Strikes.

"Let me have another shot at that too, pal, huh?" the stranger said and reached out his hand for his bottle. He began to tell all of them his life story and they listened gloomily.

"Anybody got a coffin nail?" he asked, looking at Mr. Mackenzie, who was smoking. He threw over his pack of cigarettes. "Thanks, thanks a lot, Lucky," he said, and hastened to return them after he had lit one. Mr. Mackenzie thought: Homer, you're in for a rough time.

Later that day when he came back from the library, the three were sitting in the park by themselves.

"Where's the puppydog?" he asked.

"What's that?"

"Homer Conway."

"Him," Jumbo said. "He didn't belong."

He wondered how they'd done it. Frozen him out by staring and not answering any questions, or by the direct approach: get the hell out of here, white man, this place belongs to us.

"How do you know?"

"All over him like chicken pox, hello my lifelong friend,

thank you this thank you that, can I have my bottle back? He won't be around no more. You see what he done when he got the bottle? Wiped it with his hand."

"Just a reflex action, habit," Mr. Mackenzie said.

"What I say. You got all them reflex habits, you don't belong."

"I think maybe he wanted to be saved."

"Crying for it," Jumbo said, and opened the paper to a very satisfactory account of a flash flood.

That was in the summer. Now it was the beginning of November, and when Jumbo finished reading the paper they tore it into sections and put them inside their clothes to keep out the cold. They were thinking of hitting the road again, perhaps going to Florida, although they hadn't yet decided exactly where. They asked him if he was coming. He said he couldn't tell, he'd have to think it over, he didn't think he could make it but he'd tell them for sure later in the day.

The broken-windmill leaves of the tree bent back and flopped against the wall and he thought he'd have a drink. Or two, or maybe three, because the cigarettes and the coughing made his throat dry.

He had his first drink in a bar where there were travel posters on the wall. One of them showed tall palm trees and sea of a color—he didn't know how they ever managed to get that color onto paper, it was so lovely. Didn't look like the sea he knew, the treacherous sea full of biting creatures and mines and colder than the grave. Painted or printed by somebody who'd only seen it from the shore. That was the way to look at it, from the shore.

He had a second drink and thought: maybe I'm going crazy, everything I look at making me think *that's not true*. What did it matter? Still, that was not the sea. More like eyes, blue eyes.

He walked out into the street again, coughing, and held his coat together at the throat. He passed by a laundramat and looked in through the windows. Really they were glass walls from the ceiling to the floor, and it was funny to think of the people inside like the clothes inside the machines, which you could also look into.

One day he had been sitting on a bench in one of the laundramats and seen a father with two small boys sitting one on each side, leaned up against him. All three were looking into the spinning machines. The place was crowded and the father was the only man there except for Mr. Mackenzie. Perhaps his wife was sick or doing the shopping or getting a divorce. Or dead? No, it wasn't in the father's face. That was in the summer, too, and suddenly one of the boys pointed at the machine and said, "Hey, Daddy, I got a good idea. We could get in there and go swimming." The father didn't laugh, he said he reckoned it would be a tight fit with all of them in there. But you could see, really, he thought it was a pretty good idea, too, and he didn't look so tired after that.

Before he found the park, Mr. Mackenzie sometimes used to sit in the laundramats. Not for long, because he was in the way, with the women taking out the wet clothes and putting them into the dryers and trying to keep their children under control. But he liked to sit there for a while, knowing the street was there just outside and he could get out if he wanted to. He had been told to go from several laundramats. Even in the summer. But especially now in the cold weather, the supervisors kept an eye out for tramps who came in there to sit where it was warm. He'd been thrown out of this particular one at the beginning of October.

He peered through the window. He began to cough and saw spots. He walked up to the glass and put his nose against it, cold, and leaned there, looking in and not seeing the superintendent. But somehow he no longer wanted to go inside as he had while passing.

Next to him on the street stood two women, talking. They both had baby carriages with them and one held the hand of a little girl. Ap-yap-yak-ak they talked. Why did they have to shout like that? Throwing their arms around. People stare at a crazy person muttering and shouting through the streets, but what was the difference? Just that the crazy one is alone, and maybe that's what the word meant.

The mother of the little girl had a bandana over her head and her hair tied around silver things underneath it; small poppy rat eyes, a long lip, and one of those noses that looks as if it's taking offense at what the face is directed towards. He noticed that the little girl was staring at him, sour-faced, the duplicate of the other. Suddenly she stuck out her tongue at him. He had to laugh. She stuck it out even farther and made it sound.

"That's a nice trick. Bet you learned that from your mother," he said.

The child tugged at her mother's stretchy pants and started to yell, tears running down her mean little face, and the mother turned around, shrieking, "What the hell are you doing to my child you filthy bum you dirty old man stinking of liquor too quick Mabel call a cop you lousy—" and so on. The child yelled louder and buried her face in the trousers, wishing it was a skirt no doubt, for he could see that really she was gloating, shaking with satisfaction and glee in spite of the tears. Then the mother pressed her child's head to her thigh, covering its ears with her hands, shouting at him. All those old army phrases of abuse, they hadn't changed since nineteen fourteen. He moved off.

He went to another bar, one he knew well. A daytime bar. At night it was so crowded you couldn't sit down unless you came in early, and then it was difficult to get out, easier to stay there until you passed out.

"Where's Selwin?"

"Off sick," the bartender told him, snuffling. "Everybody's got it. I'm just getting over it."

He had one drink, taking it slowly, seeing spots again and the back of his head tight at the top. He looked up at the painting, the pride of the bar. Lots of men came in to drink there because of the painting—one of the original old-style frontier bar types, a gigantic splayed nymph fully fifteen feet long and accompanied by cherubim and floral sprays. While he was looking at it a woman got up from the end of the bar and moved near him. Not right next to him, but leaving one stool inbetween in case he wasn't interested.

"Got a light?" she said. He lit her cigarette and she went on, "Haven't seen you around here before."

"I'm here now and then. Not every day."

"What's your name?"

"Murphy."

"Murphy, that's an Irish name."

"Russian," he said. "They changed it from Murkevitch."

"Oh yah, you don't say. I never met anybody from Russian ancestry before. How about that."

"Drink?" he said.

"Sure, thanks."

She was a big girl, her face too. Big nose, big mouth, big eyes, big black hair. But friendly. He'd have liked to buy her lunch but then she'd want to talk. First they ask you for your life story, better than a psychiatrist. And before you get out the essentials they're telling you theirs, lock, stock, and barrel. How then they met this really nice boy, real nice and she really loved him, oh not like *that*, nothing dirty like that. Getting weepy which was bad not getting weepy which was worse and made you think of all the men who'd kicked them in the teeth and what a miserable life.

"My name's Bubbles," she said. "Guess why. For two very good reasons, that's why." She opened her mouth and laughed, leaning towards him so that he caught her perfume or perhaps deodorant like a brisk whiff of floor polish. Big teeth too, what they called tombstone teeth.

"Want a sandwich?"

"No thanks, I'm trying to keep it down."

He wanted to go, but a silence fell and became too long for him to break.

"You live here?" she said.

"That's right. You don't come from around here, do you?"

"Nah, New Jersey."

"Long way away."

"You're telling me." She looked unfriendly all at once, slumping lower on the stool, thinking about New Jersey.

He finished his drink and she said, "So what's your line, pops?"

"Import-export."

"Gee, you don't say. What do you import and all?"

"Import bananas, export poker chips. But I'm giving it up."

"Why's that?"

"Trouble with the packing crew. Bananas are all right. It's the chips that are putting me out of business. They keep packing them upside-down."

"Yah? Oh gee, hey, you're pulling my leg, aren't you?"

She wanted another cigarette. After he'd lit it for her he kept looking at the flame of the match. Mexico. He couldn't take his eyes off it.

"Hey, look out, you're going to burn yourself. Are you okay? Let me see."

"Fine, it's fine. It's just that I suddenly remembered something. I have to go."

He hadn't remembered anything. He simply felt a need to go back to the park. On his way there he did remember that he'd meant to return the library book still in his room, and turned back. He then remembered several other things, such as telling Bessie that he would be in for lunch.

He opened the door and there she was, waiting with her arms crossed.

"Hello, Bessie."

"I got your dinner for you, Mr. Mackenzie. It's cold. You take off your coat and come on into the kitchen. I'll heat it up again."

"I'm sorry, Bessie. I just forgot. I had something to eat in town."

She set her jaw, taking a step back as he passed through the hall, and he thought: she's smelled the whiskey and she's saying to herself sure, you had lunch all right, out of a bottle. She didn't like so much any more. It was mainly the liquor that made Spellman run off.

"Save it for later," he said. "I'll eat it tonight."

"You sure you'll be to home?" When he was drunk she did not call him "sir" where she could avoid it.

"I'll remember," he said.

Sad, she had enough troubles already. He felt a pang at seeing her liking for him go. But maybe it was just as well, maybe everyone should learn as soon as possible; about all men, black or white, and women and children too and the rest, like the way little girls learn to count the buttons on their coats to see who they are going to marry—rich man, poor man, beggarman, thief, doctor, lawyer, Indian chief —and all the others, too, the ones who are organized, businessmen, unions, insurance companies, the internal revenue, the church, the government, put them all together and find out it's no use counting on them. Because when it happens they won't be there or it will be happening to them too, all over the world the management locking the doors to make sure nobody gets out without paying.

"All right. You remember now, hear?"

"I'll write it down," he said, and lurched up the stairs, holding onto the bannister and coughing.

"And Dr. Hildron call up on the telephone, about that coughing," she called after him. "He say you get right down to his office this evening. Four o'clock. You write that down, too."

"All right," he said, "all right," and reached the top of the stairs, choking. He went into his room, closed the door and leaned against it, coughing with his head down and his hands up against his mouth. He felt something like a hollowness inside him and a knife going through it. The coughing stopped and he opened his eyes, all the room jumping with spots. He sat down at the table, put his head down on it, and waited until he remembered what he had come home for.

The book. It was lying in front of his face. Plutarch. He hadn't read it, just flipped through it, catching a sentence here and there. That was the way he read everything now. He put out his hand for it. What was that on his hand, had he bumped into something? It looked like blood. How did that get there? He got up and went into the bathroom, to the basin, and washed his hands. Then seeing himself in the mirror he washed his face and rinsed out his mouth. There was blood there, too. He picked up his watch, lying next to the toothbrush. It had not been running for eight months and he had not worn it for three. He put it in his pocket, deciding to set it as soon as he saw a clock, and remembering four o'clock. Then he sat down at the table again.

He needed some paper but couldn't find any. He found his pen and a bottle of ink and thought perhaps he would tear a sheet out at the end of the book. But they'd notice it at the library and there would be a fuss.

I must do it now, he thought, otherwise I'll forget. And he opened the drawer where Bessie put his shirts and un-

tacked the lining paper, a good large sheet of it. He spread
it out on the table, took up his pen, and wrote a will.

He left something for Mitsy and something more for her
child, enough money for Bessie to get a divorce and keep
herself comfortably for the next five years. He went down
a list of people, the names all crowding into his head at
once as though he had remembered them all the time, people
who had need of a small sum of money and would know
exactly what to do with it. Then he left a fixed amount for
flood relief, some more for disabled veterans, left the mis-
cellaneous stocks and shares to be divided among relatives,
writing down the names he knew and making provision for
the ones he had forgotten or not been told of. That still left
what young Bender would call a sizable sum. He put it
aside for the building of a new library, his old books to be
installed in it. And then he thought of everything else in
storage and started to deal with that. At the bottom he
signed his name. He ought to have it done formally and
witnessed, he supposed, but it was too much of a bother
and he'd probably forget. Never mind, it would hold good
as it was. He folded it up and put it in the pocket with his
watch. Then he took up the book and went to the library.

The wind was bitter and made his walking slow. Sit in
the reading room, that was another idea, except that the
place had small windows and he didn't like the thought that
he couldn't get out if he wanted to. He had seen old people
sitting in there for the warmth, but they were not tramps,
all the holes in their clothes had been darned. If he sat there,
probably he'd be shooed out.

It was the older woman behind the counter. He liked her
better than the other one. She had grey hair and glasses
and pudgy hands with normal fingernails. She took his
Plutarch and he went over to the shelves. What he really
wanted was a book that played to him like a tune, so that
he did not feel his eyes scanning on the surface seeing noth-

ing, or leaping from word to word making him turn the pages so quickly because he was finished with the ones that could not hold him there.

He stood between the walls of books and tried to concentrate. His eye was doing the same trick with the titles that it did with the pages, gliding from left to right, from right to left, noticing the colors but not really reading. He must have stood there a long time because all at once the other one was there back from her lunch hour, standing against the shelves, her arms folded, showing the ribbed shapes of whatever wire contraption she was wearing underneath.

"Something you want?" she said, raising her metal eyebrows and drumming the orange nails of one hand against her arm. She was wearing the pink sweater today. The mouse pin was there again, with its red eyes. He wondered if she had bought it herself or if someone had given it to her, if it might be a badge of something in her circle of friends, like a fraternity pin or some other token that young people wore to indicate the state of their emotions or opinions or ideals.

"Looking for a book."

"Which one?"

He stood for a moment longer, then seized one from the shelf and said, "This one will do." When she stamped it with the date he saw that it was a copy of Xenophon and was quite pleased. He made himself promise not to stop on the steps outside and whip through the pages. Several times before he had done that with a book and in less than two minutes had the feeling that he had read it and wanted another one. Once or twice he had gone straight back into the library to get a different one. They didn't like that at the desk.

He put the book in his pocket and went to the park. The tree no longer suggested Mexico of its own accord, it looked like his hands, stiff, old, going numb in the cold weather. He had to will it into looking like a tropical tree. And then for a while he was with the flower beds and spice smells and the sunshine on them as they sat at their table and watched the people walk past through the green square.

Then he was out again, sitting on his bench with the wind blowing his hair down into his face and the others walking in through the entrance. Elmie brought a bottle and Jumbo read them an account of a disaster at sea, a ship with a burning cargo that might explode at any moment. The Captain had been told to anchor it off the coast and the nearby townspeople had complained, since should the ship blow to pieces they might be in danger. They had already been advised to keep their windows open against a possible shattering of the glass. Keep their windows open in November.

"Captain's still on her," Jumbo said. "Ain't that a thing?" He stuffed the paper back inside his coat. Spats wanted to know if the Captain was really duty-bound to stay on his ship when it went down. Jumbo said yes, Elmie said he was supposed to stay on till the very last moment, but when the utmost tip started to go under he was allowed to jump off and swim away. But did they hold it against him afterwards? They talked the matter over.

When the light began to fail, Mr. Mackenzie remembered that he had to buy a stamp, and stood up.

"Coming along?" Jumbo asked.

He shook his head and said, "Can't. When will you be going?"

"Tonight, tomorrow maybe, next week."

They stood up also and all four walked from the park, passing the guitar player and heading towards the post office.

"I've got to buy a stamp," he said and crossed the road,

waving good-bye. They waved back and he thought: that's probably the last time we'll see each other.

The post office was just about to close. He bought the stamp, came out, and remembered that he needed an envelope. He searched through his pockets and found the last month's bill for electricity. Tearing the old stamp off, he crossed out his own name, readdressed it to Bender's firm, and put the new stamp on it. Then he folded up the will and put it inside, tucked the flap of the envelope in to keep it there, and dropped it into the mailbox.

He stood looking at the box, thinking that there was something he had meant to remind himself of. Off in the distance, coming through the crowd of people making their way home from work, a voice called, "Repent." It came nearer, saying, "Repent, the hour is at hand," and Mr. Mackenzie saw a man, looking doubtless much like himself, with long hair and a beard and carrying a large cardboard sign on a stick. Written on the board was the message: *Prepare to meet thy doom.* The man came closer, and because Mr. Mackenzie was the only person in the crowd whose eyes were not turned away, singled him out, looking straight at him and finally coming up and standing next to him, shouting, "Repent, re-pent, the day is nigh, re-pent."

"What for? I'll be dead soon," he said and barged away into the crowd, thinking: what does he know about repentance—no more than I do or anyone else and that's too much knowledge to have to live with anyway. No wonder they don't look at him, a life of repentance would be a lifetime of hell, and if they believe in all that they'll have the opportunity to do all the repenting necessary after death.

He thought he would have a drink. He went to two or three bars and ended up in the one with the frontier nude. The megaphone system was playing conveyor-belt Dixieland and it became very crowded so that he was squashed up against the corner, but when he had somewhere to sit down he preferred the crowd, which made it less likely that someone would speak to him. He could still see the exit, so that was all right. He got out his library book and turned over the pages, telling himself to do it slowly or else he'd have to exchange it the next day. He promised himself not to go through it all because he liked to have something to read before going to sleep.

The pages went by and he followed Xenophon through Persia with the ten thousand. He saw them going through their hardships, trapped in a foreign country, being shot at by the Persian archers, pursued by the enemy cavalry, uncertain as to the direction in which they were traveling. He could almost smell the dust and the sunshine and see the column moving tightly-packed for protection through the brown hills, and all the time being full of fear. He seemed to be watching with them, for raiding parties attacking in the rear, for single enemy scouts that would appear on the hilltops indicating who knew what huge forces waiting to receive them and massacre every last one of them.

Then came the cold and the snowstorm and all the men falling sick and dying, lying where they dropped in the snow, and all the heart went out of the ones who were still alive. Mr. Mackenzie began to cough.

He ordered another drink and was just taking the first sip when he heard a ticking sound. The man seated next to him had an elbow on the bar, propping his head up in the cup of his hand while he talked to his neighbor on the other side. The ticking came from his wristwatch. That was it, Mr. Mackenzie remembered, and pulled his own watch from his pocket and set it from the other watch at quarter to seven. In an hour he would get up and go home to eat the dinner he was supposed to have had at noon. Remember that, he told himself, one hour from now.

He read on. Out of the snow, into lush fields green and gold, asking directions, allying themselves with this man and that. The treachery, the betrayals, the discussions. The sea, the sea, they all shouted, and beyond the sea, home. But more treachery and more betrayals and corruption over money matters and Xenophon losing his grip, having to call meetings, saying he'd give up the command if anyone could prove he'd been at fault.

It was really a pretty good book, he thought. When he'd first read it, a long time ago and in Greek, he hadn't liked it. He'd thought it wholly lacking in psychological interest, not to be compared with Thucydides or Herodotus or even Arrian, and unstylish, just plonk-plonk-plonk we did this and we did that and so-and-so said such-and-such to which Xenophon replied as follows; worse than Caesar. But now he liked it, he was even really reading parts of it and it was easy to understand, simple, only told you the important things: where they were, what was happening, where they were going, how many people were killed, what they had to eat, how many horses were left. Just the plain truth. He thought it a model book and was about to read on when he noticed how thin it was getting at the end—he was near the end and wouldn't have anything left to read late that night. Just this one more paragraph, he told himself, and I'll go back to the room and be there in time and Bessie will be pleased that I remembered. He finished off his drink and read.

A man stood up from the group and said he had a gripe against Xenophon because when the army was all lost in the snow, Xenophon slapped him.

That's a nice touch, Mr. Mackenzie thought. The anonymous man throughout history. Empires fail and governments are overthrown, dark ages come and new learning springs up and there are always these men who can say with pride: I held Napoleon's horse, General Washington hired a boat from me, I delivered a message for Lord Byron, Xenophon slapped me.

He closed the book and put it back in his pocket, looking forward to reading Xenophon's explanation and justification of his conduct. He walked out into the street and thought he must be drunker than he had imagined, for the wind blew him against the wall and he had to put up his hands against it to keep from falling over while he coughed.

He was still coughing, but not badly, when he opened the door. He took off his coat and hung it on the peg in the hall. Bessie came out of the kitchen.

"You see? I remembered," he said.

"Remembered what?"

"I said I'd come home for dinner and here I am."

"Yes, sir," she said. "Where was you at four o'clock?"

"Four o'clock?"

"Dr. Hildron called up here. You never been there."

"I knew there was something else. I forgot."

"He say he coming round tomorrow morning and you be here." She had a spoon in her hand and shook it at him.

When he'd finished eating and put his plate on the sideboard, she came in with coffee, saw the plate, and put it back in front of him.

"The doctor says he see you last week and why don't I feed you right. You eat that up."

"I'm full. Don't fuss, Bessie."

"I do all that cooking just for you and you don't eat half of it."

"All right." He ate some more, drank his coffee, took another bite, and spread around what was left to make it look smaller.

"I believe I'll get to bed early tonight," he said, and saw she was glad that he wouldn't be going out. He took the book from his coat pocket, calling out a good-night to her, and prepared for sleep. When he was ready to get into bed he noticed that she'd taken all the ashtrays out of the room. Did Hildron tell her to do that? He went into the bathroom and found a box of cough drops. The box was metal, so he tipped the contents out and brought it back and set it on the night table.

He smoked in bed and read the rest of the book. When he was through with it he smoked for a while longer, listening to the wind outside. Cold. It would be months before the tree in the park regained its tropical look. He thought, maybe I should go away. Everyone kept telling him that. And he had enough money to go anywhere. But somehow he didn't want to move. He didn't want to be where he was, either, and now that Jumbo and Elmie and Spats were moving on—he thought of the long winter, walking in the cold, not wanting to be inside any one place for too long a time, and the park having to wait for spring to bring back the allusion to Mexico.

He turned off the bedside light and lay in darkness, breathing hard and thinking about the cold.

When he woke up it was freezing. It was snowing, And someone was carrying him, walking through the snow. He wondered what could be happening. Then he opened his eyes and saw the other men, soldiers walking. They had their feet wrapped in hides and he remembered the terrible trouble they had with them because in the cold sometimes the torn soles of their feet would freeze to the leather skins and rip off pieces of their flesh. Then he saw riders and noticed the leather bags tied around the horses' hooves to prevent them from sinking into the snow. Someone passed on horseback and said an encouraging word to the man who was carrying him. The wet snow beat into Mr. Mackenzie's face and he closed his eyes again. He felt himself being let down to the ground onto the snow, so cold that it burned and made him open his eyes. The man who had been carrying him was doing something. Digging a grave, Mr. Mackenzie realized. That's what he's doing, he's digging my grave. Another man walked to where he was lying. He heard the steps vague and swallowed in the flying snow and heard a voice, saying, "What do you think you're doing? That man's not dead yet. Pick him up."

The one who had been carrying him said, "I don't care if he's dead or alive, I'm not dragging him one more step."

Then Mr. Mackenzie heard it: the slap. And he saw Xenophon bending over him. The other man said, "Well, he's dead now," and Mr. Mackenzie wanted to say he wasn't, but he couldn't speak or move. The soldier dropped him down into the grave and piled earth over him and then heaped snow on top of that. The earth was cold but the snow felt warm, like a blanket, and he thought, they're going to leave me behind, I must get out. He tried to move, to scrape away the earth and snow, but his hands moved so slowly. One of those terrible feelings, his wish to get out moving quickly quickly through him and his hands going so slowly. The way it sometimes happens in dreams. But this couldn't be a dream because he could feel everything. He could feel the snow and how cold the earth was, burrowing through it.

And then he was out.

He looked around and it was spring, the snow was melting, and down in the plain the brown was turning to green. They had left him behind, thinking that he was dead. He stood up. Away to the north stretched the great plain with its fields and villages, the hills beyond, and beyond that the sea and home. From somewhere in the sky at a great distance he thought he could distinguish a voice. *Oh Mr. Mackenzie, sir, what happened? Oh my Lord, Lord. Don't move, don't you move. I'm sending for the doctor.*

Let me see, he thought, this is sometime around the fourth century B.C. If I can make my way north I could be at the great Library before Alexander comes to burn it down.

He began to walk down the slopes. No other person was in sight, and his own people must be miles away by now, marching over the hills and plains, green now and full of growing fields, impossible to catch up to. He imagined them as they must have looked disappearing over the farthest ridge at the horizon, the winter sunshine glinting on their helmets, their eyes tired, with the winter still in them. Again he thought he heard a sound that might be water or leaves rubbing against each other, seeming to be saying something like *Charlie, Charlie, can you hear me? You hold this to his mouth, hold that there, we'll need the ambulance.*

But to walk, alone, all the way to the coast—it might take him years. Even if he kept his strength up, there were other dangers to consider, such as the undoubted hatred of the people through whose lands they had been marching.

The wind overhead made a wailing sound as he reached the plains, and a word came into his head: *Oxygen, quick, the oxygen.* A Greek word.

And that was the trouble. The army had marched off and left him, one lone Greek in the middle of the great Persian plains. He did not look like the people who lived there, he did not speak their language, and there was nowhere for him to hide among that enemy country lovely now with spring, that stretched away for thousands of miles into the horizon where the management had locked the doors to make sure that nobody got out without paying.

Early Morning
Sightseer

On the way out of town we passed a white house with an electric pink flowering vine growing over the roof and front. I got out to take a picture of it. It looked like a house wearing a hat and the morning sun made the color shout out. In the background was the ocean, stern but full of luster. This was one of the two times I ever saw it have that purplish look the epics speak about, the wine-dark color. Maybe it was caused by seaweed. The first time I'd seen it that way was at evening, so naturally I imagined it came from the sun's reflection, or the clouds.

When I got back into the car Tilney said, "You and your pictures. Why don't you save the film for something worthwhile?"

I wound up to the next number and put the camera down beside me. Tilney was sitting behind us on the back seat but he kept leaning forward when he had something to say, folding his arms over the back of the seat and putting his head forward so that if I had turned my face around to him we would have been practically nose to nose.

"If I had a good enough camera," I said, "and knew enough about light and the angle you take the thing from and so on, it might make sense. But the postcards they've got everyplace are a lot better than I could do with this. There's no sense in trying to get a good picture out of it."

"Then why take any at all? Specially that. That awful color. Garish."

"Just to remind me. To remind me of what I thought it looked like when I first saw it. Later on when the sun's up it won't be the same. And it's never the same on a photograph anyway."

"Then why bother?"

"Why not?" I said. It was going to be one of Tilney's mornings. So far, with a certain amount of strain, I'd been able to handle them. This was before I'd put two and two together. I thought it was because of the business the month before, and all that being aggravated by the hangovers, and when he'd get this way I'd try hard to remember what he'd been through at the beginning of March, and say to myself that I must try to make things as easy as possible for him.

We turned inland and to the left, passing some nice houses, mostly whitewashed and good-sized, though not really large like some of the villas you came across in town. I thought this was a wonderful place, that some day I'd really like to live here for a while.

"Oh shit, that's all we need," Tilney said.

The driver slowed down and then stopped. Up ahead five men were getting out of a pick-up truck. There was a tree down in the road.

"Jesus, what a country."

"It could happen anywhere," I said. "There was that storm last night."

"What storm?"

"You didn't hear it? Early in the morning. Or late at night—I don't know. About a quarter to four. You can see the branches down along the road."

"Funny, there weren't any branches down out by the coast."

"Maybe they get these local air current things around here. You know, raining on one side of the street with the sun on the other. You get a lot of tricky wind currents on an island."

"Seems funny," Tilney said.

I turned around and said, "Of course, maybe it knew you were going to be coming by this way and just fell down on purpose."

My nose brushed the side of his face as I turned back again. He was looking over to the side and hadn't moved.

"Well," he said, "that's what it looks like."

The driver had his window down and was talking to the men. I couldn't catch any of it. Two of them had lit cigarettes and a third was standing with his arms folded across his chest. The two others went up to the tree. One of them tested it with his foot. There was a lot of running hands over jaws, fingers to the side of nose, pulling of earlobes, scratching of heads, rocking back on heels with hands in pockets. Our driver called out something and the two cigarette-smokers laughed and called back.

"Oh shit," Tilney said again, and flopped back into the seat corner. He started looking for his cigarettes.

"I'll bet this takes all day," he said.

"For God's sake, Rick, it isn't that bad."

"What a country. They're all buddies here, too. Look, they're asking him how much he's soaking us for. That's what they all want, to have a car."

"He's okay, I asked around first."

"You asked around. Your Greek is so good."

"What I mean is I stalled them till they started beating the price down on each other."

"And this guy was at the bottom of the bunch."

"Well, almost. I thought he looked dependable."

"Wait till we get there and he starts to welsh on the price. Looks like a typical Greek chiseler to me."

The driver had lit a cigarette, too. He was looking out the window, holding a conversation with one of the men.

It wasn't very serious talking, just saying something every once in a while and occasionally laughing. He looked like a solid family man who wouldn't try to drive us over any cliffs in order to show what a hell of a man he was on wheels. He'd said his name was Spiro.

The two men in the road walked back to the truck and started to sort out axes and saws. The tree was still attached at the base and I began to wonder if all the leaves and small branches in the road hadn't come off the one tree. Maybe there hadn't been any storm the night before. Maybe I had dreamed it. But there had been a very strong wind, I was sure of that. I'd heard the shutters crashing against the outside of the hotel for a long time.

"You know what these jerks are going to do?" Tilney said. "They're going to dynamite the goddamn tree." He blew out smoke and then French inhaled.

The driver turned to me and said something in Greek and then, "Soon. They make away soon." He smiled and I said, "Good."

"Baby, you've made a conquest there," Tilney said. "Good old Barney, friend of the working man. Oh how I love the prolo-proletariat."

I turned around.

"What the hell is eating you, Rick?"

"Nothing, nothing."

I shouldn't have moved my head. He smiled from four inches away and blew smoke straight into my face, and then laughed. I got out of the car.

Three of the men were now lopping branches off the tree with axes. Spiro got out on the other side of the car and we both watched. The men worked quickly and I could smell the tree as they cut it. All the air smelled fresh, and I began to feel better and tried to remember the sound of his mother's voice over the telephone.

There were other things I didn't want to remember so

much. About taking Diane out the first times. About the time I took her back to the room and he was there. "Is that your car outside?" she had said. I'd seen one like it in Athens the week before and something in me stopped dead to look. But he'd been looking at it, too, and it hadn't even registered. "I know it's a lot to ask," his mother said, and you can hear belief in people's voices. All those pills, she really believed he had meant to do it. And I'd believed it for a while, too. When he blew all the hour exams and got drunk that time and passed out with his head over the windowsill. But that was when we were still living there, the place of the myth: the great myth of her and him. Other people were reading about it and trying to write about it and dreaming about it, but they were living it. Love in capital letters.

Spiro dropped his cigarette and stubbed it out with his shoe. I leaned over and looked through the windshield at Tilney. He blew some more smoke at me and winked. I looked away.

All five of the men were set to tackle the tree. Two of them had already sawn it clear at the stump and now they started pushing, and lifting with the chains. Spiro said something to them and they repeated it, probably whatever the Greek is for "Heave, heave," and that was what they did, swinging it clear of the road. They must have been pretty strong. It isn't that easy to do and it was a pretty big tree. Spiro and I got back into the car. He waved. The men waved back, I waved too. Everybody waved except Tilney and we started off again, past more white houses close up against the road but a couple that had flowers growing out in front. I guessed most of them must have had gardens in the back yard if they had any. I looked back and saw that one of the men had gone over to the truck to back it up, another one was sighting down the trunk with his saw, and the three others were readjusting the chains.

"Ah, the noble life of physical exertion," Tilney said.

I looked ahead and tried not to think. Going around the next corner we nearly hit a chicken. Spiro leaned on the horn and we were all right.

"Chicken dinner tonight," I said, and he laughed, but probably didn't understand. He said something that I didn't get either, so we were quits. A younger driver would have been talking our ears off, but not so sure on the road.

"That's an idea. Better than what we had last night. Tell him to stop and I'll go back and get the chicken. Tell him to try to hit the next one."

"Hell, Rick, this isn't Boston, you know. You run over a chicken here and you pay for it."

"What for?"

"Well, they aren't wild. They aren't part of the natural fauna hereabouts. You see a chicken, it belongs to somebody. Right?"

"Okay, okay. Trust a hick to know. They ought to change the ruling, make them spoils of war or something."

We turned left and down into a shady road with trees growing at the sides. We passed a golden field that had been cut recently. In among the grain were pine trees bent in windblown shapes and the crop hadn't been baled yet, just left to lie in mounds. Around the next turn the road went through an enormous field that had two or three big old olive trees standing in it, and the grass around them was knee-high and looked almost as green as barley.

When he pushed the note under my door, he knew I was in the room. He didn't knock, of course, but I never heard a piece of paper crinkle so much. And I remembered him once saying that pills wouldn't work unless you knew the dosage, because if you downed the bottle you'd just throw them all up, which was what happened. And he'd said that at least six months before.

"Beautiful," I said to Spiro, dipping my head towards the green.

"*Naì,*" he answered me, smiling.

Tilney put his arms up on the seat again. "What's up now?" he asked.

"Just said it was nice."

We had come at just the right time of year. I'd always thought Greece would be dried up and dusty, really bleached out like a desert. But then, just look at that field. This wasn't Greece, of course, but all the same—flowers, grass, bushes, and vines. The nice thing about this place was that they had a lot of water, not like the other islands.

"You just think everything's nice, don't you? Everything's peachy-pie. Good old Barney."

"Why don't you take it easy and enjoy yourself?" I said. "Take a look at it, it really is nice." I'd lit a cigarette and handed one to Spiro and I had the window open. Out in the field a breeze was going through the high grass, making waves. I asked Spiro about the distance and established almost full communication for a few minutes. The air was wonderfully clear, fresh as water, and I felt that I never wanted to get back into a city again.

"You asking him for a date or something?"

"Asking him the distance. About twenty-five more minutes to go, I reckon."

"Ask him if he's got a sister, Barney."

"Lay off, will you?"

"Wait till he tells you how he's always wanted to go to America. Drive a taxi in Chicago, that's what all these characters want."

"Look, what's eating you, Tilney?" I said, and turned around.

"Nothing, nothing at-all. I'm just great." He was laughing close to my face, and for the first time I believed what his mother had said about the medical report.

"Just I'm out of butts, that's all. You got any left or have you wasted them all on plying the lower orders? Establishing firm Greco-American relations, is that what you're doing? Remember, you are your country's ambassador. Don't sell them free enterprise, give them Chesterfield cigarettes and become their creditors."

I made a move towards my breast pocket, but he got there before me, reaching over the seat.

"That's a red-blooded American heart of gold in there," he said, and suddenly my knees shot up and I hit the window frame with the side of my elbow. Through the shirt he had put his hand on my nipple and tickled me.

"Jesus Christ," I said, and threw up my left arm, but he had already snatched his hand out of the pocket and taken the cigarettes. He was laughing like a maniac, trying to get a cigarette into his mouth, and lying far back in the seat where I couldn't get at him. When I looked, I looked at him sideways. I didn't want to see his face. Spiro had stopped the car. He asked me something I didn't catch, the cigarette I'd given him still in his mouth. "One moment," I said to him, and got out of the car and dropped my own cigarette on the road and stepped on it.

There was another open field next to the road, with a few olive trees in the distance and a ditch full of bushes beyond them. I started out towards them and heard Tilney banging on his window and saying, "Hey, where are you going?" as I left.

I had that terrible childhood feeling of wanting to get into a deep sulk: I'll walk away forever and die in a ditch and won't you be sorry then. Halfway through the field it left me. Grasshoppers jumped up from the grass and the olive leaves showed silver as the breeze turned them.

When I got down to the ditch to relieve myself a brown goat jumped up in front of me. It walked away quickly and then stood looking at me with those strange eyes Greek goats have: bright yellow, and they look as though they ought to go with a different animal, some large carnivore

like a tiger. I kept my eye on it because the only animals I
know about are cattle and pigs and chickens, and though I
didn't quite believe it could happen, I didn't want to be
charged by a goat with my pants down, or even just undone.

The hell with you, Tilney, I thought. And with your
soft-spoken mother and her bank account, and with your
medical reports and your imminent total nervous collapse
that let you out of exams. And with your Grand Passion
like the olden days that let you out of everything else for
the rest of your life. The hell with you for your damned
romantic agony and suicide notes and spoiled brat grand
gestures. And all your beautiful clothes for sailing, riding,
tennis, opera. And for giving them away so carelessly, for
giving away lots of things you don't need so you can take
away other things that you don't need. Like taking away
my girl the first time I introduced you, taking her out and
getting engaged and the whole House the audience to this
white-hot young love, though whether you ever slept with
her I don't know to this day.

When she crashed in his car she was going a hundred
miles an hour, and after tearing out through the metal center
strip had plowed into another car coming in the opposite
direction, killing a man and woman and their two children.
That was how little she had cared what happened.

And that was what I couldn't understand at first. She
was a very careful driver. Not cautious, but completely
efficient, sure, and self-contained about her driving, the way
she was about everything. I wondered a lot at first, but
only the way people do when they keep thinking over and
over again, "How could it have happened?" But since seeing
that other car in Athens and seeing how he hadn't even
noticed, I was really wondering why. Why it had happened.

There was a shaking and then a lurch in the bushes and
a second goat put its head out. The first one wheeled away

and trotted up the slope. I climbed up and began to walk back.

It was still early morning and fresh, even cool if you weren't in the sunlight. A beautiful day, and I liked the country. The only thing I'd missed on the mainland was trees. I liked olive trees all right, but as far as I was concerned they were only large bushes. What I mean by trees are high oak and beech, chestnut, elm, ash, maple, sycamore, willow. Big trees with lots of limbs and branches and leaves. But you don't find them in very old lands; the trees are the first things to go. All the ancient navies, all the houses, and those winters thousands of years ago needed them. And everybody's always hungry, so they put down crops before new trees can grow, and by that time they're building their houses out of stone or bricks or concrete. Pretty soon they aren't even building the boats out of wood any more.

As I reached the car I was thinking about whether trees might some day disappear from the world altogether, or that there might be only a few left and people would come to look at them the way you go to art galleries and museums. They might even come to be thought magical again, beings connected with the gods. Not because they attracted lightning, but because they would be very rare, snobby objects.

"What were you doing all that time?" Tilney said.

"Took a leak."

"You need that long, you should see a doctor." He lit another cigarette. I looked around for the knapsack and realized he'd had it in the back with him all the time.

"Reach that over, will you?"

He handed it up and I got out a fresh pack of cigarettes. Spiro started up the car.

"From tomorrow looks like we'll be smoking something local."

"Oh Jesus," Tilney said, "those lousy Greek coffin nails."

"You smoke so much."

I put the pack in my pocket. Tilney began to talk about what a lousy country it was: the animals all had mange, the rooms had bugs, the food was lousy, everybody was a liar or a cheat, you couldn't drink the water. And all the money came from tourists—that was the only reason anybody would come to the godforsaken place, and if the tourists didn't pay to see all the old stuff you could bet it would be all crumbled away by now. And it was a damn good thing the English got the Elgin marbles off the Parthenon when they did. This was a country of greaseball runts and barbarians who'd sell you anything including themselves and they were all ugly as hell, not a trace of the old Greek look left; it was like being in some place like the Lebanon.

"In fact, the only reason the roads on this island are any good is because they were built by the Italians, did you know that? That's what they need here, another occupation."

"Do me a favor," I said. "I don't know how much he understands, but I don't want to get thrown out on my can in the middle of nowhere."

"You think any goddamn Greek is going to mess up a chance of collecting his money? Man, for two cents he'd sell you his grandmother."

"If I were in his place and could understand half of what you've been saying, I'd just cut our throats and take the money without asking."

"Oh he wouldn't hurt you, Barney. You're his pal for life. He's taken a shine to you. Why don't you ask him what he's doing tonight? Say, 'What's a nice kid like you doing in a joint like this?' "

I'd had about enough. I thought about the last trees in captivity and three thousand years of history and how it doesn't help you to handle your own life. As calmly and quietly as I could I said, "Look, Rick, it's a nice day, we're going to see this place, everything's fine."

"Oh everything's hunky-dory. Everything's nice-nice-nice."

"Sure. So just take it easy. And quit being so—hateful."

"Hateful? Oh boy. Wow, can you pick them out of a hat. You really are going to be a poet some day, aren't you?"

"Sure, why not?"

"I bet they say that all the time back home, bet they even say 'picayune.' They probably say 'I opine.' Barney, buddy, I can't wait to see your complete works bound in burlap."

"Send you a copy some day."

"You do that. You do that," he said. He was working up to something more, and I didn't want to hear it.

"All through now?"

"You'll never write anything good, you know," he said.

"Maybe not. I'm giving it a try."

"It isn't going to get you anywhere. You don't have what it takes."

"How would you know?"

"I just know. You don't."

"Thanks for the information," I said, and started to turn around, but he went on.

"Tell you why. Because you're still back on the farm. You don't see, you don't hear. You don't even know the place you've got to get to before you can start. You're so naïve."

That was one of his favorite words.

"And you're still a real old Puritan block of American granite, aren't you? Nothing touches you. Like the man says, to move you've got to be moved. Bet you wouldn't even feel it if I put this cigarette out on your arm."

I had my sleeves rolled up and my left arm was lying across the back of the seat.

"Like this," he said, and calmly stubbed his cigarette into

my arm. It didn't occur to me that he would. I didn't really believe it when I saw him start to do it, and when I pulled back I fell into Spiro's right arm. He swerved and stepped down hard on the brakes, and we all went forward. Tilney still had the cigarette in his hand.

"Did it hurt?" he asked.

Spiro gave a little sigh, straightened his shoulders and turned to the back seat, looking at Tilney as though he'd like to knife him. Then he said something in a loud, firm voice.

Tilney appeared not to notice. He said, "You tell your boyfriend I'm paying for this ride and he can shut his dirty peasant mouth or I'll knock his teeth down his throat."

Before the tone could get through to Spiro I tapped his arm, indicated Tilney with my head, and touched my temple. He grunted and turned back.

"The hell I am!" Tilney shouted at me.

"Why was she driving so fast, Rick?" I said.

"Not about me you don't say that."

"I said why was Diane driving so fast? The cops said she was doing a hundred."

His face went stiff.

"What are you talking about?"

"Why was she driving so fast?"

"What are you trying to do to me?" he said. "Just when I'm trying to forget." Tears came up in his eyes.

"Try to remember."

"How can you? My God, Barney. How can you?" He closed his eyes and hung his head. I made a motion for Spiro to start the car again.

Nobody spoke until we arrived at the town square. It was a tiny place and I was glad we had come early. We got out and I told Spiro that we would be gone about two hours, allowing for the climb up and back, and tried to show him on my watch. He took my wrist, bent down into the watch-face and suddenly beamed at me.

"Timex!" he said. Then he shot back his cuff and showed me his, also a Timex.

"Small world," I said in English, and we batted the idea back and forth. When I tried to go through the "when the big hand is here" routine again he brushed my efforts away, telling me something that I hoped meant it was all right because in any case he would wait till we got back down again.

"This looks like it," I said, looking up. "All the postcard stands seem to lead in this direction."

Tilney followed along behind for a way and then came up beside me. The path was narrow with houses built to-gether on either side, no front steps or anything, like a theatre set. At some places large colored pebbles had been put down to make mosaics in the stone-paved ground.

"I guess that's instead of rosebushes or flowerboxes," I said, and then wished I hadn't tried to make peace. Rick muttered something.

Several houses had the usual identical tourist junk set out in front of them: genuine home-made cheesecloth peas-ant blouses tied at the neck with string, plastic ballpoint pens with the name of the place and a picture stamped on the side, postcards everywhere, belts with the old square wave pattern embroidered on them, badges, glass beads, shell necklaces, scarves, paperweights, worry beads, don-key beads, penknives. And standing near them were the owners, heavy women in black, telling us what special treasures we could buy. I murmured the word for no a couple of times, and decided that if Tilney pulled an Ae-gina on me I'd just walk away and let him stew in his own juice. On Aegina he had waved his hand at them and said in a perfectly normal tone of voice, "Piss off, piss off." And he'd told the man who wanted to sell him a sidesaddle donkey ride, "Not on your life, Mac, I don't want any fleas."

But he stared straight ahead. The path kept rising and went around a corner.

"Just tell me honestly," he said, "as an objective observer, have you ever seen such hideous women in your life?"

I shrugged. We went by one house that had a songbird in a cage hung out from one of the windows. It wasn't singing, but you could see it through the bars, a brown bird about the size of a small thrush.

"I mean, look at them. How can they stand to let themselves get that way? Even the young girls here—I haven't seen a really good pair of legs in the whole country."

"You haven't been looking."

"A really good pair of legs, I said. Not just passable. Come on, admit it; have you seen one single pretty girl since we got here?"

"That girl at the travel bureau was beautiful. Just like an icon."

"Maybe," he said. "That isn't what I meant. I hate all that Byzantine crap anyway. It's so wooden."

We kept climbing. The grade was getting progressively steeper and at the corners you wondered how the houses kept from falling in on each other. They all looked piled together. But I liked it. Coming around the corner I got the sun smack off all that whitewash, like the glare of a snow field, even though we were so low down and it was still pretty early in the morning.

"It's just such a disappointment that they don't look like the statues," he said. "Now, Italy is different. You can still see it all, Renaissance and medieval. And the Romans still look like the Romans, by God. They even stand the same way. It's great."

We came to a corner again and stopped. There was the

wall, covered with bougainvillea like a blanket hung out to air, and you could look down over.

"A real sock in the eye, isn't it?" Tilney said.

"You can say that again."

"Do you have your famous camera in there?"

I had the knapsack on my back, but I'd purposely left the camera in the glove compartment of the car.

"Not for this place. The postcards are always better for the big guns."

"Sounds crazy to me. I don't know why you brought it at all."

"You ready for the next lap?"

There was a flight of stairs and we started to go higher even more steeply than before. Soon the houses gave out and it was just mountain rock with a wider path like a country road and it leveled off.

"Seriously, though, I think maybe we should have gone to Italy instead." He was huffing a bit because I'd stepped up the pace. I didn't want to talk any more.

"Italian girls don't have very good legs either, not on the whole. But they have beautiful breasts. When they're young, of course. They're mostly built top-heavy. Too many years of spaghetti and it's like a landslide, all seems to go at the same time. But the faces there, Barney—you'd go ape. Everybody's got these incredible faces. Maybe we could change the tickets and leave here earlier."

"Not go to Delos? That's supposed to be the really interesting place. The groundworks of the whole thing are left, all the private houses and the theatre box office and market place. Everything. I thought Italy was supposed to be rainy this time of year."

"It's good even in the rain."

"And you've been there once."

"Three times. With my parents, on my own, and last year with Keppel."

"Who's Keppel?"

"You know, that Kirkland House jock I roomed with freshman year."

"Oh. Him."

"He's okay."

"If you like them that way," I said.

"What do you mean?"

"Well, he's queer as a three dollar bill."

Tilney collapsed with laughter and came to a stop. He was falling all over himself. "Is that right?" he said. "Who told you that?"

"Guy I know. I believe him, too."

"The things you come out with. I didn't think you noticed that kind of thing, Barney. Not coming from R.F.D. land like you do."

"Well, it's true, isn't it?'

"Hell, I don't know. I always thought he was just sort of a mindless jock."

"What were you doing, traveling around with a dope like that?"

"Oh, it was before I got the car. He had this car to get to some big Italian soccer game. What's that up there?"

Up ahead at the top of the rise, in the corner of another hairpin turn, a bench was let in to the mountainside. Above it and to the right the rock looked dark, and as though it had been formed in a design. I looked up and then I realized what it was.

"Hey, I've read about that. It's a famous thing. Come on."

"Wait up, I'm winded. I guess I'm not in such good shape as I thought I was."

"Let's face it, you've been drinking like a fish the last few days. And you smoke like a fiend. That's why we only have three packs left."

"I know, I know. I don't take karate lessons, either. Or ju-jitsu, or whatever it is. Let's set a spell, pardner."

He dropped down on the stone bench and I got the guidebook out of the knapsack. I had read about the carving before, but I had forgotten.

"Here it is. It's a trireme, dedicated to Athena."

"What's it of?"

"Well, look. It's a boat. This place was a big center for sculptors. And all those really big pieces—if it's got that sort of flying, nautical look, chances are the sculptor trained here. The Laocoon is supposed to have been done by a sculptor from Rhodes. And I think I remember something about the Winged Victory, too."

"That's Samothrace."

"I mean where the sculptor trained. I think I remember reading something about it, but I may be wrong. It may be another statue. Anyway, it has that look."

"The Winged Victory looks like a boat, huh?"

"You know what I mean. Let's say like something that's sailing, not just standing there. They did all right."

"Who did all right?" he asked.

I was thinking about the statues and why people build them, about boats and why people should carve them on the side of a mountain, sailing where no ship can sail. And why people make pictures and why they look at them, or make them in words and listen to them. All these occupations of making things which, when they are made, turn into something that never was before. And then they have the power to call forth an action in you, to do something to you that changes you and changes time. It was a kind of magic, and one of the reasons why I had always wanted to come to the country. I thought it would be all around, like something in the air, like the story about the Greek shepherd who said, "Where I come

from there are more gods than men." Ideally, if you looked
at things the right way, you ought to be able to work out
this business of time and magic so that you wouldn't have
to depend on any particular sight or object. And if you
finally understood it, you ought to be able to hold it, to
retain it in yourself. Then you wouldn't need beauty or
strangeness to call it into being, and you could use it to
live. It wasn't really a question of art or aesthetics; I was
sure that somehow it all had to do with religion, that at a
certain point you could achieve a kind of revelation, like
breaking the sound barrier, and from then on you would
have a special certainty that would never forsake you. But
I didn't really understand these things. I only knew that
when I thought about them I would get so excited that it
almost made me feel sick.

Tilney was saying my name. When I heard him I realized
that I must have blanked out for a couple of moments.

"Barnes," he said, and then called me by my first name,
which nobody ever used, not even my parents. The only
time I ever saw it was when I wrote checks and signed
myself on letters to people I didn't know.

I sat down next to him on the bench.

"What happened to you? Staring at the wall as if you
were going to go straight through it, muttering 'They did
all right.' Who did all right?"

"Oh, all those ancient Greeks. Damn those Greeks. I told
you about my cousin Sukey and her art school, didn't I?"

"You've got more cousins than anybody I ever met. If
you ever syndicated, you could put the protection rackets
out of business. Sheer force of numbers, wipe them right
off the map. Cigarette?"

"Okay."

He offered me one from the pack he'd taken from me in
the car. My arm felt bad in the sun, but the walk had made

me feel too hot to want to pull the sleeve down. He gave me a light and faced me. The bad temper had gone from his eyes and mouth, and he looked relaxed.

"The way you look when you like something," he said. "I can see it in your eyes. As though you wanted to eat it."

"Don't you like all this stuff?"

"Sure, but not the way you do. You never should have majored in economics. You ought to be in classics or archaeology or something. Or fine arts."

"Well, I did audit those courses."

"No, I mean really go into it."

"And end up as a teacher someplace, like all the other humanities majors who don't have a private income."

"It doesn't have to be like that."

"I can get a good job with what I'm doing now. And then I can have the money to travel around and learn things, see things, for pleasure."

"You wouldn't rather do that all the time and skip the economics?"

"Economics is interesting, too. Very interesting. See, I don't have the feeling I'd be giving anything up. I mean, the other things are always there."

"But you wouldn't have the time for them."

"Time enough. It isn't as though I could paint myself, or sculpt or build things, you know. I'm just good at appreciating, that's all."

"You could be an art critic."

"That's right. Why didn't I think of that before? That's what I could do. And dabble in Tibetan translations and slip in a little brain surgery in my spare time."

I stubbed out my cigarette and started to get up. Tilney held me back by the arm.

"Hell, I really did burn you."

"You did."

"Does it hurt?" He was holding my arm with both hands and peering intently at the burn.

"It just stings, the way they do. Like when you pop a blister."

"You ought to cover it up with something. This country is so damn dirty."

"I'm all right. Let's go."

"No, let's stay on here a couple of minutes."

"I want to see this place before the crowd gets here."

"We've got plenty of time still."

"I can go on ahead." I pulled my arm away and stood up.

"Look, Barney, I'm sorry I said that about your poetry."

"It doesn't matter. You aren't the only one who thinks it's funny."

"It's just that I've been feeling so rotten. You know." He gave a deep sigh. Now comes the monologue, I thought. Or the soliloquy. If only he would stop acting. I started on ahead, so he wouldn't have his audience.

But he got up and followed. He started talking about Diane. It didn't matter to him that I wasn't answering him or even looking in his direction. He went on and on, saying the most unbelievable things. There wasn't anything he wouldn't put his mouth on. I shut off all the valves and kept walking, and heard the sound only. Sometimes I could tell by his tone of voice how much he was just acting and how much there was of something real behind it, some emotion which probably had nothing to do with whatever he was saying.

We were getting near the top. One more bend and I figured we'd be up by the ruins. Tilney began to wind up the hearts and flowers.

"Well," he sighed. "But you understand already. It's just that I have this constant feeling that if I can put it into words, it won't be so bad. That's what Dr. Thornton says: verbalize it."

I thought of telling him that his lousy psychiatrist was out of his mind.

"You loved her, too."

I didn't answer. He stopped walking again.

"Didn't you?" he said, in a muted voice. I stopped, too, but didn't look at him. I didn't want to see those actor's tears again. I could hear them in his voice.

"I don't know, Rick."

"You told me, you always told me that—"

I started walking, and said, "Let's quit talking about it."

I couldn't tell him, because he wouldn't be willing to understand it. But sometimes I had almost hated her. I remembered the way she looked, down to the smallest detail. Every dress she ever wore, every blouse and skirt, her coats, clothes for warm weather, and snow, and for wet weather. She had even more clothes than he did, and they all looked brand new. She, too, immaculate, every hair on her head in place. That was one of the things I loved most about her—the breathtakingly inhuman way she looked, like a girl who had been made by a machine: perfect.

"I understand," he said, catching me up. "If she hadn't met me, I mean—I know how she felt about you, but it just wasn't the same. She needed somebody who really understood her."

"She wasn't hard to understand."

Just hard to get.

"Oh, Barney, she was so screwed up. All that stuff about her family. You wouldn't know about that."

Why not? Hadn't he told me about it over and over? Two o'clock in the morning, four o'clock in the morning, come in and tell Barney. Who needs a newspaper if you've got Tilney for a roommate?

"Maybe you have to live on the East coast for a long time to know how it can be. Or have the experience of growing up in New England."

"Or have a Porsche." That got him.

"You think that would make any difference to a girl like Diane?"

"I know it did," I said.

I remembered the day he first met her. She was in the room and I had heard the car outside—he always revved it up around every corner—and I heard the door slam. I went to the window to look, and saw the car parked down below, and knew that he'd be coming up the stairs in a minute. "That's Tilney," I said. "You can meet him now." Diane came over and put one knee on the windowseat and leaned over to the window. One of her shoes was loose.

She had shoes with high heels, and walking shoes, and stadium boots, and fancy boots for winter which she'd bought in Europe before anyone else started wearing them, and evening shoes, and three pairs of flat shoes. The flat shoes were made in red, blue, and black leather, one pair of each, and inside they each had a striped lining. The red ones were striped red and white, the blue ones blue and white, and black and white on the insides of the black ones. All of them were comfortable, so she said, which meant that every once in a while they fell off at the heel. That was how I first noticed the linings, and it seemed wonderful to me that the makers had taken the pains to put a design where no one could see it except whoever wore the shoes.

She leaned over to the window and one of the shoes fell away so that I could see the blue and white lining, and she put it back on with one hand and looked out the window. Her hair slid forward as she looked down, and she said, "Oh! Who owns that car?" All the time I had waited to hear her voice do that, and it had never done it for anything connected with me. "That's Tilney's," I told her. And I hadn't finished speaking before he was at the door.

"You son of a bitch, you didn't know her at all," he said.

"I don't know why she was driving so fast. I've asked you once. You want to tell me?"

We had both stopped walking.

"Well, why do you think?" he said.

I don't know what I had expected, perhaps the same reaction as the first time I'd asked him, only stronger, maybe strong enough to get the truth out of him.

"I don't know," I said. "That's why I'm asking you. Because you know."

"What makes you think that?" He started walking again, and his face had one of the many indifferent looks he had in stock, the one which meant he had something up his sleeve.

"I just know it," I said. "It was something you said, or something you did, or something she found out."

"About me?" he said lightly.

"Maybe."

"Maybe," he admitted.

I felt the strength go out of me. This was something I had believed I could win. From the time I first began to wonder, I thought I could finally get it out of him.

"I've been thinking about it a lot," he said. "I suppose it never occurred to you that it might have had something to do with you?"

"Me? In what way?"

"Oh, I don't know."

"Shove that, Tilney. What are you getting at?"

"Just what I said. It might have had something to do with you."

"But how?"

"Hell, I don't know. Just as much as it might have been me. Or it might have been something about her family. We just don't know what she was thinking about. I mean, if it wasn't an accident."

So there it was, out in the open, and it didn't get me anywhere.

"I still think it was one of those freak things," he said. "Like blacking out for a second or two on a long drive. It happens all the time to truck drivers."

"But it wasn't such a long drive. And anyway, that wouldn't explain why she was going so fast."

"If she was in that sort of blank stage, she might not notice how fast she was going."

"I just find it hard to believe."

"Sometimes she took sleeping pills, you know. And she had a bottle of dexadrine she got from somebody."

"That would have showed up in the autopsy."

"Not necessarily. Let's say she was taking something for a while and then stopped. It would be the reaction, a long time afterwards. Suddenly make you sleepy or forgetful, or lose your judgment."

"I see. Is that what you think?" I said. He wouldn't look me in the face.

"I just don't know. I don't suppose we'll ever know. Let's drop it, Barney. Come on, let's go. I can see somebody up there. I think this is the place."

It was the place, all right. And although it was so old, it didn't have any of the archaic starkness, none of that massive, Aztec look. It looked delicate and civilized, up on top of the world, and not small like the postcard photographs, but a huge pure white and pale honey-colored dream city from a ruined age. And it was all there, the whole acropolis, with the ocean scintillating beyond and below it, and nothing else but the sky.

We stepped out into it and I felt as though I were in a trance. I forgot my tiredness and suspicion and the bitterness that kept coming back like a taste in the mouth after eating something bad. A strange feeling came over me of finally being at home.

We wandered around and then took the first flight of stairs and stood where we could see the other staircase to the left and the standing columns of the temple below, and the temple of Athena on the other side. Without saying anything we began to aim for the columns, but then both noticed at the same time that an elderly couple was already stationed there.

"Hell," Tilney said.

"Isn't that something?" the old man was saying over his shoulder to his wife.

"You watch out you don't get too near the edge," she said. "You're making me nervous."

"Let's move on a way," Tilney suggested.

I looked off to the right. There was another old couple looking over the wall at that end. Tilney saw them too.

"We can move on back till they've had enough," he said.

We went back down the stairs and came out beyond the first set of columns, where there were broken pieces of marble and stone lying around in a lot of undergrowth. The ground was full of stumbling places. Tilney took the lead.

"Look out, I think those are probably thistles or something," he said, pointing down. We came to a couple of standing broken columns that had spiderwebs strung everywhere between them. One of the webs was complete, like an overgrown doily with the spider sitting in the center, yellow with dark spots on it.

"Look out for the spider," I said. Tilney jumped a mile.

"Jesus! If there's anything I can't stand!"

I could see that he wanted to kill it but was unwilling to take the chance that it might touch him.

"Leave it. Then at least you'll know where it is."

"I suppose the place is crawling with the things."

"I doubt it. They won't want to build far down. It's interesting. I wonder if they build to the average flying-height of the local flies."

We got to the wall and half sat on it, and looked over. Down, down, down, the sea. And you could follow it up, higher and higher until your eye reached all the way out and up to the horizon, like looking across the world.

Tilney took off his jacket. Underneath it he had on one of those tennis shirts with a tiny alligator, green with red stitching around it, sewn over the left breast. And he was wearing white ducks. He looked like a vodka ad in the *New Yorker*. We'd had a long argument about the best clothes for traveling. Tilney had maintained that white was essential because it didn't absorb the sun. I had tried to tell him that in Mediterranean countries the local people wore suits and kept their cuffs and collars buttoned when it was hot. And he had said no, white was the answer and also never to wear a hat unless it was a light-colored straw hat with a very loose weave, because you got heatstroke that way, and that was why the British had really lost the Empire, because of trying to govern from under a pith helmet. Also, he had assured me, they had all gone bald as a result. "It isn't going to be all that hot in April and May," I had said. And that had turned out to be true. It was just beautifully warm and comfortable. Later on, of course, and down on the Peloponnese, we would see how far the sun-repelling property of whiteness was to be trusted. I just had on a pair of ordinary khaki summer pants.

"Nice breeze," I said. "I wouldn't mind living on this island for a while."

"For how long?"

"Oh, a year."

"You'd get sick of it in three weeks."

"I don't think so."

"Well, maybe you wouldn't. I would. That's the trouble with the beautiful places. No people, no life. Let's go see if the senior citizens' committee has decamped."

We made our way back, past the spider, mounted the

staircase again, and looked from the central plateau. They were still there.

"We can sit down here," I said.

"All right."

I unslung the rucksack and sat, and got out the guidebook. We had the whole view of the place but were sitting looking to the side, so that you could see the landspits going out into the ocean like islands.

"You want to hear what the guidebook has to say?"

"Not just yet, Barney. Let's just enjoy it for a while." He was leaned back against the stone with his hands behind his head and his feet crossed in front of him.

A man and a girl came up the flight of stairs we had just left. They stopped on the top step and looked. The man had on a red shirt, sunglasses, and brown trousers. He was carrying a newspaper. His girl was wearing one of those madras cotton skirts, a pink blouse, and a brown suede jacket. She had her hair tied back in a scarf, and had a pair of sunglasses the exact copy of his. They must have been just behind us on the path coming up.

The man pointed his nose at the temple of Athena, swiveled his gaze around once, turned around, and sat down with his back to the whole works. The girl sat down beside him. Then he opened the newspaper and began to read aloud in French.

"What the hell," Tilney said.

I couldn't understand all the words, but I could hear that he was reading prices in francs out of the paper and quoting dates.

"What's he reading?" I said,

Tilney listened for a minute.

"Christ, it's a list of secondhand cars."

"You aren't serious."

"That's what it is, all right. The god-damned French."

"Maybe he's Swiss."

"Not with that gall. The only tourists worse than the Germans are the French. But with the Germans it takes at least three to make the place intolerable. With the French you only need one. Let me tell you about the French."

"I've heard it."

He had a set piece on the French, about how good propagandists had kept alive a myth about France being the head of the civilized world, whereas in reality, if you took it century by century, or book by book, cathedral for cathedral and so on, through science, painting, music, novels, poetry, and plays, and compared each example with instances from other countries, you discovered that they didn't have the best of anything. Furthermore, most of the time they were outclassed all along the line, not even breaking even. The Russians and English had better novelists, the English and Spanish had better playwrights, the Dutch and Italians had better paintings, the Germans and Italians had better music, the English had better poets, and so on. The Renaissance had passed them by, and even in the age of the Song of Roland, the Germans had just as much to boast about. He wound it up saying that the only things they'd ever had were clothes, food and wine. As for the clothes, in the past English clothes had been better and in the present Italian clothes were better, and they'd never even been as good as Spain on making footwear. And as far as cooking went, if you wanted to consider it an art, Chinese cooking was just as great; but now that French cooking was going down the drain, it was the Italians who were the best in Europe now. And that left wine, which admittedly was the best, although it didn't entitle a nation to brag about being the head of world civilization. And anyway, the Romans had planted all the vines.

He had trotted this rigamarole out once at a party given by the Comp. Lit. department just before Christmas. A lot of section men and graduate students and their wives had been invited, and there was a Swiss woman sitting near him whom Tilney had suddenly taken against. So he launched into the book for book, cathedral by cathedral harangue. In the middle of it the Swiss woman stood up from her chair, grabbed her evening bag, and said loudly and patriotically, "France does not need your love!" Tilney had answered, "Oh, don't go yet—I haven't even started on Switzerland. I *hate* Switzerland."

He could do it with any country. He could also do it for America, of course. That was the most involved one. And it took me a long time to see that they were meant to be funny. It took me even longer to think it was funny when he did it about Indiana.

"A nation of line-jumpers, shoplifters, collaborators and backbiters," he said. "And concierges."

I tilted my head back and closed my eyes for a few minutes. Then there was a slapping flurry of paper and I saw the Frenchman standing up. He stuck the newspaper under his arm and moved off. The girl followed, and I watched them taking a turn around the ruins. Every once in a while the man would point his nose right and then left, then turn on his heel and keep going. The girl followed along behind. She walked with a very easy gait, which was both demure and enticing, and nice to look at. I thought she looked much too good for him, and how sad it would be if they were already married and she wouldn't have a chance to find someone better. They did the complete circuit and came back our way, passed us, and went down the stairs again.

"So they've seen it," Tilney said.

"At least he took the trouble. For a while I thought he'd just read his paper and then take her home."

Tilney spread out his jacket on the ground and lay down full length, leaning on one elbow.

"The way your hair goes blond," he said. "If I didn't know you better I'd think you'd dyed it."

"It always does that in the summer. Not so good here. It's all right for you."

"Why?"

"They think I'm German. Spain, Italy, Greece—if you're lighter than average brown, they think you're a German. And Germans aren't exactly popular."

"It looks better now it isn't so short."

"I'm going to try to find a barber tomorrow. It's getting over my collar."

"No, leave it," he said. "It looks better like that."

"Want to move?"

"They're still there, aren't they? Dug in for the duration. I'm feeling lazy."

"I'm just going to take a look," I said, and got up. I walked around and went up the staircase. The feeling was still there, of a marvelously remote and foreign place where I felt at home. I thought that this was why people traveled, why they had a mania for different places. And probably you could only experience the sensation if you had left your own home for good, or if you had come to notice how much it had changed, so that when you were away you found yourself feeling homesick for things that weren't even there any more.

When I went back to join Tilney, he said, "You were going to tell me about your cousin Sukey."

"She went to art school where they put you through the whole thing. So many weeks drawing letters, so many weeks doing something else. They had one class where the instructor came in with a paper bag, and he'd crumple it and throw it on the floor and say, "Draw that." After twenty minutes he'd pick it up and crumple it into a different shape and get them to draw it that way, every wrinkle. The whole of the first term was like that. And then they went on to bigger and better things. History of painting and sculpture and architecture, and they had this slogan when they used to meet each other in the mornings. Instead of saying hello, they'd say, "Damn those Greeks." Because they all wanted to be sculptors and architects, but the Greeks had done all that, and done it perfectly, and they were learning enough about Greek art to know how hopeless it was to try to match it. It's true, too. They could do anything. Especially the terra-cotta things. Hands and birds and people and animals. Anything. You see them in the museums, and they've just got that extra thing that changes you when you look at them."

"They didn't have the paintings, though."

"The vase paintings are wonderful."

"Give me Rembrandt every time. I like perspective."

"We agreed Rembrandt and Shakespeare were out as comparisons."

"Some day I'm going to own a Rembrandt," he said.

"And pigs will fly."

"No, I mean it. There's one in the family. Chances are it'll come to me sooner or later."

"You're kidding."

"God's truth."

I pounded my fist on the stone.

"Can't you take it? Never mind, I'll let you come look at it."

"Tilney, I'm shocked. Jesus God, it's enough to make you join the Party."

"Not you. You're a dirty capitalist swine from way back when. Economics major and all."

"Only because it's the only way to survive. If they'd split it up fair, I wouldn't mind."

"Bull."

"I wouldn't. Except for land ownership."

"Oh my God, Barney, that's the basis of the whole she-bang."

"I just meant agriculture, not real estate and penthouses.

I mean land you grow things on. That's where it breaks down."

"I can see you tilling your iceberg up in Siberia. I can just see it."

"We've been through this before."

"Okay. Tell me some more about back home in Indiana. Tell me about your Uncle Gus, he's my favorite."

"I don't make these people up, you know. They're real."

"I know," he said. "That's what makes it so funny."

"You're always making cracks about my relatives."

"I don't mean it that way. I envy you your family."

"Sure you do."

"I mean it. My family, now. They're not funny. Not at all."

"They sound just like everybody else. Except I guess it's different being an only child."

"They say it does something really bad to you to be an only child. Dr. Thornton was telling me all about that."

"Haven't you realized your Dr. Thornton is off his rocker? It's bad to be an only child or to be the oldest, or the one in the middle, or the youngest. What happens if you're brought up in a large family or a small family—it's all bad, you can't win."

"But it's true."

"Then how come they keep changing the theories every few years? Hell, at least you've got two parents, even if you hate them. Supposing you'd been brought up in an orphanage? Then you wouldn't even have anybody to hate."

Tilney snorted through his nose. "I'd really be stuck then," he said.

The sun was pouring down and felt wonderful, and the cool wind, and the quietness and space. I could hear the sound of birds coming from somewhere near.

"Are those people still there?" Tilney asked. I stood up and looked, and sat down again.

"Yes. They're taking pictures."

"Take them back home and bore the pants off of anybody who comes to dinner. Jesus, I wonder how they got up here? They couldn't have walked. Pathetic old biddies."

"Come on, Rick. It's great. What are you going to do when you're that age?"

"Shoot myself."

"Remember that old gal on the boat going to Aegina? Eighty-five if she was a day, and still going strong."

"Completely ga-ga and making everybody wait on her. It isn't fair to other people."

"She didn't ask for a thing."

"No, she just kept falling over all the time, so people had to come hold her up."

"I thought she was great. A real game old lady. Who knows, maybe it was a once-in-a-lifetime thing and she'd never been away before. All on her own, too. That takes something at any age."

"You know, you really are nice. You've got the nicest disposition of anybody I've ever met."

"Look at it this way. Most people spend all their lives playing safe. But if you were near the end of it and knew it—well, wait till I'm that age. My God, I'll make them sit up. Cross the road where there aren't any traffic lights. After all, what can they do except kill you? That's more than they'll do for you in the hospital even if you're asking for it. I'd do just anything I wanted to. I'd feel I'd earned it."

"You can do anything you want to now."

"No, I couldn't."

"Sure you could. That's the time for taking risks, when you're young. The older you get, the more cautious you get."

"What about that old lady on the boat?"

"Man, she was senile. Probably didn't even know what

country she was in. Couldn't see, couldn't hear. What do you think she got out of all that besides making a lot of trouble for other people?"

"Well, I guess that might be a pleasure, too. But I don't believe it. I was watching her, and she was having a good time."

"Everybody over the age of thirty-four ought to be shot. Before they get ugly and boring."

"I'm not biting, Rick. What are you going to do when you look old and feel old?"

"I'm never going to be old," he said. "I'd rather die first. What's so funny?"

"I'm never going to be old, I'd rather die first," I repeated, and then he saw it and laughed too.

"Why save it up till your old age?" he said.

"What?"

"Jaywalking and all that. Listen, I'll tell you something. People who give good advice almost always advise against, but I can give you advice for, and it's the one thing I really know about. It's if you see there's a risk, take it. It always pays off. Always."

"Not always. I don't think so. And anyway, I'm not in a position to."

"What the hell is that supposed to mean?"

"I couldn't afford to."

"You mean money?"

"In a way. I mean I couldn't take the kind of risks you do."

"Like what?" he said, looking at me closely.

"It's hard to explain," I said. And it was. It's what you can never fully explain to a European when you try to tell them that in America there is no such thing as a class system but that we have something else which operates just as effectively; it's called Success and Failure. Sometimes it depends on money and sometimes on whether you are liked, but the thing is really unaccountable. It can make a future in the most unlikely places or it can be allocated or withheld because of the combined efforts of the ones who have been lucky and who can only stay that way if they keep on living in a certain manner. It isn't always money, but so much of the time it seems to be, especially if you haven't got it yourself. Tilney was one of the successes, it was all over him.

"Well," I said. "Just some of the things you've been doing recently—getting drunk and yelling at people, acting crazy, or let's say something quite simple like being rude. If I tried it, I'd be in the clink in no time flat, and somebody would be telling me to shut up because they'd never heard of habeus corpus. If anybody ever nabs you, five lawyers would materialize out of nowhere and suddenly people would be apologizing all over the place to you. You'd probably even be awarded damages."

"Stick to me, kid, and we'll rule the world."

"God forbid. I wouldn't want to rule anything."

"Okay, we'll hire somebody to do it for us, and then we'll sail away and go on vacation for the rest of our lives. Like this."

"That wouldn't leave any kicks for our old age," I said.

He wasn't right in what he had said about risks. They probably only paid off if you took them for fun. But if you did it for fun, then it wasn't really a risk.

"Wish I'd brought my bathing trunks along," Tilney said, "but these damn foreigners are such prudes they'd probably throw me out for indecent exposure. Let's go to that beach this afternoon."

"I don't know if you're allowed to unless you're staying at the hotel."

"Not that one, that's a pebble beach. I mean the one on the other side of the island."

"Isn't that a pebble beach, too?"

"Damn. I'm not sure. I just assumed it was going to be sand."

"You can get all that at home."

"I guess so. I've got the feeling I could do with some exercise."

"Walking up the hill at Delphi wasn't enough?"

"Don't remind me. But that was a long time ago."

I sat up and looked around.

"How's that burn?" Tilney said.

"It's okay. I'm putting it out of my mind."

He ran a finger down my arm.

"We should have a fight some day. That would get me back in shape. We've never had a real fight. Let's see your biceps."

I made an elbow.

"Not bad," he said, feeling the muscle.

"Now you."

"I don't think I can lift my arm."

"Come on."

He made an elbow and I put my hand on his arm. "What have you been doing, lifting weights?" I said.

"Punching the bag. That's the trouble. If you stop doing it, you feel terrible."

"What did you want to go build yourself up like that for?"

"Feels great."

"Until you stop."

"We should have a fight. I want to see just how much that karate crap is worth."

"I told you, it isn't that kind. I'm not splitting bricks with my hands or breaking people's necks by jabbing them with a rigid toe. I don't even think that stuff works anyway unless it's under contest conditions."

"Sure it does. Everybody says it does."

"I think what they mean is what they teach you in the

army. But that's pretty much free style, just unarmed combat. They give you all the lethal moves and drill you till they come automatically, and then if you need them you use whichever one is fastest. But that's free form, not a science."

"What about all that black belt mystique?"

"My cousing Will—"

"Here we go again."

"No, listen, this is a true story."

"Aren't they all."

"It's about karate. My cousin Will was in the Marines with this guy who was standing on a street in Hawaii one day with a couple of friends, and they saw this M.P. come walking down the street with a couple of his buddies. There were a lot of Hawaiian kids standing around, and one of them—just a shrimpy kid about sixteen years old—yelled something at this beefy M.P. And he stopped and said, 'Now listen here, kid, don't mess with me, I'm a black belt in karate.' And the kid just took a swipe at him and laid him out flat. Smeared him. He hadn't seen it coming. So I don't think it works unless you're a professional or unless you're all set to fight. Old fashioned street fighting will win every time, specially if you know how to use your feet."

"So that's what they taught you back home. How to fight dirty in street brawls."

"Be serious, Rick. You know we don't have any streets back there in Indiana."

"That's right, I forgot. And the nearest thing to culture you had was that gas station attendant who could whistle in two octaves at once."

"Herbie Skinner."

"What a life."

"The one I'm learning isn't even offensive, let alone killer-type chops." I started to explain about it, and how all the exercises were supposed to be a mental training.

"I get it," Rick said. "Karate is a way of life. Happiness is a warm karate chop. That's all bullshit. It's a waste of time. If you're going to play around with that kind of thing, you might as well do it right. If you're going to learn how to fight, then learn how to fight. If you've got something, you've got to use it. No sense in having a gun unless it's loaded."

"And no sense in having a loaded gun unless you're going to fire it, and there's no sense in shooting a gun unless you kill something. One of these days they're going to find you tied up in a knot, and the verdict will be death by logical argument."

"You never should have taken that course."

"I needed the credits in humanities."

"It's all useless. Totally useless. All these mental training things are. They start you out on one of those neat tricks like the one about all goldfish living in a body of water, and a full bathtub being a body of water, so therefore all goldfish live in a full bathtub. And then before you know it you're proving that the Socratic method doesn't work and Hegel doesn't prove anything, and Kant is full of holes, and then you get all the way up to Wittgenstein till you've defined your definitions into ten volumes, and what the hell good is any of it? It still doesn't help you."

"What does?" I said.

"Nothing."

"Religion, maybe. If you could believe it."

"You really do, too, don't you?"

"I wish I did."

"I think you really do. Otherwise you wouldn't always be wishing so hard about it. It's that old black Puritan magic still got you in its spell."

"No, no, just the opposite. It isn't Puritan. It has to do with a kind of freedom. I can't explain it—sometimes I feel

it, but it always comes from outside. What I want is to get
to the point where it's inside me."

"Oh! Oh! Oh!" Tilney said. "Please, God, make me the
Pope."

"Go to hell." I'd made so many promises to myself not
to talk to him about poetry or about religion, and he could
still make me think he was the only friend I had ever had,
and still always get a rise out of me.

I sat up and dusted off the side of my shirt.

"Give me a cigarette," he said.

"You've got nearly a whole pack in your pocket, Rick."

"I want one of yours."

"I'm keeping count. From here on in we smoke them
fifty-fifty."

We both sat with our backs against the stone. I gave him
a cigarette and lit one myself, and looked out at the sea.

"Those French people have gone for good," I said. "Want
to walk around?"

Tilney took a long drag on his cigarette.

"I just remembered something," he said. "Diane's ring."

"Her engagement ring?" I knew perfectly well what he
meant. She had been wearing the engagement ring when
she crashed.

"No, the wedding ring. Do you remember where it is?
Didn't I tell you to put it somewhere?"

He had told me to keep it safe until the wedding, otherwise he would lose it. I was going to be best man.

"You told me to hang on to it till the wedding."

"You haven't lost it or anything?"

I took out my keychain and unfastened the ring from the
clip. The sun sparkled on it.

"Is that it?"

I put it into his open palm, and the moment my hand
left it I realized how much I had been hoping that he would

forget all about it and I'd be able to keep it. She had worn it on her hand in the shop. I'd tried it on my little finger but it wouldn't go even halfway down.

"You carried it around with you all this time?" he said.

"You told me to keep it somewhere safe."

He stayed looking down at the ring in his cupped hand. I had a sick feeling that he was planning to throw it over the outer wall into the sea as a romantic gesture.

"You go ahead and walk around a while," he said. "I think I'll read some of the guidebook."

"Okay."

I picked up the rucksack and strolled off across the plateau. The wind blew my hair down over my forehead and back again when I turned and went up the steps.

I sat on the wall with one knee up, and smoked and looked at the sea. Somewhere or other in one of his books, Joseph Conrad has a statement to the effect that the sea has many moods, nearly all there are, except one, and that one is gentleness. Nobody should know better than Conrad, but he ought to have added "from the deck of a ship." From where I was sitting the sea looked as sweet and gentle as a spring meadow. It had the lovely, calming look of pasture and parkland.

Over to the right a flight of birds was flying and circling around the cliff face below the level of the wall. I began to think about Diane. At the end of the summer and in the fall and winter, and in the spring of the year before, when I had first met her. All the seasons, one year exactly. And the places and weather of New England. How fast everything had seemed, and how special and different and sophisticated and rich. All the things that had struck me at first—the odd formality that would have been unfriendliness at home, the attitudinizing, the orgies of talk, the tension and snobbery—seemed to make life so complicated. But then you acquire a taste for complicated things, nothing simpler will satisfy you. Go back home, and it's a let-down, there's something missing, everything is slower, duller, the conversation makes you want to bang your head against the wall.

And all that excitement, which I had longed for, had come true. There had come a point during school at home when I had suddenly thought: wouldn't it be terrible to get out and away into the thick of things and then find out that it was just as dull as Indiana, and that all the wishing and longing had been for nothing? But it hadn't been. The first week I knew that it was just what I had wanted. The look of things, the houses, streets, the names of all the streets I memorized, the way people looked, even their faces looked more alive. Everything striking sparks off everything. And the work, long hours of work, eating it up. And then Diane and the way she looked, the way she talked, and Tilney with his maniac jokes, his clothes and his car and its speed, and his easiness and arrogance and thoroughbred look. And then his so-called insanity, although I had seen insanity before and it didn't look like what Tilney had.

I thought about Indiana, and felt homesick. It was strange. This beautiful place which I had been longing to see, and it was perfect, perhaps even better than I had imagined it, and it made me feel right, as though I lived here, and yet it also filled me with even more longing. It had me right there, pinpointed in the present so that I knew that I would never forget this day or this place, the way the sun felt, the color of the shadows, the feel of the air. And I would have liked not to think about anything, but I kept wondering about my life and what I was looking for, and looking out at the sea made me yearn to know what it was.

The feeling was almost like those early summer nights back in highschool when I would thrash around in bed until I couldn't stand it any more, and go downstairs and out into the back yard and throw myself down on the grass and roll in it, and then lie there until I felt better, hearing people come back from being out late, the doors opening and closing, voices echoing and then the screen doors slapping shut and the screen twanging. I remembered how my mother had once tracked me out into the yard. *Good gracious, heavens to Betsy, what on earth are you doing out here in your pyjamas?* (It's so hot, I just thought I'd like to sleep outdoors.) *You'll catch your death of cold out here.* (For heaven's sake, Mother, I've told you, colds are caused by germs.) Aunt Sue came out onto the porch and told Mother to leave me alone, it was just spring fever or growing pains, or one of those euphemisms for being sexed up all the time and having nowhere to put it. *I'll get you Charlie's sleeping bag.* (Oh no, Mother, just leave me alone, please.) And Aunt Sue came to the rescue: leave him be, it's just his age, wonder who the lucky girl is. Everybody at breakfast repeating who's the lucky girl tee-hee, but it wasn't that. At least, that was part of it but there was more to it than that. I guess there always is. The sleeping bag was unearthed from the attic and dusted and presented, though what I really wanted to do was to take off the pyjamas and lie out there without anything on. But of course that would have hit the headlines.

I finished the cigarette and snapped it over the wall and moved on, up to the better view where the old people were. One of the couples hadn't moved since we had arrived, or rather, the wife hadn't. Her husband had been wandering off a way, but he always came back to the same spot. The wife was sitting down on a little folding chair. She had on a straw hat with a large floppy brim and a scarf tied around the top of the hat and down under her chin so the wind wouldn't blow the hat away. The scarf was a souvenir from somewhere, but tied in a way that made the names unreadable. She was knitting something where she sat. The ball of yarn was inside a quilted bag down on the ground.

Her husband had stationed himself up at the wall, looking over it. He was a big man who had been in good shape once. He had large shoulders and stood up straight, but he had gone to fat and most of it was in his paunch. He, too, had his head protected, by a peculiar white cotton hat which looked like a baby's cap. The brim had been turned down at the back to shield his neck and up at the front to keep his eyes clear. I thought for some reason, maybe because of the way the hat looked, that he was bald. His arms were very red from the sun.

As I crossed over in back of them, the other couple strolled in their direction. The husband wore a camera around his neck and a natty little fishing hat on his head. The wife wore saddleshoes and carried a pamphlet of some kind in her hand. Her head was tied up in a scarf and she wore a pair of sunglasses with such large lenses that she appeared to be goggling at everything.

She hesitated for a moment as they approached. The other woman smiled, and there was a pause when they both weighed up whether to talk or not. It was interesting to watch. Strangers meeting react differently according to the sex and according to whether they have somebody else along, and according to lots of different factors: age, nationality, and so on.

"Isn't it grand?" the woman knitting said.

"It sure is," the other one answered. Then she came closer and said, "Say, didn't we see you on the boat?"

They started to make friends. It turned out that the woman in the hat was Babs, her husband was Earnie, and the woman in the scarf and glasses was Marge, and her husband was called Truby or Struby or some name that I didn't quite hear.

"C'mon over here, you two," Earnie said. "You've got to see this." Babs murmured something about "heights make me dizzy" and stayed where she was.

"This sign over here, it just gives me a kick," Earnie said. "Look, it says 'danger, death,' nothing else. These Greeks don't mess around when they want to call a spade a spade, just 'danger, death,' couldn't be plainer than that. Back home I bet that sign would start off with the name of the company that couldn't be held responsible for lost articles, injury, drowning, and you name it. But this is the best part, look here."

He guided them to the place where he had been standing before. They seemed to be watching the birds flying around the cliff down below. After a while Marge left the two men and sat down near Babs. They began to talk about what they had seen and where they had been. They had been to many of the same places. Then Babs asked, "Where do you come from in the States?" and I didn't hear, though I guessed later from the other things she said that it was Ohio.

"And you?" said Marge.

"Oh, we've moved around a lot," she said. Her husband laughed at something he was saying to Truby and she looked up at him. "I come from Kansas, and Earnie is from Illinois, and we've lived in both places, but we've been in Massachusetts and Ohio. Dayton, right near you, and Florida, that was for three years. Then New York and New Jersey, and Wisconsin and Connecticut, oh all around."

"Gee," Marge said perfectly seriously, "you've been just about everywhere."

"Yes," Babs agreed. "You could say that, I guess. I guess you could say we've been just about everywhere. We thought we'd take our vacation down in Florida this year, but then these people we know told us about a cruise they'd been on." She began to talk about vacations, and Marge joined in. I turned around and looked at the view.

And it was while I was standing there, not thinking of anything particular or trying to listen to the talk going on behind me, that I began to feel some sort of answer to what had been troubling me. There was no sudden revelation, just the beauty and peace of the place and the sound of the birds, the talk and the sunlight, which all combined to make me happy.

In back of me I heard Earnie say, "Excuse me for a moment." Out of the corner of my eye I could see him pick up a white airline bag with a shoulder strap, and walk away with it. Truby started to aim his camera in different directions and the women were comparing recipes. Marge said, "Apple crumble," and Babs said, "Apple brown Betty," and was told that apple brown Betty was a different thing altogether. I turned back. "Now just hold it like that, ladies," Truby's voice said.

I felt a deeper and deeper contentment. I thought I could never get enough of the place.

Earnie returned to the party, and Truby had disappeared to find some shade where he could change the film in his camera. Lifted on the breeze I heard Marge's voice quite distinctly saying, "What I really miss are those Sara Lee krullers."

I could feel that my face was smiling. I closed my eyes for a moment and then opened them again, and it was as though I could see all the rest of my life, the possibility and strength of it, all the things I could do with it, and I felt certain that I would know how to live it, and that I could be in control of it. The feeling came straight out of the scene, like a personal message to me, and I didn't have any fears that it would fade when I turned around. I had no thoughts about its being a false state of mind that I had worked myself into because I needed it. Just the contrary, it was as simple and direct as though someone had breathed on me and I could feel the breath.

"How about over there?" Babs said behind me. I turned around and saw her walking away, the chair folded up in one hand and her knitting bag in the other. Marge was walking in front of her. They sat down away from the wall, not far from where I had been before. Beyond them I could see Tilney with his nose in the guidebook. I moved over to where the two old men stood. Truby had just finished taking a picture with the new roll of film.

I looked over the edge of the wall and saw what the attraction was. There was a huge hollow cave in the cliff face and a large flight of twittering swallows, closely pursued by about a dozen hawks, kept zooming in one side of the cave and bursting out the other entrance. They always flew in the same direction, clockwise, and the hawks kept right on their tails, swooping and darting. But the swallows stayed just ahead. In and out of the cave they went, in and out.

"Ain't that something," Earnie said, beaming with enthusiasm. He noticed me standing there, and I smiled agreement and moved a few steps closer.

"You wonder why one of them doesn't turn the tables," I said.

"How's that?" Earnie asked.

"They keep going in the same direction. But if the hawks reversed all of a sudden or just lay in wait inside the cave, they could catch as many swallows as they wanted."

"Maybe the air current's against it," Truby said.

That sounded sensible but somehow implausible. I thought the reason might be that when you are in a panic, as the swallows were, or almost winning, as the hawks were, you just don't think of changing direction. I wondered if they could keep it up all day.

"Sure is a thing to watch," Earnie said. Truby leaned over the wall and then pulled back again. "There's a cove down there," he said. "You can't see it because of the incline. Isn't this where St. Paul landed?"

I said, "He sure picked a good spot for it."

"For what?" Earnie said.

"Oh, for just about anything. But he must have had quite a climb. Maybe faith got him to the top."

Earnie laughed. Truby sighted with the camera for a while and then told us he thought he'd try a few shots of the part below the staircase, and left us.

"Zingo! Just look at him go there!" Earnie shouted out into the sunny air. "I do love to see a hawk chasing something. The way they kind of swoop—look, see how they fold up their wings, just like a bullet. There, he's almost got you—Jehoshaphat, what a thing to see! Did you see that?"

He took a handkerchief out of his pocket and wiped his face, still grinning. Then he turned and gestured to his wife and Marge and yelled, "Hey, come on over here and look at this." They shook their heads from where they sat. Babs made a go-away motion at him with her hand. The two of us looked at the birds for a while longer and Earnie told me what to watch for to see how the hawks worked together and how the swallows kept in formation. Every once in a while he would become exhilarated to a pitch where he'd shout something to the birds. "Zoom, zoom!" he yelled. "Wow, look at that!" he'd say, as one of the hawks folded its wings to streamline into a dive. He wiped his face again and took a roll of lifesavers out of his pocket and offered me one. I thanked him but said no; I didn't want the sweetness lying on my teeth. He began to eat them, several at a time. Sometimes when he yelled out at the birds I could catch the smell of peppermint. Then after a few minutes he picked up the airline bag and said, "If you'll excuse me for a moment?"

"Sure," I said. " 'Bye."

I watched the birds alone, and then I moved back to where I had been before, and turned my face into the breeze and looked out to sea. For a long while I stayed there, still feeling completely happy. I forgot everything: the guidebook, the other people, Tilney. It even seemed as though I had forgotten myself, or rather, as though my life had come to a special point and I could see everything balanced and calm.

Earnie rejoined his wife and her friend while I was standing there. He talked with them for a few minutes, offered them lifesavers, strolled off around the parapet, helped them to take some photographs with a camera that had been in the knitting bag, talked about cameras, and then excused himself again, and the two women sat down in a different place, about fifteen yards away. I turned to look back and saw them settling themselves on the stone stairs, and beyond them saw Tilney walking towards me with his jacket over his shoulder and the guidebook in his right hand.

I turned back to the sun to take a last look on my own, just for luck. I wanted to fix the feeling of happiness so that nothing and nobody, especially Tilney, would be able to spoil it.

He came up behind me, and at the side of my vision I saw him drop his jacket and throw the book down on top of it. Then he put his hand on my shoulder and stood next to me.

"It's okay," he said, "but I'd like to know about the drainage before I make a firm offer. What do you charge for the month?"

"Oh, you've just been outclassed. I've rented it out to that Frenchman. Says he's going to set up a secondhand car business here."

"Yup, a choice location for secondhand cars."

We both laughed. "Well," he said. "All this communing with nature. Have you decided what you're going to be when you grow up?"

"Not exactly. What about you?"

"Oh, me. I'm going to be a dilettante, naturally. A few

select monographs bound in red morocco and a life of pleasure and sin."

"You ought to be an actor, though. Seriously, you'd be good at it."

"No, that's a rotten life. I wouldn't mind being a director. But then you've got to get the backing and the theatre, and after you run through the old stuff you've got to get a good play. There'd be a lot that would be just wheeler-dealer stuff."

"Wouldn't you like that? On the cocktail party circuit?"

"Maybe."

"Come here," I said. "I want to show you something." I took him over to the sign. He read it and then looked beyond at the view.

"You see, the laconic spirit lives on in spite of everything."

"It would be a long drop," Tilney said, smiling. "A long drop." He began to horse around, shadow-boxing, and then pretending to throw me over the wall.

"Undergraduate sinks without trace in wine-dark sea," he said. "Dramatic duel between the good old classic art of self-defense and insidious inscrutable karate methods. I thought they were just fucking around, claims Mrs. Elmira Fudd, shocked onlooker of Happydale, California."

"Cut it out, Tilney," I said. He had me in a bear hug around the waist. I'd put my hands back and had a moment of panic as I realized that the wall didn't even come up to my belt.

"And which one will win?" he said.

"Quit it, Rick."

One of the women had seen us and called over, "Hey, you boys, watch out, now. That's dangerous over there."

I swung to the side and kicked at his knee, and put my arms up to get his head. But he was trying to lift me, to get my feet off the ground and turn me so that I had my back to the wall.

"You don't believe I could kill you," he said.

"Leave go, will you."

"You don't think I would."

He'd gotten me turned around again. The strength coming out of his arms was unbelievable. I was heavier, but I'd never realized just how much stronger he was.

"You think I wouldn't?" he said.

There were one or two basic moves I could make to break out of the hold he had me in, but if I used them he'd flip straight over the wall. And it was Danger Death, all right, no doubt about that. He was latched on to me as though he'd never let go. And suddenly I was terrified that my feet might slip out from under me and it would happen anyway by accident. Over his shoulder I could see that both women were standing up, watching us.

"Jesus, Rick, you'll push us both over. Stop it."

"You think I wouldn't?" he shouted.

"I think you just might," I said. "Just for the hell of it."

He stepped back, loosened his hold, and let me turn my side to the wall. I took my arms down from his neck. He straightened up and laughed.

"You were practically strangling me. Did you really think I was going to kill you?"

"I don't know."

"Whenever I ask you something important, you say 'I don't know.' "

Babs and Marge had decided that the excitement was over, and had sat down again. Their faces were turned away.

"I could still do it, even now," Tilney said. "Look, I'll show you."

He stood in front of me, turned my shoulders around, and had me backed up against the wall again.

"I don't want to see."

"Just to show you," he said. Then he put his hand on my neck.

"Like this. This is one of the things they should have taught you in karate," he said, and pushed.

"Okay, I get the idea. Now you can let go. You'd be in real trouble if I lifted you over."

"No, you couldn't," he said. "Look." He got one of my arms pinned across my chest and held the other one down by the wrist against the top of the wall. His right hand was still on my neck.

"You see?" he said, and pushed again, not too hard. My head went back and I looked into his face.

"See?"

Then he shifted his weight, leaning closely against my legs so that I couldn't kick to the side.

"See?" he said. My head kept going back and back and back over nothingness, the sun came down on my eyelids and cheeks and mouth, the wind moved over my hair.

"You see?"

And all at once, I did see. I saw the whole picture: about Diane and the last year, and why she was driving so fast, and what it had to do with me, and what Tilney was trying to do to me. I was looking into his face and I couldn't move. He was smiling.

Then he took his hand away from my neck.

"You're so nervous," he said. "Relax."

I closed my eyes, waiting for him to let go of my wrist and move away from me. And finally he did. I opened my eyes and looked down at his feet. It was the first time in my life I had ever seriously thought of killing someone, not at a distance from hindsight or in anticipation, but at the moment. It would have been easy to grab him by the knees and just dump him over.

"It really is quite a view," he said.

I walked away, pushing him aside where we still touched and going to find the knapsack. I picked it up and started to put it on as I went. I passed the two women, climbed the steps, went over the top and down the other set of stairs, and through the ruins, taking the path to the entrance. On my way I passed two or three ruined places set about four feet below the stone flooring I was walking on. They looked like bombed rooms, and in the center of one of them stood Earnie, with the airline bag at his feet. He was drinking out of an upended liquor bottle. The bag was unzipped and there were two other bottles inside it. As I went by he heard me and brought the bottle down. He looked in my direction and at me as though he had never seen me before. Then he turned his head and lifted the bottle again.

I got to the entrance, went out past the ticket place, and kept on going. I hit the path and started downhill. Tilney was coming after me, calling my name.

"Hey," he yelled. "Wait up."

I didn't stop or turn around. I took the first bend and the second before he got near.

"Hey," he called to me, "you didn't think I meant it, did you?"

I walked faster.

"Barney—" he said.

I could hear him breathing.

"What the hell? Why are you going so fast?"

I turned the corner and sprinted for a way. We were going downhill quickly. Ahead was the bench in the wall with the ship carving.

Tilney kept up about six feet behind me.

"Are you crazy?" he said.

I stood it for another few yards while he called my name behind me, and then I turned around.

I knew my face must look terrible. I knew it for certain when I saw his expression.

"Jesus Christ, Barney, what is it?" he said.

I was so mad I couldn't speak. My throat was going like a snaredrum.

"Why are you looking like that?"

I was afraid that if I didn't say something he'd come closer and try to get near me. But my throat had closed up.

He came a couple of steps closer.

"What—" he started to say.

I hit his face. It was a very light blow that sliced him across the nose. I was furious that I hadn't really connected. And I was scared, because all control had left me. It was like trying to fight something in a nightmare. I didn't have the sense of my right arm; it felt heavy and unmovable, with no force, like a heavy arm made out of paper. I thought the only way to get out of the feeling would be to get him solidly by the throat, but I didn't want to touch him close to.

I hit him again in the face, near the eye, with the same horrible lightness. I was panting and making a strange noise with every breath.

"Look," he said, and when he saw that I was going to try a third time, he looked as though he might start to laugh. That helped me. On the third time I connected. I busted him on the chin and felt it on my knuckles and up my wrist and forearm. His face went back and he took two steps backwards and sat down in the dust. He shook his head twice and his nose began to bleed.

I turned around and left him there, and walked on past the bench, not looking at the carving, around the corner and down the next slope. A few yards from the place where I could see another bend in the path, I stopped. I was drenched in sweat and gasping. I didn't know where I was, or even who. It was as though I had died or gone out of my mind. For the last few yards I hadn't even known I had been walking.

I put my hands over my eyes and tried to breathe deeply, like trying to cure myself of hiccups. And at last I got my breath back. Then I started shaking. All the muscles in the back of my neck and across my shoulders began to twitch. I was shivering like a dog. I took a deep breath and waited. And finally it left me. Everything left. I felt as though ten years had gone by.

I started walking again. On the next slope I met five people walking up the path, a man and two women and two children. At the lookout where the bougainvillea grew over the wall I stopped and lit a cigarette, and looked at the whitewashed houses down below, at the flowers, at the view. All the colors were clear and sharp and all the shadows behind them had lost the morning blueness and were black. I decided what I was going to do, and continued on down through the alleys, between the houses, past the tourist stands, and into the square. I bought two postcards and got two stamps out of my wallet and stuck them on. Leaning up against a wall, I wrote one card to my parents. And I started to think about the other one. To my right I could see people sitting down at tables in a café. I felt thirsty and went in.

I went up to the counter and ordered a beer. Behind the woman who served me, a picture of the king and queen hung on the wall. Everybody in Rhodes seemed to be pro-Monarchist, not like Athens. And not like Delphi, where we had met two men in a café, one of whom came from Salonika. They were both Communist and hated the royal family almost as much as they hated the Church. The one from Salonika wanted to be a writer and told us that a famous Greek writer, whose name I had heard of but kept forgetting, lived just down the road from the café. He said that he was interested in all kinds of writers, not just Communist writers, but what he really wanted in life was a house, and he described this imaginary house in great detail.

It would have a large, very large picture window. About the window he was insistent. Then he told us about the famous Greek writer's house. It, too, had the large window, and beautiful paintings. Modern paintings. While we were talking a priest walked by outside, and the young man from Salonika hissed, "Look at it, just look at it. That terrible old woman. Can you believe it? Just look." Watching him looking at the priest was like seeing the hairs go up on a dog's back. I had been very impressed by his self-assurance, by the way he knew exactly what he wanted out of life, and also by the things he had told us about Salonika and what he had been through up there although he wasn't any older than we were.

I drank half the beer at one go while I stood at the counter. Then I looked around and I saw Spiro sitting at one of the tables. The tables were tiny, almost like large plates, so it was hard to tell if any of the people were sitting alone or at someone's table. But he nodded to me, and so I went over to him and found a chair and sat down. He asked me something which I took to be a question about how I'd liked the beautiful ruins, and I smiled and did my best, and showed him the postcards. I asked him if he'd like a beer, and he smiled, so I went up to the counter again and bought him a beer. He asked me if I spoke French. I said, showing with my hand, a very little bit. He told me in French that he had four children and had an uncle in New York, and I told him how much I liked his country and especially Rhodes, which was more beautiful than the rest of Greece, and had trees and water, and was green. He said yes, and also beautiful beaches. Then he offered to buy me another beer in return, and I said no thank you, but a coffee, perhaps. When he brought it back to the table he asked me who the postcards were for. I said, "Relatives." Then I addressed the second card. And I wrote, "Dear Mrs. Tilney, Rick has had a good rest these past few days. I can really see what an improvement there has been, and I know he will be all right from now on. He wants to go on to Rome to visit some friends there and says he will be fine doing the trip alone. So I will be flying back home now. Rick sends his love and says he will write to you from Rome. Yours sincerely, F. Barnes."

Spiro finished his beer and I drank up my coffee. I asked him if there was a post office. He stood up and beckoned to me and we went outside, where he took me over to a mailbox. I dropped both cards in at once. That's that, I thought.

"*Voilà,*" Spiro said.

I thought he was talking about the cards, but when I turned my head I saw Tilney walking into the square. He had cleaned himself up, but you could see that there had been blood on his face, and see where it had dried around the nostrils. There was also a look about his chin and mouth and his left eye. No bruises yet, but he'd have a black eye in a few hours. He looked like a man who had been in a fight. Better than that, he looked as though he had lost.

Spiro said nothing, but I sensed his approval.

"*Allons?*" he said.

"*Oui allons.*"

We walked to the car and Tilney trailed after us. I got into the front seat again and we started off. He sat well back in the seat and didn't speak for a while, and then after a few minutes I heard him sigh.

"Well," he said. "It may not be karate, but you broke me up, all right. Tell them back home, don't mess with killer Barnes."

I kept looking straight ahead and didn't answer.

"Do you have the guidebook, Barney?" he asked.

I lit a cigarette and rolled down the window.

"Do you have any more cigarettes in the pack? I've gone through all mine," he said.

I fought down the urge to tell him to shut up. He was quiet for a little while. Then he said, "Look, Barney, I know I've been acting a little crazy. I'm sorry. I don't know why you didn't knock my block off before. It'll be different from now on."

If he starts leaning over the seat, I thought, I'll get Spiro to stop the car and I'll punch his teeth in and stop him talking for good. I was calm now, and I could do it. And I didn't think Spiro would mind. He thought Tilney had had it coming to him.

"It's just, you know how it is. I still haven't gotten over it yet. Sometimes I can't help it."

He went on for a while, and I let him. Finally he said, "I get it. We're not on speaking terms. We're going to teach me a lesson. What a hell of a day," and quit. We drove the rest of the way in silence, except for once or twice when Spiro said something in French. On the way back we passed the tree that had been down in the road. The truck was gone, and the men too, and they had lopped all the limbs off and sawn it so that it was lying in three pieces. I found it hard to believe that it was the same tree, and it seemed a hundred years ago since we had driven past it going the other way.

Spiro let us out in the main square. I paid him off, and shook hands. He said, *"Bonne chance."*

I started walking to the hotel.

"Well," Tilney said, "where do we go from here? I feel like hell. I don't suppose they've got a piece of steak on the whole island. I can see myself trying to get down a black eye with goat's meat."

Outside the hotel door I said, "I'll be back in five minutes," and left him standing there.

"Where are you going?" he said.

I walked back the way we had come, and headed for the bank. I'd remembered that I'd taken all my papers out of the suitcase and put them into the rucksack. Tilney hadn't liked the look of the hotel management.

At the bank I cashed all the traveler's checks I had with me except two that would get me home from New York. They didn't want to give me the full amount in dollars, so I settled for large amounts in drachmas and liras.

Then I went back to the hotel. Tilney was already up in the room. He was lying down on his bed with his arms over his eyes. I took off the rucksack and got out my keys. Then I unlocked my suitcase and put in the two suits I had hung up, and got shirts and socks and underwear out of the drawers and packed them. It took hardly any time at all. I didn't think Tilney even noticed what I was doing.

"I feel so rotten," he said.

I locked my suitcase, put it near the door, and took out my wallet. I counted out enough money to get me to the airport and some extra in case I had to spend a night in Athens or New York. Then I checked the ticket, got my raincoat off the hanger, and put the wallet and ticket in the inside pocket, and put the coat over my arm, and picked up the rucksack. In my right hand I held all the rest of the money wadded up in a rubber band.

"This is where we say goodbye," I said, and tossed the notes at him. They landed on his shirtfront. "What do you mean?" he said, and took down his arms. He took the money in his hand and sat up.

"What's this?"

"That's all the money your mother gave me to hold your hand. All except enough to get me to the airport and buy my bus ticket from New York. I've sent her a postcard saying that you're so much better you don't need me any more—"

"I do need you," he said. "Look, Barney—"

"—and you want to go on alone to Rome and meet some friends of yours there. And you're going to write to her as soon as you get to Rome. You'll have to pay the bill here. I didn't leave out enough for that."

"We can both go," he said. He dropped the money on the bedspread beside him. "I don't want all this, Barney. Let's forget—"

I turned to the door, opened it, and picked up my suitcase.

"Where are you going?"

"Indiana," I said, and I walked out, and down the hall, down the stairs, and out of the hotel. The man behind the desk tried to stop me getting to the door, but I told him firmly in English that my friend upstairs would pay.

And that was the last I saw of him for a long time. He wrote to me from Rome, but I didn't answer the letters. Then I moved to a different House in the fall, and he phoned me up a couple of times, but one of the few natural gifts I have always possessed is an ability to put people off over the telephone, so I avoided him that way. The first time I saw him on the way to classes I knew I was going to have to make it stick. I went into it like jumping into cold water—looked past him and kept walking. He said, "Barney," and I pretended I hadn't heard him. One or two times more it happened like that, and then he didn't try to speak, and after that I wasn't worried about it. We didn't have the same classes in any case, and those were the only times I saw him until graduation.

Then my mother saw the announcement of his marriage, and so I knew about that. The girl was another girl like Diane, only a bit more so, registered pedigree and snot boarding school and debutante, a year in Paris to learn cordon bleu, and six months of charity work in New York, and then the full-scale wedding. The paper had pictures. And that let him out again. I guessed that they would have two model children and he would be let out of even more, and go on to become another of America's brilliant younger generation whose dinner parties and political views, and charming young wife . . . and all the rest.

But a month later the papers carried the news of the suicide, which they called "a tragic yachting accident." Maybe it was, and maybe his family and her family had thrown money around to make it sound good. There was an inquest and everyone was bereaved but good-looking. After the first spread somebody saw to it that there were no more photographs.

It made me feel something, but not enough, and not in a definite way. I just thought that finally Tilney had been let out altogether. And I went ahead and was living my life and not thinking about him.

Then it was lunchtime, and eight years later, and I walked into a bar in town with Jack Halsey. We were meeting to put together the last pieces of a tax swindle pulled by somebody named Horowitz, and I'd asked Jack to look up some information on it at his office. I'd spent the whole morning running around town because none of us working on the thing had wanted to use the telephone at that stage.

We sat down at the bar and after a few minutes I recognized Tilney sitting over at the other end, big as life, whispering and laughing with some television actress who was wearing a fur coat. Luckily I saw him before he saw me, so I was prepared. I drank up and nudged Jack, and told him to finish his drink because I'd just spotted somebody I knew, and we were getting out. But Tilney looked up, in our direction, and suddenly knew me. Well, well, well if it wasn't Barney. How was economics, I was looking great, what was I doing that night, what was my telephone number? And so on. I said that I was moving house, so he couldn't get hold of me, but that I'd call him at his hotel. And who was my friend? I introduced Jack under a false name before he had time to open his mouth, and got out of the place quickly, saying that we had to get to a business lunch. Tilney kept telling me not to forget to phone him.

Afterwards, when we got outside, Jack asked what the hell, what the hell had that been all about? "I'll tell you later," I said. All through lunch I felt sick, but I didn't want to talk about it. We went over the Horowitz thing the way we had planned. Once or twice Jack asked, and that night when we were out at a party he asked again, "What was all that stuff about at lunch? About that guy in the bar?"

"I'll tell you later," I said again. And later, after a couple of days, I did try to tell him. But no matter how I began it, I couldn't get it right. There was that year at college, and the part about Diane, and then there was the day on the island, where everything came to a head. When I thought about that day it seemed to shift in my mind. Memory is very strange. If you look back to a time when you thought you suddenly saw the truth about something, or about someone, it can happen that your own later knowledge does something to it. It's almost as though people were made with an automatic mechanism for dispelling truth. The hardest thing to remember is the truth about yourself.

When I looked back on that day I remembered all sorts of things that might not really have struck me at the time. I remembered the carving on the rock face, the tree down in the road, the driver who had a watch like mine and a relative in America. I remembered the Frenchman reading his newspaper. And Tilney, through all of it. I remembered the look of the ruins, and the sea full of light and sweet as a growing field. I remembered the intense feeling of complete happiness I had known, which I had never had so strongly before and have never had again, when I saw the freedom and power of my future and could almost taste the fullness of my own life stretching out before me. And looking into Tilney's face with his hand on my neck, and his smile as he shifted his weight and pushed my head back over into the empty air.

And then I remembered very clearly the old man watching the birds and bellowing with enthusiasm, drunk as a coot at quarter to ten in the morning. And I could recall exactly how his wife had looked at him as she said in her flat voice, "Yes, you could say that, I guess. I guess you could say we've been just about everywhere."

St. George and the Nightclub

After dinner we decided to have coffee in the town and to walk around for a while. It was still light outside, although the sun was gone. Dusk was just beginning to accumulate, making the distances look different. And sounds, especially footsteps, were altered and had an echo as they do early in the morning. My wife buttoned her cardigan at the neck, but didn't put her arms in the sleeves.

We walked around the little garden plot outside the hotel and after we had gone by I remembered that I had meant to take a closer look at the statue in its center. We passed the old graveyard where some of the tombstones were crowned by turbans and the grass was growing wild. Then we came to a place where it looked as though a new villa was about to go up.

"You don't think it could be an excavation of some kind, do you?" she said.

"I don't think so, but you can never tell around here. Might be."

We turned the corner and came to the building whose function I hadn't been able to guess. It was stucco and had arches cut into the sides, which lent it a South-of-the-border look. I still couldn't determine whether it was the post office or the jail. In any case, no one was on duty.

We came out into view of the harbor. Two large tourist

cruise boats were tied up at the quay. There were people strolling around between the beds of hibiscus flowers, and three taxicabs still parked to the side of the café, with about a dozen men standing near them and talking.

I stopped, and tried to figure out the view we had had from the beach that morning. If you had your back to the sea, you could look towards the harbor and see a mass of houses and other buildings. That was what we had seen when we stood up to leave the beach before lunch, and then we had watched a large schooner, white as a swan, come sailing in from the ocean towards the buildings. It had looked just as though it was going to crash into them, but as we watched, it went straight through the middle and you could see that there must be water between the houses. It was one of the most extraordinary tricks of eyesight I had ever experienced. From where we stood we had seen the white sails riding serenely forward above the rooftops. It was as if I had been on the way to my job in the middle of the city and seen, a few streets off, a boat sailing past the office where I worked. Just to see such a phenomenon, to have had the ability to see it, convinced me for a moment that I had participated in the workings of the supernatural. It had made me feel transported, as though I had seen into another dimension, or been granted a special freedom or a miraculous talent not normally available to mankind. But my sense of perspective had altered now, and I doubted the fact that we had been able to see the thing happen.

"What are you looking for?" my wife asked.

"I'm trying to think of where that schooner could have come in this morning."

She pointed.

"Right over there, I'd guess."

"But there aren't many buildings around there. You remember how it looked? It seemed to be going through the center of a town full of buildings."

"Maybe it has something to do with the level we were standing on. Maybe the buildings we saw were farther away, like over there."

I looked, and she looked, and then I gave it up. We went up the café steps and sat down at one of the tables outside, and ordered coffee. While we were sitting there the café began to fill up fast. The light was still good, but suddenly we saw both tourist boats leap into different shape as the party lights, strung up high over the decks lengthwise and crossways, came to life.

"Want to stay here, or walk around?" I said.

"Let's walk."

We set out in the only direction there was to go, back into the town. There were people wandering around everywhere, some even taking photographs in the darkening air. All the shops were still open: copperware, rugs, jewelry. They all had their doors still open and someone standing in the doorway. We turned off onto a side alley, up stone stairs, and through several similar streets, and didn't seem to be getting anywhere.

"There's a shop," my wife pointed out to me.

"Where?"

"Up those steps, where those people are going. Listen."

There was music coming from inside.

"I think it's a private party."

"No, there's a sign. Let's go see."

"Do you want to buy anything?"

"No," she said, "but we might just take a look."

We climbed up the stairs. Two people came out of the door as we reached the top, and the rooms inside were loud with voices. There were three rooms full of rather better quality tourist wares than we had seen so far: icons, bedspreads, blouses, records, ashtrays, cocktail trays, and so on. There was even a collection of marble eggs. The music came from a portable phonograph, and all the talk from the people who had come inside to buy and had either struck up conversation with each other or with the owner.

The owner was a large man in his fifties, with a moustache and the sort of beard which had had a name given to it in the nineteenth century. Most of the beard was on the chin and the moustache was cut to grow down around the sides of the mouth to meet it, but the cheeks were bare. It suited his face. Sitting down at a table in a corner of the first room was a woman who might have been his wife or a sister, or a more distant relative. She had an account book and pencil beside her on the table and a metal cash box next to them. She nodded to us as we came in.

My wife said good evening in Greek. I said it in English. The woman replied to both of us in English and Jean said, "May we just look around?"

"But of course," the woman said, and made a graceful gesture with her hand as though she were giving us the whole house. My wife headed for the hand-printed materials in the second room, where the owner was talking to two couples. One of the couples was American, the other was English. The Americans looked married and neat and relaxed. They were both deeply tanned and gray-haired. The English people looked as though they might have been a heavy industry salesman and his secretary on an illegal expense-account holiday. She had incongruously platinum-blond shoulder-length hair held back with a scarf which was tied like an Alice-in-Wonderland headband, and she made frequent use of the kind of laugh that let any man within hearing know that she would be a heavy drinker and game for propositions and got a lot of fun out of life. The man was in slacks and a sportsjacket, without a tie, and spoke with one of those English accents that's only just off around the vowels. He had a moustache, too, but on him it seemed more a matter of habit than adornment, and didn't

do much to tone down his expression of happy lecherous-
ness.

The American woman had forgotten the name of the
cruise ship she had arrived on. She asked her husband, who
told her the name.

"That's right. It's one of the boats in the Epirotiki line.
They're quite good."

"Epirotiki?" the Englishman exploded, slapping his thigh.
"Christ, I don't believe it! Epirotiki," he repeated, and grabbed
his girl, who broke up, hanging on to his arm.

"That's what we thought, too," said the American husband.

"Really," his wife added. "It's a real name."

The owner began to tell them all a story about a woman
who had been on a cruise with a line which had given all
its boats names like Aphrodite, and Agamemnon, and Homer. Then she went on a tour to Mycenae, and when the
guide explained to her how Agamemnon had brought his
conquering army back from Troy through the Lion Gates,
she had said, "Gee, how did they get a big boat like that
through such a little place?"

Then he told them a story about a woman who had been
in his own shop, looking at the icons. He made a brief
digression to discuss the kinds of icons he stocked, and told
something of the history of the monasteries from which
they came, or in some cases, from which the wood came.

My wife had wandered into the farthest room, but I
stayed to admire the owner's technique. It seemed to be
wasted talent in such a small place. On the other hand, the
shop looked very prosperous.

"So I was explaining to her, and she picked up one of
the icons and wanted to know the date. I told her it was
seventeenth century. And she said, 'Gosh, B.C.?' "

The American couple laughed a lot. And the English

couple joined in, but they had considered Epirotiki much funnier. I wondered if the owner changed the nationalities of the characters in these stories to fit his hearers, but on second thought I doubted it. Most good tourist blunder stories are about Americans, and American tourists always enjoy hearing them.

I joined my wife in the third room, and the others began to move off to see the icons. She was looking at cocktail trays.

"Well," she said, "they're all nice, but there are just as nice ones at home, and I don't know how I'd ever get it back."

"You could say it was one of your suitcases that got run over by a steamroller."

"Yes," she said absently, and fingered a rack of dresses all made in the style I call "hand hewn." I went back into the second room. Three more people had men was saying, "But honey, what would you do with it?' I didn't see what the object under discussion was. I wandered on into the first room. The two couples had gone and been replaced by three white-haired Frenchwomen. The owner had changed the record on the turntable and was speaking French to the women.

I looked at the icons, which ranged in size from one big one as wide as an arm, to a few tiny ones about three inches by four. Most of them were about the size of a large book. The prices were marked in pounds, francs, and dollars as well as drachmas, and ran from three hundred and fifty dollars down to eighteen. I was looking at some of the smaller ones just larger than playing cards, when one of them caught my eye.

It was a picture of St. George slaying the dragon. The saint himself was dark brown, with lighter brown hair, and his horse was pure white. George's expression wasn't very interesting, but the attitude of the horse's raised hoof and flowing mane and the posture of its head, all gave an impression of near-foolish innocence which was rather endearing. What I liked best about the picture, however, was the dragon underneath. It was shaped vaguely like an alligator, and bright green. Up above, St. George was leaning on his lance, which went straight through the dragon and out the other side, bringing with it a runnel of lovingly painted blood that ended in a pool on the ground. The dragon had his tail curled into loops and his ears laid back like a cat, and the one visible yellow-brown eye shone with a look of furious glee.

The owner came up behind me as I bent over the icon, and began to talk to me about all the different ones that I wasn't looking at. I admired his technique even more. My wife joined us, and I asked what was the reason for the difference between the prices on the three small ones I had been looking at before, and he gave me a condensed history of the rarity of certain portraits. I didn't listen very hard. My wife was trying to catch my eye.

"I like the St. George," I said.

"Yes, yes. An English saint."

"But the dragon is international."

He laughed, and picked the icon up in his hand. "Yes," he said, "it is nice," and then he put it back on the shelf. This was not a shop where you tried to knock the price down; if you didn't buy it, somebody else would.

"Will you take a traveler's check?" I asked.

"Yes, certainly. You want to buy it?"

"Yes."

My wife made a sort of hissing noise, and I glanced at her and smiled. She was looking fed up with me.

The woman at the table told me how to make out the checks, and I gave her a twenty and a ten, and got the change back, eight dollars in drachmas. There was a pile of other traveler's checks under a spring clip attached to the side of one of the compartments of the metal box. She wrapped the icon up in pink tissue paper and put pieces of scotch tape on the corners.

The owner said, "You have had dinner?"

"Yes, at our hotel."

"There is a good nightclub, if you don't go back yet. Music and wine, and dancing."

He handed me a card like a calling card, with the name of the nightclub printed on one side, and a street map on the other. There were five piles of cards and a ballpoint pen on one of the shelves. One card for the shop, one for the nightclub, and the others presumably for restaurants and hotels. Before he handed it to me he had marked it with the pen.

"We are here, you see?"

"I see," I said. "Well, fine. We might give it a try. Thank you."

"Not at all. You will like it. Everybody goes there."

"Does the name mean anything special?"

"It is a Turkish word. It means a—hob-goblin." He searched with his fingers in the air for another word. "A bogey man. They are night spirits."

I thanked him again and said good night to him and the woman at the table, and my wife was polite in saying her goodnights, but furious when we got outside.

"Don, those things are all fakes. It was probably painted last week and the varnish has just dried."

"I know that. I just like the dragon."

"Oh, for heaven's sake."

"I'm not interested in whether it's genuine or not. I think it's worth it for the picture."

"It's a waste."

"But I like the dragon. Do you want to go to this place?"

"Not specially."

"We could just look in and see what it's like."

"If we ever get out of here. I'm lost."

The night had gone dark while we were inside the shop, and there weren't many lights. I decided that if we kept walking downhill we'd reach the harbor.

"There it is," my wife said after a while. "I can see the lights on the boats."

The lights on the tourist boats reminded me of something, but I wasn't sure what. Not exactly of Christmas trees or of ferris wheels, but of something just as definite which I couldn't for the moment recall.

We came out two streets to the right of the café, and looking farther to the right I saw the nightclub. The name was written out in electric lights over the door and the painted letters underneath the lights had the bulbous, cur-licue shape of circus poster writing.

"Let's have a look," I said.

"All right."

There was a knot of people entering as we came up. We followed them into a sort of cloakroom and I saw that you had to buy tickets as a cover charge. The door into the club opened and the sound of the music came through, and I could see lots of people sitting at tables.

"What is it?" my wife asked.

"Just a cover charge."

"Let's go, then."

"Don't be so stingy. It looks like this is the only nightclub in town. We might as well see it, and hear some of the music."

I paid, and we were pushed through the door. The people who had gone in ahead of us were still standing up, waiting for a table. There was a circular dancefloor in the center of the room; it was about ten feet in diameter, raised up, and the surface looked as though it had been covered by a special material to insure against slipping. No one was dancing on it.

Looking from the doorway, the building was a reversed L-shape. The foot of the L was very broad and branched off to the left. Everyone sitting in it would be able to see the little wedge of dancefloor. About three-quarters of the way across from the door, the part of the room in the longer upright of the L was raised three feet up, and there was a white open-work fence like a stair railing across all that part of the room except for the middle passage, where there were stairs going up. The whole floor, not counting the dance circle, was bare wood and very scuffed. Two carpets ran across it like trails, one up the stairs, and one over to the left. To the right of the door, backed up against the wall, a sitting band played, and a statuesque girl was singing at a microphone.

We were bullied along the carpet and then halted.

"You don't mind you sit all at one table?" the waiter asked me. He seemed to be including several other people in the request.

"We don't mind," I said. Two of the people turned around. It was the English couple from the shop.

"Do you mind sharing?"

"Not in the least, old chap," he said.

The other couple were very young. The boy was saying to his girl, "I don't think there's a table for two."

"Are you American?" I asked him, and he turned around. A big, beefy boy in a seersucker suit, with a light crew cut and a face full of freckles. He smiled sheepishly.

"Yeah," he said. "What gives here, anyway?"

"They're doubling us all up. Do you mind joining us?"

"Oh. No, we don't mind, do we, Linda?"

The girl looked at me and gave me a come-on smile.

"We'd love to," she said. She was small, but wearing very high heels. Her eyes opened all the way up like a doll's so that no lid showed.

"It looks like they've got plenty of tables up there," the

boy said, indicating the raised part of the room behind the railings.

"Reserved for a party, maybe. Or maybe the Greek navy's arriving at midnight."

"I'd like to see that," the Englishwoman said. We all started to introduce ourselves. Her name was Betty and the Englishman was Graham. The waiter darted forward and began to shoo us along the carpet to the left, and sat us down at a table not far from the wall. Another waiter was hanging over us with a notepad in his hand before we had even sat down. I ordered a bottle of retsina. Graham wanted to go through the wine list. I said to the American boy, "I'm sorry, I didn't catch your names."

"Linda Whiting," the girl said, and then corrected herself. "Linda Butterworth."

"Rocky Butterworth," he said, and held out his hand. I shook it and introduced myself and my wife and Betty and Graham, whose last names I hadn't heard distinctly.

"Honeymooners, or I miss my guess," Graham said to them.

"Give the poor kids a chance," I said. "Everybody and their grandmother has been asking them if they aren't on their honeymoon."

"They certainly have," the girl said, and Butterworth grinned self-consciously. I told him that I didn't think there would be much sense in ordering a cocktail unless they were really dying for one. It would be a lot better, and also cheaper, just to order a bottle of the local wine.

"I can't bear the local wine," Graham said.

"What I'd give for a snowball," Betty told him.

"What do you say to some champers, old girl?"

Linda looked up. "What's champers?" she asked.

"A spot of the old bubbly."

"Champagne," I said.

"Do you want some?" Butterworth asked.

"No, let's follow Mr. Coleman's advice," she said, demurely flicking her doll's eyes in my direction.

My wife lit a cigarette and blew a long jet of smoke across the table. Then she looked as though she were about to smile, and murmured, "My goodness." Butterworth started to turn around. "No, don't look just yet," she said.

I glanced quickly to the side and saw what she was looking at: the table to the left, up against the wall. It was like a tableau out of something by Zola. A local tart, perhaps attached to the club, was being treated to champagne by a family man out on the town. He looked very respectable and was wearing Sunday best with a stiff collar. And he was very, very drunk, but quietly so. As I watched, the waiter poured out the last of the champagne, upended the bottle in the bucket, and went for a new one. He seemed to be working for that table only. And the whore was fabulous. She was squat, well muscled but not fat, and wore a nineteen-twenties type of sleeveless black evening dress with glimmering black beads or sequins sewn on it. Her bushy short hair was parted in the middle and dyed a dark orange-red, and underneath it her face—low forehead, deep-set eyes and a prominent nose—had the stony, libidinous look of a gargoyle. She might have been any age from twenty-five to fifty, and she was the only clip-joint girl I had ever seen who actually drank. She was belting back her champagne as fast as the man.

Their fresh bottle of champagne arrived at the same time the English couple's did.

"No, leave it here," Graham ordered our waiter. Nobody was going to wrap a towel around his bottle and turn it upside down into the bucket while it was still half full.

"Chin chin," he said.

"Cheerio," Betty laughed.

"Christ, I hope he thinks it'll be worth it."

"He probably won't be sober enough to find out," I said.

"Always sober enough for that, old boy," Graham said, and leered in the Butterworths' direction. Butterworth looked into his glass as though searching for a fly. Linda asked my wife what resin was.

"It tastes like leather," she said. "But it's some kind of gum, isn't it?"

The girl at the mike started on another song which I thought was probably Turkish. She was getting a lot of appreciation out of the two big tables to our right, where about fourteen men dressed in unpressed dark suits were drinking together. They might have been dockworkers or taxidrivers, or waiters on their time off. None of them was out of hand, but the pitch of their talk rose, and they were looking at the singer with increasing approval.

"Can you understand any of the words?" Butterworth asked me. His wife and mine were carrying on their conversation across us.

"I have a feeling this one is Turkish," I said. "All the Greek ones have words like *monos*, which means alone, and then there's another word that means pain. As far as I can figure out, they're all about some boy standing on his girl's doorstep and feeling out in the cold."

"Would you say this was very authentic music?"

"I don't know. They haven't played 'Never On Sunday' yet, or that other one."

" 'Zorba,' " he said.

"Just taking a guess, I'd say it's like American and Scottish folksongs: the more off-key it sounds, the more authentic it is."

The singer was doing a lot of sexy death-of-the-breath business around the minor notes. I took a long drink and began to feel high.

"Does it excite you?" I asked him.

"I don't know. It just sounds so foreign to me. And a little monotonous."

"It makes me feel excited," I said.

"Oh, don't go there," my wife was saying to Linda.

"I like the ones they dance to," he said. "The faster numbers. Like balalaika stuff."

"Yes, I like those, too."

A waiter sped past with another bottle of champagne for the two against the wall.

"You can look now," I told Butterworth.

He turned his head slowly, saw them, turned back and was laughing.

"Gee, is he going to be sorry in the morning," he said. "They're going to have to carry him out."

Graham was making toasts to Greece, to Rhodes, to the nightclub. A man sitting at the table to our right had been included in the toasting and given a glass of champagne.

"I wonder who that is," my wife said. Linda turned around, and I looked, too. At a table just below the raised part of the room sat a man in a white dinner jacket, a red flower in his lapel. He had his own private waiter. While we were watching, the waiter presented him with a tiny gray tiger-striped kitten.

"Oh, how cute," Linda said. "I guess that's the local millionaire or something."

He was middle-aged and looked rich, healthy, civilized, and as though he were enjoying himself.

"All alone, too," Linda said. "Do you suppose he's waiting for somebody?"

"Maybe he's the owner," I said.

"Oh no, I'm sure he's sailed here in his yacht."

"You romantic," I said, smiling.

"Oh yes, I sure am. I'd hate to be anything else."

My wife was taking small, discrete sips of her wine. She wasn't enthusiastic about retsina. The song ended, and Graham leaned over Betty.

"This chappie says the bloke's the chief of police from one of the other islands."

"The guy with the gargoyle?"

"That's the one. If they knew about it at home!"

"And he probably has a wife and five children at home, too," said my wife. "I bet that's his year's salary. And what do they get?"

"If she knows what she's about, she gets the milkman while he's away," Betty said, laughing.

Graham pinched her under the table.

"Now then, none of that," he said.

"Not a chance," my wife said. "In Greece they probably lock them up before they go away."

For a moment Graham had the look of a man about to unburden himself of a story about chastity belts, but he changed his mind and took another long look at the visiting policeman and his incredible child of joy.

"What a perfect situation for blackmail," he said. And not for the first time in the evening, I wondered what his work really was. There was something spurious about him.

"Oh look," Linda said, "they're going to dance."

A man from the band had come forward, leading the singer with the dark hair. Behind them walked another woman, with auburn tinted hair. She was big, but lovely looking. Both women had the same teased-up hairstyle that fell into a curl at the base of the neck. The auburn girl wore a skin-tight bronze dress. The dark one was wearing green. A second man joined them on the dancefloor as the music began.

All four joined hands and began to dance around in a circle. Every once in a while one of the dancers, still holding hands, would crouch down and twist, first into the center of the circle, then out to the side, and then jump up again.

"The one in the gold dress is beautiful," my wife said.

"My God, what a body," Graham said. "Have you ever seen anything like it? She's like one of those jars—what do you call it—"

"Like an amphora," I said.

"That's it, like those wine tubs. I say, it's solid. Isn't she marvelous?"

"She is," Betty agreed.

"You couldn't dance like that, could you?"

"Why not? I'll take you on for the challenge match."

"That's very sporting of you," he grinned, and kissed her neck while she laughed.

I said to Butterworth, "Tell Linda not to clap when it's finished. It's considered an insult."

He whispered to Linda. From the other side of the room where a group from the tourist boats had been seated, came rhythmic finger clicks. At the end of the dance they applauded wildly. Linda turned around and made a smug face, and said, "They don't know any better."

The policeman's waiter scurried past us with another bottle and the next dance began. The men dropped out this time and left only the two girls.

"I thought Greek dances were only for men," Butterworth said.

"I think they're supposed to be," I said. "But the regular crowd obviously comes for the girls."

The policeman was so drunk that he didn't know there was any dancing going on. He remained looking across the table at the woman. They were getting so drunk that it was almost painful to watch, although it was also funny. I was slightly tight myself. Not very, but enough to feel good.

When the dance had ended, the two girls went back down the carpet to the band. Then the man in the white evening jacket stepped forward. He was holding the kitten in his hand. The band began to play again, and he stepped up onto the dancefloor, putting the kitten on his shoulder. And with the kitten sitting there, and a lighted cigarette in his mouth, he did the slow leap and jump and handclap dance, his shoulders back, his arms loosely out to the side, and pivoting from the hip.

"Oh," Linda said. "Oh, isn't he wonderful?" She had clasped her hands together over her collarbone.

Still dancing, the man handed the kitten out to a waiter. He got a round of applause for that. Then he took the cigarette out of his mouth and stuck it into his left nostril, and danced that way. The steps became more complicated and the leap more dramatic, but the dance hadn't changed in quality or pace. It was still a combination of casual sloppiness and iron muscular control. The other people in the club did not matter to him. I'd seldom seen anyone who could enjoy himself alone like that without actively ignoring others around him. Most people need a group or another person. This man clearly was happy without needing anyone or anything. He was dancing for the sake of the dance and for himself. I was glad we had come.

When he had finished, Linda started to applaud and caught herself just in time. My wife wanted to, too.

"That was great," Butterworth said. We all agreed. The light-haired singer began a song in Greek. Graham and Betty had their arms around each other's necks. The Butterworths finished their bottle. She lit a cigarette and beat him to the draw with a miniature lighter which might have been a going-away present.

"Let's go soon, okay?" he said to her.

She blew a lot of smoke in his direction and looked straight through him.

"What for?" she said. Just like that. Then she covered up. "I'm having fun," she said. "Aren't you having fun? I want to see the millionaire dance again. He was terrific."

"Sure," he said. "Anything you like."

He lifted his glass and as his head turned I could see the

tight little smile on his face. Graham and Betty burst into laughter at some private joke. It occurred to me that of the six of us they were having the best time, although they were so obviously not married. And they seemed to be lovers of long standing. There must have been some story to it. One of them was probably married. Perhaps they were both married to different people.

"What do you say, old girl," he said.

She downed her champagne and said, "Righty-ho. Mm, that's good."

He signaled to the waiter and made motions of writing on paper. "Well," he announced, "we'll be pushing off. The little woman needs her beauty rest, you know."

"I'm sorry we couldn't stay and see the Greek navy arrive," she said.

The waiter brought the check and Graham looked at it carefully. Then he put his finger on it. The waiter bent over, took out his ballpoint and changed a few numbers. Graham took out his money.

"They fiddle the bills here," he said. "Word to the wise."

"I know," I said, "I could see it coming. You wouldn't think they'd have to with the cover charge and everything."

Graham's change came, and he counted that, too. When he was satisfied, he stood up and hauled Betty to her feet.

"Night all," he said. Butterworth and I stood up, and we all said goodnight.

As they left, the dark girl came out onto the dancefloor and did a solo routine between snatches of a song. She had a portable microphone around her neck and made the attached wire form part of the dance.

"I want to see the millionaire again," Linda said.

I said, "I want to see the cop get out of here under his own steam."

Two waiters had converged on his table, and he was laying out lots of banknotes. When they had gone, the female gargoyle snatched up her bag and stood up. The policeman rose as though breaking to the surface from a great depth. He seemed to see the door, faced it, and moved towards us. On our side of the room all attention was focused on him. It was like watching a dying man. His face looked as paralyzed as the face of a man who had had a stroke. And his body was rigid. Very slowly, with the dignity of a man in pain, he went forward. The woman let him pass, and followed along behind him. There was nothing wrong with her walk, in fact she was full of zest in spite of that fixed, gargoyle look. The two waiters walked behind her and she talked and laughed with them as the policeman maneuvered his stiff and poisoned body all the way to the door.

"Well," Butterworth said. "I guess this is one of those places where you could just sit at a table and see the whole of life."

"It's quite a joint," I agreed.

We waited until the dark girl had finished her number and left the dancefloor, and the other girl had begun another song standing up by the band.

"What do you think?" my wife said.

"Had enough?"

"Yes."

"Me, too." I waved the waiter over.

"Let's go," Linda said.

"Okay," he answered, and signed to the waiter that they wanted to go, too.

"Where are you staying?" I asked him. They were staying at the hotel we were at.

"Well, we can walk back together," I suggested. "Unless you want to wander up and see the fortifications by moonlight. There's enough of a moon tonight."

"I'm too tired," Linda said.

I checked the count and took a look at Butterworth's tally.

They had charged me the wrong price and added an extra bottle to his. The waiter didn't seem upset at having to change the numbers. I supposed that later in the evening, or the morning, nobody noticed much of anything.

We walked out along the quayside, and I felt better than I had for a long while. It was a beautiful balmy night and I was just the right amount drunk. Just enough to feel relaxed and lighthearted. The lights on the two tourist ships reminded me more than ever of something, but I still couldn't remember what. As we walked, my wife and Linda fell into step together ahead of us.

"Can I ask you about something?" Butterworth said.

"Sure."

"Something important."

"Money?"

"No, no. Nothing like that."

"Okay." I called to my wife, "You two go on ahead. We'll meet you at the hotel."

"All right," she said, and they kept walking.

"Do you smoke?" I asked.

"No."

I took out a cigarette and lit it. We stood still for a while, until the women were far enough away. Then we saw them turn the corner past the café. I could hear the waves hitting up against the quay and thought I could hear them against the boats in the harbor.

"Let's find someplace where we can sit down," I said.

"All right," Butterworth mumbled.

We walked past the café. All the chairs were fitted into each other and the stacks turned upside down on the tabletops so that the top chairs had their legs pointing up to the ceiling. It looked like a shop for large Chinese puzzles. Now that the tablecloths had been taken away, the tables and chairs looked worn, and centuries old.

"It's about Linda?" I said.

"Sort of."

"And marriage in general?"

"That's right."

"The honeymoon's got you both a little on edge."

"That's it in a nutshell."

"Well," I said.

"You see, I'm not sure exactly—I mean . . . now she's . . . um."

I didn't look at him because I'd only just become aware of the extent of his embarrassment.

"Let's go up here," I said. We turned off into a side street. There was another empty place which looked as though it might be a construction site, but later I thought it might have been one of the real excavations. There was a wall next to the minute sidewalk, and a creeper growing over it. I sat on the wall and Butterworth sank heavily down next to me. There were some flowers on the vine, but no scent of flowers, just a fresh smell of leaves.

"Did you have any other girls before you got married?"

"No, that's just it. See, I was brought up kind of strict."

"And Linda, too?"

"Not so much, but there wasn't anybody serious before. I mean, she never—you know."

"She never slept with anybody either."

"No."

"And it isn't working out so well?"

"No, that's just it."

"Have you read any books about it?"

"Not exactly. Um. You see, I was brought up kind of strict and back home—well. It was considered not right to read those kind of books, if you see what I mean."

"I don't mean pornography. Just a medical book, or Reproduction and Society or something like that."

"No. Well, we had biology class in highschool, but you know. I mean, it was all about frogs and starfish and things. And that isn't the same."

I laughed. "No, that isn't quite the same."

I heard him draw a deep breath. He was shaking, but not with laughter. I thought that he probably wanted to back out of the conversation, but couldn't. It was more than embarrassment. It was all over him and around him like an emotional blanket. My own son was old enough so that I had given him the "Momma fish and Poppa fish" talk and it hadn't worried me. I had handed out the euphemisms, knowing that all they need at that stage is to know you're not nervous about it yourself, and to know you aren't using foreign, secret words, and to hear that your voice is steady and see that your face is normal. I thought that if my son had been this age, it would be all right. Not that I'd have let him reach Butterworth's age in such a state, but at least I'd know his reactions.

I realized that I was sweating, and was glad that the light was so bad where we were sitting.

"But surely you have friends who've talked about it," I said.

"Oh, yes. But I tried not to listen. I mean, it starts off and then it's all dirty jokes, and I just don't think that's funny."

"Well," I said. I was exasperated. And I was beginning to catch his inhibitions. For one appalling moment I considered plunging in at the deep end and asking him point blank whether he couldn't get it up or couldn't get it in.

"Can I just ask you one thing?" he gasped.

"Yes, sure."

"Are all girls . . . Do they all have . . ."

"Have what?"

"I mean, is it usual for . . ."

"Come on, spit it out."

"Are they all so hairy?" he blurted out.

"Hell, yes," I said quickly, and gritted my teeth so that I wouldn't laugh. "Rather nice, when you get used to it. You've never seen a girl without her clothes on."

"No. Just paintings and stuff."

"And that's different. That's the trouble. All these things are different."

"Exactly," he said.

"Okay," I told him. "I'll give you a short description of what the average girl should look like in the natural state."

I gave him the description, and he listened, but he was still wound up like a spring. Then I let him have a short list of steps that could be taken to get a girl into a good mood. It was fairly explicit but there was no Latin in it.

"Another thing you can try is to make her laugh."

"Oh my God," he said. I couldn't see his face, but it sounded desperate. The whole shape of him in the dark looked defeated and thrown away.

"All right," I said. "Let's get technical."

For about ten minutes I got technical. That seemed to cheer him up. He started to ask one or two questions. Then I got less technical, and he was asking "is that usual?" and "is that normal?" I kept saying, "Hell, yes." Once I made him laugh, just once. And then he sighed, and said, "Well," and stopped, as though really nothing had been resolved. So I asked him to tell me what kind of person this girl of his was. Was she very bossy, did she have a sense of humor, was she easily frightened?

He began to tell me about her. Not much, but just enough to let me know how he felt. He was obviously very proud of her, and a bit sentimental, too. He would start to tell me about things she had said, or ways she had shown how wonderful she was, and then he would trail off. He didn't really want to talk about her to another man. But then, he wanted other people to know that there never was such a girl. During this part of the talk he sounded much more relaxed.

"Have you two talked about it at all?" I asked him.

"All the time, that's all we do. I mean, not exactly talk about it. But, you know, arguing."

"What I meant was, just sit down and ask each other if you're willing to work it out."

There was a long pause while he took this in.

"If you've decided you want to live together and be with each other all the time, for the rest of your lives—well, you're grown up now, and you've made it legal, and you can do anything you like. You can go to a doctor or a marriage counselor or Swedish sex movies, or you can skip the physical side of it altogether for a while and just see how you get along living in one room for a month and trying to be nice to each other. As long as you're willing to have it work, you'll be okay. As long as you really want it to turn out right."

"Yes, I know." It didn't sound completely confident.

"Okay. I'll tell you a couple of stories."

I'd never had such an audience. Once he said "wow" and one or two times he said, "That's terrible," and when I paused, "What happened then?" The stories were more or less true, although I was making them all end well, and that hadn't always been true.

"Of course other people's stories are never the same, but you see what I mean."

"Listen, I want to thank you."

"No need."

"You don't know what a difference it's made. I feel a lot clearer about everything."

"Good," I said. I slapped him lightly on the shoulder and got to my feet.

"You'll be okay."

"I believe I will," he said.

We turned the corner and came in sight of the hotel.

"It's quite a place, isn't it?" I said.

"It's huge. It must have hundreds of rooms."

"I expect they cover their losses with the summer months. This is really the best time to be here."

We passed by the round garden plot with the statue in the middle, and I saw that my wife was waiting down below in the lobby. She was sitting in one of the chairs and just preparing to stub out a cigarette. The girl must have gone straight up.

She looked in our direction when we came in, and stood up. The difference there is in a face when someone is glad to see you—not even the posture of the body is the same.

"Well, goodnight," Butterworth said. "Goodnight," he said to my wife, and started for the stairs.

"Do you have the key?" I asked.

"They're in your pocket. You always do that."

We walked slowly towards the stairs.

"Did you have a good long talk?" she said under her breath.

"Did you?"

"Did we ever."

I looked up and saw that he had turned to the left. Our rooms were up the second flight, to the right, and then down a corridor. It was a fine hotel, one that I should have liked to stay in for a long time. And under different circumstances.

The stairs were marble, and the long carpet fixed on with stair rods had a Persian design. On every third step stood some kind of palm in a large tub. The palms went all through the corridors and must have meant a lot of work. I hadn't seen anyone sponging the leaves, but I thought that was what you were supposed to do with potted plants. There must have been hundreds of them if the other floors were like the first two. It should have been called the *Hôtel des Palmes*.

"Well," she said as we started up, "I hope you gave him the benefit of your vast fund of technical tips."

I ran my hand through the fronds of one of the plants. They had a pleasant feeling, not cold or sticky like many leaves, but dry and clean. When I brushed my hand across them they spread out like feathers.

We came to the top and turned right, down the passage to the next flight of stairs. I touched a few of the palm trees as we passed. I was still a bit high. I looked at her, but her mouth had gone sour.

"My God, he spends an hour necking with her and then he leaves her high and dry and says, 'I'm happy just cuddling.' That was never your trouble, was it?"

We're not going to get into a fight again, I thought. Not if I can help it.

"You just had to do it with everybody," she said.

I got the keys out of my pocket. She took hers out of my hand.

"You can come in through my room," I said. I opened the door. As soon as she stepped over the threshold she asked, "Do you want the bathroom first?"

"No, you take it."

She opened the bathroom door. All the curtains blew out and the door on the other side of the bathroom, the one that led into her room, slammed shut with a loud, high crack like the sound that accompanies a direct hit by lightning. One of the shutters outside was banging.

"Close the window," she called, and leaned into the door.

The rooms didn't seem to be on a corner, but the draft couldn't be explained in any other way unless for some reason, incomprehensible to me, two opposite air currents met just outside the windows. Even one window open in one of the rooms was enough to set the place rocking if a door to the bathroom was open. I suppose there was a certain amount of suction from the corridors outside, too. On the first afternoon, when we had come up from lunch, I had opened the bathroom door and for five minutes it had sounded like blasting exercises in a quarry.

On the other hand, it was exhilarating, and while I was busy closing doors and windows, I regretted having to. I'd have liked to weight down everything in the room and open up the works. It would have been like being on shipboard, or even like flying, since we were just that much above the ground.

I had no desire whatever to go to sleep. I started to pace the room, flipped through a few books, and smoked a cigarette. After a while I heard the bathroom door open and close on the other side and the water running. I gave it a few minutes and then opened the door. She was standing at the sink, brushing her teeth.

The bathroom was like a vault. Marble basin, marble bathtub like a sarcophagus but bigger, and a tiled floor. Even at midday it was cool.

"I'm sorry," I lied. "I thought you were through."

"I'll be finished in a minute," she said, the toothbrush still going up and down. Nobody I had ever known could whip up so much foam from toothpaste or do it so fast. Maybe those early years taking piano lessons had created the perfect wrist muscles for brushing teeth.

She rinsed out the foam and spat it into the sink and started to clear away the brush and glass and to roll the tube up from the bottom. She did it meticulously, knowing that I was watching her in her nightgown. When she had screwed it up to bursting-point, she looked up at me angrily.

"That poor girl. She doesn't know anything about it and now she's married to that homo for life."

"He isn't."

"Of course he is. You can see it a mile away. He's queer."

She said it in an unpleasant way. We had several friends and a couple of relatives at home who were queer in one way or another, some in just the ordinary way, and it had never seemed to make a difference to her before. Now she was furious. She began to slap cold cream over her face.

"I don't think so," I said.

"The best thing she could do would be to get an annulment right away."

"Is that what you advised her?"

"You bet I did. And she can do it, too. All the proof is still there."

She finished with the cold cream and screwed the lid on.

"There," she said.

I touched her arm with my fingers.

"Jeanie—"

"Oh no. Not on your life. I am so very sorry, but I still do not think it should be just your nice way of ending the day with whoever happens to be handy." She whipped around and left the bathroom through her door, saying as she closed it, "You can ring for the chambermaid." I heard the bolt shoot home, and then nothing.

If I'd thought I stood a chance of getting it, I would have rung for the chambermaid. Poor Butterworth, I thought, if you only knew. I ought to have offered to give his wife a fatherly heart-to-heart talk for a couple of days.

I took the cap off the tube of toothpaste and squeezed some onto my toothbrush. Up and down, up and down. It's so much easier to brush them sideways. Then I washed my face, used the toilet, and went back into my room. This time I remembered to close the door. She was always telling me that I left doors open. I had probably left the cap off the toothpaste again, and squeezed the tube in the middle, too.

I paced the room. The wind roared up against the building, clattering the shutter. It cut out the sound of the sea.

I sat on the bed and began to undo buttons. In the morning we would go down the stairs together to breakfast in that enormous dining room where a dozen waiters stood against the wall like sentries and the sun filled the place, making the white tablecloths shine. And I would order a cheese omelette because the one I'd had that morning was one of the best omelettes I had ever tasted. It seemed a shame not to enjoy everything, everything it was possible to enjoy. But of course people can never enjoy enough, or at the right times, and certainly nobody ever learns.

There was a knock at my door. The wind distorted the sound so that at first I thought there was someone at the door to the hallway. I called, "Come," and the bathroom door opened.

"I can't find my murder mystery."

She still hadn't put on her bathrobe.

"I'll have a look," I said. "Come in and sit down."

"No, thanks. All I want is to find the book."

She frowned. Evidently the missing bathrobe hadn't been deliberate. She fidgeted her hands together and apart.

"You stay there. I can look for it. Where did you put the books?" she said.

"There are some on the dresser. I don't think it's there. And then a pile on the windowsill right next to you."

I got off the bed and looked over the books lying on the lace cloth on top of the big chest of drawers standing next to the wardrobe.

"Not here," I said. She was bending over the windowsill; like the ones in the bathroom it was marble and massive. And she had her back to me. The nightgown was one of those long nylon ones made with two layers of material which make you think you can see more than you actually can, or sometimes that you can't see as much as you imagine. They must hire sadists to design the things. Even the color was indistinct and mysterious, a sort of creamy, bluish gray. She leaned back on one leg and held up a book.

"Here it is," she announced.

And I couldn't resist. I stepped forward and grabbed her from behind. And then it happened so quickly: she shrieked "Oh!" and pushed me aside, and was out through the bathroom door, slamming it behind her, and I had tripped over the rug and gone headfirst into the marble edge of the windowsill.

At first I thought that the sound of the door was the sound of my head cracking open. Then there was another slam, the other bathroom door, which she was probably bolting again.

But I was sure that my head had split open. I fell back on my knees and looked at the stone edge. The whole of my head felt hot and searing and, at the same time, frozen. I was scared of trying to touch it, to see how badly I was hurt. Then I also had the feeling that my sight had gone. I knew I was looking straight at the window frame above the sill, but something was wrong with my eyes. Then I was sick, and for what seemed a long time I sat there looking at where I'd been sick.

I got up and turned around, and felt very strange. Maybe I was bleeding, I thought. Or something else. My left leg buckled and I staggered where I stood. Then I thought something really must be wrong and I'd better get to the wardrobe over against the wall, to look at my face. The wardrobe door had a mirror on it. So I started off. The floor went up and down. The door began to move away. Everything started to go prickly and the light changed and broke up into pinpricks, and the room made a zinging noise. The door went away, the floor went away. Then I went away, too.

When I came to, I wondered whether I might have been out for twenty-four hours. My head felt heavier and larger than I would have believed possible. First of all it felt as though someone had put a bowl over it, and secondly it was as if there was another projection of my head in a different place, about six inches in front of me, and that these two heads were joined by pain and I had to carry both of them with me.

"I've got to do something," I said out loud. It sounded peculiar, not like my own voice.

And finally I managed to get up, clean myself up, find my wallet, put on my coat, get out of the room, lock the door and start down the hallway, holding on to things as I went.

The whole place was deserted, of course. My watch said two-twenty.

Once I almost passed out again, stumbling into one of the potted palms and bringing down two branches. At the top of the main staircase I sat down for a few minutes and then took the descent slowly, crossed the lobby, and got to the desk. There was no one in sight. I banged the little service bell.

Nobody came. I thumped the bell less politely. Still no one. I was hitting the bell for the third time, a long series of pings, when footsteps started up.

Two men came out of the back room: one small, dark bear-like man looking not very pleased, and behind him what I thought must be the bouncer. He was at least a head taller than the first man, but so unnaturally muscular that he was almost square. It was freakish. I'd never seen even a Japanese wrestler built on such a scale. I hadn't seen him until he was actually standing behind his friend, and looking at him I doubted that he could move. I felt a sort of pity at the sight of him, as though I were looking at a cripple whose magnificent, disproportionate torso had been caused not by his own intention but by some glandular ailment. Above the bull-like neck his face looked back at me with the absolutely placid, relaxed gaze of a baby.

"Monsieur?" the smaller man said.

"*Je cherche*," I panted. "I search for the hospital. A doctor, a medicine. I am bad."

"Ill? Monsieur is ill?"

Oh God, I thought, they think I'm just a drunk who's wandered into the lobby. And my highschool French wasn't made for this.

I fished the key out of my pocket.

"A dream malicious. An evil dream . . ." I wanted to say I'd had a nightmare and banged my nose against something. But I couldn't remember the word for nightmare. The only word I could think of was one I vaguely remembered meant a mare's nest. Then I realized that my mind had telescoped the words in English, not in French.

"A dream, monsieur?" Then he said the word which must have meant nightmare.

"Yes, yes," I said. "In the dream, I battered—" I hit out with my arm to illustrate the nightmare battle. The bouncer looked at me with friendly interest.

"And then, when I opened the eyes—crash! And my nose, the nose . . ."

I'd forgotten the word for broken. All I could think of was *couper*, but that meant to cut.

"The nose," I said, pointing to it and being careful not to touch it, "the nose is destroyed."

"Ah?" the desk clerk said. He put his hand towards my face.

"No, no. The hospital, doctor, medicine," I said, and repeated, "the nose is destroyed, the nose is destroyed."

The clerk said something to his friend, who went behind the desk, got out a key, and moved out towards the front doors. He walked in an odd way, quite easily and yet slowly,

so it looked as though it gave him pain, as though he really
were musclebound. But perhaps it was my pain I was thinking about. And maybe he wasn't a bouncer at all, in fact
in such a respectable hotel he was probably just the other
man's brother-in-law or something, keeping him company
on the night shift.

Suddenly I had to sit down.

"Is there a chair?"

"But certainly, monsieur," the clerk said. He took me by
the elbow and walked me over to a chair. I put my head
down in my arms and he stood beside me with his hands
folded in front of him. I thought that when I finally got to
a doctor I'd ask him to amputate. Not the nose. The head.
I just wanted to be rid of the whole thing.

The clerk started talking. His French didn't seem at all
perfect, but was certainly better than mine. He was asking
me about the nightmare.

"Oh," I said, "I dreamed of the war."

"Ah, the war."

After a few moments he said, "But, monsieur is too young
to have served in the war, is that not so?"

"*C'était une autre guerre,*" I said. That was a different war.
"Not here." I made another hand signal, indicating far coun-
tries, and miraculously came up with the word *outremer*.
"Overseas. Far, far. In Korea."

"*Comment?*"

"The war against the Koreans."

There was a silence. He hadn't understood. He didn't
believe it.

"The war," I said, trying to give a near substitute, "against
the Chinese."

"Ah," he said. "The Chinese. But yes, that is formidable."

"Yes, formidable," I told him, and I think he said something about that being enough to give anyone nightmares.

I wondered if I ought to explain that I hadn't seen much active service and was in Tokyo and Hawaii a lot of the time, but the complexities of the French would have been too much for me, aside from the two heads, one like a bucket and the other one throbbing out in front of me.

After a while I heard a car pull up outside. The night clerk helped me to my feet, saying something sympathetic and patting me lightly on the back, and he and his friend both got me into the taxi outside. We drove off straight away.

"*A l'hôpital?*" I asked, and the driver said, "*Oui, oui,*" and added a lot in Greek, or perhaps it was Italian. I was too exhausted to know.

It was a short drive and we pulled up by a building that looked like the goods depot back home. Not a soul around. Everything looked the vague almost-color of moonlight, which makes your eyes strain after things and wonder what color they would be in daylight. The taxi driver hammered on a door until a light went on and someone came to open up. Then he explained the situation in Greek.

I thanked the driver, paid him, and tried to make him understand that he was to wait. But it was too difficult, and both men waved hands at me, telling me to forget whatever was bothering me and go inside.

There were one or two bare lightbulbs in the hallway, and several turnings. I tripped over a stepladder as we came around a corner. The next corridor had just been painted cream-color and there was paint-spotted canvas down on the floor. I couldn't smell paint, but it must have been in the air, because though normally I like the smell of paint, I wanted to throw up again.

"The physician," the doorkeeper said, opened a door for me, and continued on down the hall. A thin, neat man with a goatee walked towards me, shook my hand, and took me into the room. He sat me down on a chair and himself on another. I pointed to my head and told him that the nose was destroyed.

"*Ici?*" he said, and before I knew what he had in mind, grabbed my nose in his fingers. I fell backwards in the chair and screamed.

The next I saw of him, he was washing his hands in a basin across the room, a different room, and I was lying on a couch, with a sort of mask across my face and over my nose.

He gave me a bottle of pills and spent about ten minutes filling out forms, and I paid him on the spot and asked how long the splints and bandages had to stay on. Then he wrote an extremely beautiful letter of explanation which, apparently, I would be able to present to a doctor in Athens. It looked just like the lefthand side of the Loeb Classics and I was fascinated by the speed with which it was done. He put it in an envelope, which I was to keep, and then he gave me change and settled the costs. It seemed quite reasonable.

Going back in the taxi to the hotel I couldn't believe it was the same night. I didn't take the trouble to look at my watch. No time shown on it could match my impression of how late it was. To look at it would have given me the feeling of being cheated by reality, which I had had when I looked in the wardrobe mirror and did not see my head gaping open in front of me.

The desk clerk and his bouncer friend were full of admiration for my changed appearance. I tried to look happy about it, too, and said thank you to them, and made my way up the stairs.

The first flight was all right. The second flight was like the ascent of the Matterhorn. My eyes were beginning to get shell-shock from looking at so many palm trees and so many Persian patterns on the rug. But coming into the lighted, empty room was the worst of all.

I took off my jacket, and remembering by the weight of it that the icon was still in the pocket, took it out and unwrapped it and stood it up against the window on the ledge, like a wayside crucifix where an accident has taken place. So much for a patron saint, I thought. Then I went into the bathroom and got something to clean up the floor. It hurt to bend down.

I slept on top of the bed in my shirt and pants, not even bothering to take off my socks. I slept and woke and slept and woke again.

One month to see if the pieces could be put back together again. And then if not, back to the court. "The expense!" she had said. But what did it matter? If it was going to be final, everything would be ruined anyhow. And afterwards the lawyers, and the price of two households, and when would either of us afford a vacation again?

This is the end of the line, I thought. I remembered Butterworth and thought how little he knew of what was in store for him, for both of them if things worked out. They hadn't come to the stage of having children, worrying about money, schools, false friends, being thirty with nothing to show for it except the feeling that you would soon be forty. And then you're forty and still nothing to show for it. But that hadn't happened to me either yet, not quite. Would it happen to them? Eleven years falling into the machinery and being caught in it with all the wheels going around and tearing you to pieces, and then one day instead of being rescued, the factory suddenly closes down. There you still are, caught in a monster machine, but all motion has gone out of it.

In the morning she knocked at the door. "Are you there?" she called.

No, I'm somewhere else.

She knocked again.

I answered, "Yes." The sound went clanging through my head, the voice totally different. She opened the door.

"It's still all dark in here," she said. Then she noticed that I was lying on top of the bed with my clothes still on. She came closer.

"What's happened? What's that thing on your face?"

"You broke my nose," I said.

"I what?"

"Last night. You pushed me away and sort of lashed at me with your arm. I fell right into that stone thing. The edge of the shelf there, under the window."

"What?" she said again. I had been mumbling because it hurt less. She came to the bed and I repeated the story.

"Oh," she said. "Do you want to come down to breakfast?"

"No, I'll stay here."

"I can get room service to bring it up."

"I don't want anything. You go on down."

"All right," she said. "Did the hotel doctor do that?"

"No, the hospital."

"What hospital?"

"I don't know. The city hospital."

"When?"

"I don't know. Two-thirty in the morning or something."

"Why didn't you wake me up?"

"What for?" I said. I might have asked, "Would you have answered the door?" but that was her tactic, she always won at that one. My eyes were not seeing very well. From her voice I could tell, though, that she was upset and a bit at a loss with the situation.

"Well," she said. "I'll see you later, then."

Later she came up. She hadn't taken very long over breakfast. I heard her go through her own room from outside, and after a few minutes she came in to mine and opened one of the shutters. The light made me feel worse, but I was too tired to complain. Then she opened the rest, and opened one of the windows.

"They were worried about you at the desk," she said.

"Which one was there?"

"King Umberto's uncle. You know."

"I guess the night staff must have told him."

"I didn't see our honeymooners. Maybe they've checked out."

"Maybe they're having breakfast in bed." I hoped so.

"I doubt it," she said. "Not with his problems."

"He'll be okay."

"If he finds the right man, maybe. At least he could have thought about it before getting married to a normal girl."

"Have a heart, Jeanie."

"Oh I do, I do. For her, though. Not for him."

"For both of them. Poor kids. After all, you and I were lucky that way."

"Really?" she said softly. "We were lucky, were we?"

"Hell, yes. The first time, I had somebody who knew what was going on. And so did you. Imagine what it would be like if neither one of you knew what the hell was supposed to happen."

"I think it would be nice that way."

"Jesus, it would be a nightmare. It would be hell on wheels."

"I don't think so at all."

"Of course you do."

All at once I wished I had been more of a help to Butterworth. Remembering our talk now, it seemed one of the saddest things I had known. I thought about them both caged up in their room together, each one expecting so much from the other and knowing that a lot was expected in return. They wouldn't know exactly what you were supposed to feel, or whether what was happening meant it was going all right or all wrong. Then they'd get embarrassed and blame themselves, and blame the other person. And the next time it's worse. How long would it go on like that? Would they see a doctor? If it had been two years ago, I might have helped him. Something had changed during our talk, and I knew that he had been relieved, so I'd helped at least that much, but he needed a lot more than what I'd given. Maybe if my reactions hadn't been in the way, I could have straightened him out. And maybe not. Probably not. When people break down that way it really takes someone else's lifetime to change it. The thing is so simple that only someone's patience or understanding or personality, handed over as though forever, is enough. If he had lied to her, then of course they could have broken up and found other people. But he hadn't lied, at least I didn't think so. It was just ignorance with both of them, and they were both stuck with it.

"I think it would be wonderful like that—both discovering each other for the first time. If you really loved each other it would just come naturally."

"Just sort of spontaneous combustion?"

"You know what I mean. You don't have to be so sneery about it."

"And he said he was brought up strictly, too. Maybe one of those hellfire churches lurking in the background. Telling him he'd go blind if he touched himself, and all that. Stay out once after midnight, and they take your name out of the family Bible."

"Oh, that's his trouble—strict, pious upbringing?"

"And being nervous. And a touch of the John Ruskins."

"What's that?"

"He'd never seen a girl naked before. Didn't know about pubic hair. It was sort of a surprise."

"What?" she said, and suddenly began to laugh. I hadn't heard her laugh for months.

"You can't mean it."

"Well, how would he know? He isn't the kind to go flipping through medical dictionaries, and I don't suppose it was in his school curriculum. No sisters or cousins, I guess, or if he's got any they're as buttoned up as he is."

"But he would have seen pictures."

"Haven't you noticed? It's always covered up in the pictures."

"No, paintings and statues."

"Go on."

"You're right. I never thought about it. Only the men. I wonder why."

"Because it's so sinful and exciting."

"Maybe because—"

"Like you in your nightgown," I said.

She stopped talking. It almost seemed as though she had stopped breathing. I wished I hadn't said anything. Her self-consciousness and my head; the whole room was full of pain.

"I'll be all right here if you want to go down to the beach or something," I said.

"Yes, I might do that. I'm sorry about your nose, Don. How do you feel?"

"Like the man in the iron mask."

"Are you sure you don't want me to ask them to send you up some breakfast?"

"Well, some coffee, maybe."

"All right."

She went through the bathroom and into her own room. I closed my eyes, and heard her soon afterwards locking her door out in the hall and tiptoeing past mine on her way to the stairs.

About half an hour later a boy came up with a tray for me. I fumbled in my pockets for change and then couldn't decide which was the right coin. I shrugged and held out my hands for him to choose one. He took one only, and I thought that out of politeness he hadn't taken much. I made him choose a second coin.

It was terrible to sit up. It was almost as bad lying down. It even hurt to swallow. I went into the bathroom and took two of the doctor's pills. When I got back into my room I thought I heard my wife opening her door. Then the bathroom door opened and three doors slammed, one after the other. From the neck up I died and died and died.

It was the maid, come to clean out the rooms. She gave a little gasp when she saw me, and I moved to the table and chair and explained in what sounded like French, not to mind me.

She remade the bed, quickly dusted the top of the dresser and the front of the drawers, ran a cloth over the wardrobe mirror, and went back into the bathroom to do a more thorough job in there.

The pills started to work. I began to float. I finished the coffee and lay down on the bed and looked through the window at the sky.

I slept. When I woke up, I heard someone walking quietly down the hallway as if trying not to make too much noise. Then I heard the key at my wife's door. I sat up, and realized that I felt better.

Then the bathroom door on the far side closed like a gunshot. I heard her in the bathroom, swearing, and shutting a window. Then she came through into my room, closing the door gently behind her.

"How do you feel?" she said. She had some postcards and a book in her hand. She was looking worried.

"All right."

"Your eyes look terrible."

"I know. It must have been the impact when I hit. It forced the blood up. Did you go down to the beach?"

"For a while. I walked around the town a bit. Do you really feel all right?"

"Yes. I took some pills. They made me feel wonderful for about an hour. It's probably something pretty strong." I thought it might be morphine. I had never been given morphine before. I'd thought it had gone out with the First World War. But from the effect it had, my money was on morphine if that was what it was. I wondered what would happen if I took the whole bottle full. Perhaps I'd float straight out the window. Out and away, like that white schooner coming into the harbor.

She looked at her watch.

"Do you want to come down for lunch?"

"All right," I said, and got up. "The light hurts my eyes. I think I'll wear my sunglasses." I got out the glasses and tried them on, standing in front of the mirror. They wouldn't sit straight because of the mask.

"Do you have any adhesive tape in that emergency kit?" I asked. "And for Christ's sake watch out for the door."

She came back with the tape and I managed to stick the glasses on.

"Now I look like Claude Rains in that movie," I said. "Maybe underneath I've disappeared."

"Oh please, Don," she said. "I didn't do it on purpose. I didn't know. How could I know?"

"Let's go."

"Let me get my postcards. I need some stamps."

There were three other tables occupied in the dining room. I shook my head as the waiter started to lead on to the table we usually had, and explained that we didn't want to sit in the light. He gave us a table nearer the door and about twelve feet away from an old gentleman with a large pepper-and-salt moustache, who looked as though he'd been left over from the British Raj. We had flowers on the table again. Every day there were fresh ones and every table, even the empty ones, had them. It really was a marvelous hotel.

"Wine?" I said.

"I will if you will."

"I'd like to, and I need it, but I think my head would come right off if I did."

"Then I won't."

"How about something beforehand?"

"All right."

I ordered for us, and looked around the place. The room was as pretty and open as a ballroom. At the far end the windows were all French windows that opened out onto a terrace. There was a double curtain like a theatre curtain for that whole side of the room. At noon they drew both sides nearly together. Some of the other curtains too had been drawn against the sun, but where it came in, it fell on the white tablecloths and silver, and made the bright water in the flowervases sparkle and flash.

"Are those for the kids?" I said, touching the postcards.

"Yes."

"Can I add a note?"

"You can send them some others. I'll show you which pictures I've got, so we won't duplicate any."

"That wasn't what I meant."

"Don't you think it would be getting their hopes up? Bobby knows. I practically told him."

"You didn't actually tell him the word divorce, did you?"

"No, I said something about how you'd be working away for a while, like last year, and we wouldn't see so much of you. But he has friends at school whose parents are divorced. He knows, I'm sure of it."

She started to touch the flowers in the vase. She loved flowers. She probably even knew the name, though all I could see was that they were pinkish and like sweet peas.

"It isn't complete custody," she said.

"I know. Weekends and vacations. It would break my heart. It would be better never to see them again at all. If I thought I had the strength, that's what I'd do."

"Let's not talk about it."

She looked up and away from me, towards the door. The waiter came up with our food and she remained looking off, like a giraffe scenting the air, in the way that meant she was trying not to cry.

There are so many different attitudes, like different lives, in a face and in a body. So many lines and forms, so many strengths and weaknesses. The expression of health, of nervousness, even the expression of truth, are things you can look at. How long it takes to know them all. And you never do, not completely. A body or face is never the same even in a single day. And the mind, that's even more difficult.

"If only you hadn't looked at the photographs," I said. "That's what did it."

"Talk about pubic hair," she snapped.

Quickly I put a finger to my mouth and said, "Shh."

She went red and looked over her shoulder. The British Raj saw her and also went red. He hadn't heard, but now he was suddenly aware of us.

"Oh my God," she mumbled, and started to stab her fork at her food.

I began to eat, too. When I swallowed, it hurt in my ears.

"If we gave it a try—"

"How much would you try?"

"As much as I always have."

"You mean, it would be the same as it was before."

"And it would have been all right if it hadn't been for all our wonderful friends."

"At least they told me the truth."

"And how they enjoyed telling you the truth, and then telling you that I was the one who was hurting you."

She put down her fork.

"But you'd resent it if I did it, wouldn't you?"

"Of course. But it wouldn't be the same."

"It's never the same for a woman—are you going to give me that?"

"What I meant was that if you did, you're such a stickler for propriety, you'd marry him. You'd drop me like a hot potato."

"Would it be better to have somebody on the sly every afternoon for years?"

She started to eat again.

"You probably wouldn't even have minded," she said, biting vigorously.

"Of course I would have. You're my wife."

"What does that mean?"

"I mean you're my wife. Look, I've been in a lot of different places—waiting at bus stops, in airports, been out to parties. I've eaten meals in restaurants and had drinks at bars, been to people's houses, been in people's rooms. But if somebody asks me where I live, I don't say in a bus stop or on the eight-ten or in a bar, or in a strange room. That isn't where I live. Don't you understand? You're my wife. Christ, I'm tired."

"So am I," she said, spacing the words.

"Do you want coffee?"

"No, thanks."

I looked for the waiter.

"He's in back of you by the doorway," she said. "About five of them have been standing there for the past few minutes."

I turned around and saw the group of waiters standing there trying not to appear too curious about something that was going on in the lobby. I looked, too. Just before our waiter broke away and came towards us, I saw uniforms come in through the lobby and go in the direction of the stairs with a man I'd never seen before, who might have been the manager.

"It's the cops," I said.

When we reached the lobby, they had gone.

"I think I'll take a stroll around for a couple of minutes," I said.

"I'll go on up."

"See you later," I said, and watched her go up the stairway. Then I went to the desk. The clerk we called King Umberto was there. I asked him for stamps which he produced from a drawer under the desk. Then I said, "The police are here?" and his English vanished. I had a bad feeling about it. I said, "Would you tell me the room number of a Mr. Butterworth?"

"Butterworth?" He looked behind him at the board full of keys and said, "I am sorry, Monsieur Butterworth is not in his room. He has taken the key."

"What's the number?"

He had to look at the board again. For a Greek, he wasn't a very good liar. For a hotel clerk, he was an even worse one.

"Four-one-eight," he said, still looking imperturbable. "Monsieur is a friend of Monsieur Butterworth?"

"My wife and I met them last night."

He counted up the stamps and told me the amount. I put them in my wallet.

"I believe," he said, "an English monsieur has lost his passport. The maid looks, but he asks the police to look."

"I see," I said.

I walked outside into the sunlight, and kept to the shady side of the street. There was very little shade except directly under the trees, because of the time of day. I walked all around the side of the hotel, crossed the street, and moved over to the back entrance where the police car was parked. I waited, wishing that I could smoke, or even sit down. Fifteen minutes later they came out with Butterworth.

"Rocky," I said, and he turned his head. He didn't know me with all the bandages. I went up to him. "It's Don," I said. "Coleman."

"Oh, hello, sir," he said. "What's happened to you?"

"Broke my nose. What's happened to you?"

"It's Linda. She's in a coma or something, but they won't call a doctor. I don't understand it."

The man who looked like a manager came and took me by the elbow and pulled me back. Another man, in a business suit and carrying a doctor's bag, took Butterworth in tow and steered him over to the car. He didn't look back. They got into the back seat with a policeman, and the two other policemen got into the front and closed the doors. Suddenly Butterworth leaned over and started to rap on the window. He was looking at me.

"Just a minute," I told the man holding my arm.

The doctor rolled down his window and Butterworth leaned over him.

"Mr. Coleman," he said, "she can't get an annulment, can she?"

"Annulment? Did she say that?"

"Not after you get married, can you? It wouldn't be fair."

"Don't worry about it."

"That's what I told her," he said. "They don't do it any more nowadays."

"It'll be okay," I told him, and waved. The car started up. As soon as they began to move, he lost interest in the window and and looked straight ahead.

"Monsieur is staying at the hotel?" the manager-figure asked me.

"Yes. A lovely hotel."

He inclined his head very slightly in what might have been a bow.

"My name's Coleman," I said.

He told me his, which began with Pappa-something. Then he said, "Ah yes, the nose. Last night."

"Yes," I said. "The night staff were very helpful."

We started to walk away from the doors and towards the main hotel entrance.

"You are a friend of Mr. Butterworth?"

"Not exactly. My wife and I met them last night at a nightclub and we walked back to the hotel together."

"Ah, yes."

"While we were walking, he talked to me. He said he needed some advice."

"Yes."

"About his marriage."

"Yes, I see."

"I tried to talk to him like a friend. Or as a father would talk to his son. He seemed rather young for his age."

"Yes."

"I think you'd better tell me about it. Has he killed her?"

"Yes," he said.

I thought he would leave it at that, but as it turned out, he decided to tell me about it, starting from the point when the maid had run to the floor waiter.

When I got to my room I found my wife sitting on the edge of my bed.

"I got your stamps."

"Oh, thank you. I forgot." She handed me the postcards. I sat down next to her on the bed and stuck stamps on all of them.

"One thing about a broken nose, you can't taste the glue," I said. "Does it really matter if I add something?"

"No, go ahead."

I took out my pen, and on the one to Ginny I put a plus sign after the signature and wrote, "Love from Daddy." On Bobby's it was "Love from Dad." He had taken to calling me Dad two years before, because it sounded more grownup, I suppose. I put the pen back in my pocket and felt lousy. Then I turned the postcards over and looked at the pictures.

"We haven't even been here yet."

"I thought they'd like it anyway."

"I like it, too. We should go there. Maybe we could go later this afternoon."

"Would you feel up to it?"

"I think so. I'm going to take another pill. Is the door closed on the other side?"

"Yes."

I went into the bathroom and took two of the pills. Then I unstrapped the sunglasses and went back into the room.

"Did you find out what all those policemen were for?"

"Some Englishman couldn't find his passport and thought the maid had stolen it. One of those types that wouldn't take the manager's word for it."

"Oh. What an anticlimax. I was sure with so many of them it must be a jewel thief at least. Or maybe a bomb."

"They wouldn't notice a bomb with all the doors slamming around here."

I took off my jacket and shoes.

"Well, I'll go read my book," she said, and stood up.

"Stay here and read it. Maybe you could read it out loud to me. My eyes aren't good for much."

"All right."

I lay down on the bed.

"I can use that chair," she said.

"If I move over a little, you can sit on the bed. Unless your back is going to get tired."

"Oh. All right."

She sat on the bed near my knees.

"What's happened so far?"

She explained the plot. A body had been found in the library and everyone in the house had a good motive and lots of opportunity. Things were just coming to the point where she was sure there was going to be a second murder. It had said on the blurb that there were two.

"All right?"

"Bring on the corpses," I said, and shut my eyes.

She began to read. The second body was found, shot this time instead of stabbed, and all the members of the house party were having a sticky time getting through breakfast without hysterics.

I began to feel happy listening to her voice. And I thought about poor Butterworth who would never be lying in bed listening to his wife reading a book to him. It was just like being home again, with everything all right. I started to cry.

If it always hurt so much, no one would ever cry. The salt in my eyes, the nose broken up and held together with splints and bandages. With every breath the pain knocked me over. I turned my head away, but couldn't help making a noise.

"What is it?" she said. "Oh, Don. I'll call the doctor."

My nose was broken, my head was breaking up, my life was all broken up. And I couldn't even cry.

"Oh hell," I sobbed. "Oh hell. Oh God damn it to hell!" I grabbed her hand and made whooping noises, trying to stop.

Finally I got it under control and lay back.

"Does it hurt real bad?" she said, in the accent she hadn't used or heard for fourteen years.

"It's all right now, I think. I just started to think how nice it was to hear you reading to me. Can't even cry in this damned thing."

She rubbed her free hand over my hair.

"Do you want me to go on?"

"Let's rest here for a while." I pulled her forward carefully and she put the book down on the floor and took off her shoes and let me settle her on the bed. We were lying the way we lay after love.

"Tell me something," I said.

"What?"

"Anything. A story, anything, anything that comes to mind."

"I can't think of anything."

"All right. I'll tell you."

I told her about going down to the lobby and meeting the night staff, and tried to make it sound funnier than it had been. When I got to where I claimed to have fought in a war against the Chinese, she started to laugh. Her hair was by my mouth and I missed not being able to smell it. I told her about the doctor and his goatee and the letter he had given me, which had been so interesting to see being written, and about getting dizzy from looking at the palm trees as I came up the stairs.

"Now you. Tell me."

"I just can't think of anything."

"Tell me about what you did this morning while I was dead to the world."

"I went down to the changing room and got into my bathing suit. And I sat on the beach. There were only one or two other people there and one or two boys from the hotel raking the pebbles. I tried to read, and I got more and more sort of nervous. That huge, empty beach full of pebbles. So then I got up, and changed back into my clothes, and went and bought postcards. And that was all."

She started to cry. I smoothed down her hair with my hand and held her with the other hand around her waist.

Butterworth had held on to his wife, too, but too tightly. And he had also managed to make love to her; whether before or after her death was something I didn't want to know, though no doubt the hotel manager had known.

She stopped crying, and sighed. I smoothed her hair back

and put my arm around her shoulder. Butterworth had held his wife by the neck and held her too tightly, for too long. But I held my wife close and carefully, by the waist and shoulders, and shut my eyes. And then the doctor's pills began to work, and I floated and I floated, and I slept.

Something to Write Home About

The big tourist boat was about to dock and most of the passengers were standing up on deck to watch. John and Amy Larsen sat inside on a bench in the lounge where the evening before they had listened to music and drunk wine.

"I don't have any more postcards," she said, and rummaged through her purse. From the outside pocket of it she took out three postcards, already written on and stamped. All were addressed to the same name and place, and at the top lefthand corner of each she had conscientiously put down the day, and the month, May, and the year, 1965, as though the cards were intended to be saved for posterity.

"Don't worry about it," her husband said. "We can buy some more as soon as we get off."

They had been married for eighteen months, although they did not look married. To look at, they might even have been related by blood rather than by law. They looked like students, and John Larsen was one; his wife had graduated the year before. She had majored in English, he was in his last year at business school.

Standing near them was another American couple, who were on their honeymoon. They came from New York, and, in contrast to the Larsens, looked well dressed, sophisticated, and as though they were either not married at all or had been married for several years and were taking a break from the children and a life of suburban cocktail parties. Their name was Whitlow. And they were on their honeymoon, all right. When the boat had put them ashore at Crete for the day, the Whitlows had had a quarrel of some kind and John and Amy had found Mrs. Whitlow alone, standing as though posed, with the sun on her shiny hair, and her tropically flowered sleeveless dress looking brand new, like a magazine ad for winter holidays in the Caribbean. She had walked forward towards them, peered this way and that into the other sightseers among the reconstructed ruins of King Minos' palace, and recognized them.

"Lost your husband?" John had asked.

"Well," she had said, "he went off in a huff, but I think maybe he's lost now. I've been wandering all over the place."

That night they had laughed about it as they drank with the Larsens. Another couple named Fischer, a New Jersey businessman and his wife, had joined them. The Fischers were already grandparents, but were throwing themselves into the spirit of things with more zest than the younger couples. They had all begun to talk about the places they had visited or would have liked to see. The Whitlows had been to Nauplia.

"Oh, we were there, too," Amy had said. "That's where we couldn't get any artichokes."

"We sat down on the terrace of the hotel restaurant, you know, facing the harbor—" John had said.

"That's where we were, too," Whitlow had told them.

"And two tourist buses drove up and parked. We started to order dinner and the waiter handed us the menu and said, 'With group?' "

"With group?" Amy had repeated, in the voice the waiter had used.

"So we said no, not with group, and started to order."

"And there were artichokes on the menu, which I just love."

"We were okay till we hit the artichokes, and then it turned out that they were all for group, forty-seven darn orders of artichokes. That just about finished the place for us."

"Did you notice what a funny kind of butter they had there?" Amy had asked. "It was white. It tasted just like Crisco."

"I told you, it was some kind of margarine," John had put in.

"Not tasting like that. I'm sure it was Crisco."

"Did you go to the island?" Mrs. Whitlow had asked.

"Yes, we had tea there."

"So did we, but we made a mistake about the boat. Tell them about the boat, Hank."

"Well, when Sally and I got there, we saw this beautiful boat tied up at the landing stage."

"A yacht, really, but a small one—"

"And later we wanted to get out to the island, but the boat was gone. We went and looked at the sign, and it had the times of sailing on it."

"So then—"

"Do you want to tell it?"

"Oh, go ahead."

"So then later in the day we saw it there again and barreled down to the jetty to get on board. My God, it was somebody's private yacht. Nobody on board but the English mate. The real boat was a rowboat."

"Then we got into the rowboat and this girl who was staying on the island climbed in too, and dropped a paperback she'd been carrying, and Hank handed it back to her—"

"*Fanny Hill*. No kidding. Sort of broke her up. She'd been reading it with the cover held back."

"The rooms out there were gorgeous, weren't they? If we'd known you could stay on it, we'd have booked in there."

"That boat was a beauty," Whitlow had said. "Some big wheel owned it and chartered her out for the season. The mate said it was built in Holland."

"Never mind," Sally Whitlow had said. "One day we'll have one."

"Diamond-studded," her husband had agreed, and they had shaken hands on it.

"Did you get to Delphi?" John had asked them. The Whitlows had been all through the Peloponnese and driven up to Delphi from Athens. They had really wanted to go all the way up into Macedonia too, but there was only so much time. This was the fifth and last week of their honeymoon. The Larsens had missed Delphi, which they regretted, but they had hired a car and driven through some of the Peloponnesian cities. The Fischers had seen Athens, taken a day's excursion to Hydra and Aegina, and that had been all.

The boat they were on had stopped at Mykonos, with a side trip to Delos, and at Crete. Mrs. Fischer had liked Mykonos best.

"Well, I know it's supposed to be a photographer's paradise," John had said, "but that whitewash and bougainvillea and arts and crafts just leaves me cold. I think you either like Mykonos or Delos."

"And you liked Delos," Mrs. Fischer had said, smiling at him.

"Yes, maybe the best of all. What I'd really like to do is go back there and stay a couple of days."

"But there isn't any hotel."

"Yes, there is. At that tourist pavilion, they've got about four rooms they can rent out. I asked them about it. Friends of ours stayed there last year."

"They loved it," Amy had said.

"They said that at ten o'clock the caïque from Mykonos pulled in with all the sightseers who spent a few hours scrambling over everything and climbing up the hill, and when the boat pulled out again the island was covered in shoeprints and sneaker marks. Then it took about an hour, and when you looked after that, all you could see on the ground were lizard prints."

"And the starlight is bright enough to see by even when the moon isn't out," Amy had said.

John had touched her hair and told her that they would go back there some day.

But now the boat was docking at Rhodes, and they had their luggage ready, because they were leaving the group in order to be able to spend two days on the island. Then they would fly back to Athens, and from there would take a plane home. The tour leaders had allowed them to reclaim a small part of their tickets. They had even given the Larsens the name of a good, cheap hotel they could recommend. But the Larsens would be joining the group again for lunch at the luxury hotel and might go along on the guided tour of the city in the afternoon, since that had all been paid for and couldn't be refunded. Only the morning would be different. In the morning the other passengers were going to take buses to Lindos and then visit the monastery of Philerimos. The Larsens were to visit both places the following day when they would be able to take their time. Amy had liked the cruise, but John was beginning to tire of constantly being hustled along from one thing to the next.

The boat was almost at a standstill.

"There's that creep again," Sally Whitlow said to her husband.

One of the passengers, who had started off the tour standing with the German-speaking guide and had changed to standing with the English-speaking guide because of Mrs.

Whitlow, shuffled into the lounge. His eyes were always on her, and he had been attempting to strike up a friendship with both the Whitlows all during the voyage. Mrs. Whitlow turned her head sharply away. Her husband glared at the man, who tried to start a conversation about what a nice day it was. Whitlow didn't answer. The man sat down. The boat struck against something.

"Feels like we've landed," John said.

Mrs. Whitlow stood up and walked out. Her husband followed. The German-speaking man stood up and began to walk behind them. Whitlow turned around and shoved him in the chest.

"You stay right here," he said, and turned his back and walked off.

The Larsens went up on deck, carrying their bags. The Whitlows were leaning against the rail, and Sally Whitlow was saying, "It just makes me nervous, that's all. You could knock him down ten times and he'd come up like a rubber ball. There's just something missing. Really, somebody ought to lock him up, you know."

"Oh, I think he's harmless enough," Whitlow said.

"For God's sake, Hank. He's out of his mind. He ought to be in an institution."

The Larsens passed along the deck under the strong sunlight, and joined the line that had already formed.

"I don't like her," Amy said.

"She's all right. She didn't realize, that's all."

"Just the same, I don't like her."

"Be fair, Amy. How could she know?"

She watched the men working with the cables and preparing the way for the passengers to step ashore. Her husband looked at her: short in her skirt that was too long, and her long-sleeved blouse that she wore sloppy Joe art-major style outside the skirt. She had a small-nosed, intense face like a terrier, and her ordinary brown hair just hung to her shoulders instead of billowing out in a wave like Sally Whitlow's hair.

"You just can't stand it about her hair," he said.

"Well, I don't see how it can look like that. It looks like she just came out of a hairdresser's. But we've been on this boat for five days."

"Some people don't have to wash their hair more than once every two weeks."

"That's what's so annoying. I bet it always looks like that."

"But otherwise she's okay?"

"I guess so."

"You know, I like you just exactly the way you look."

"Somebody ought to lock you up," she said. "You ought to be in an institution." She opened her mouth and laughed and laughed.

He set down his suitcase and took her by the arm.

"Look," he said. "The line's starting."

It took them quite a while to work their way forward. When they were at last standing on the quayside, the other passengers were beginning to form up in front of the three guides. They walked past the French-speaking guide and came to the English-speaking guide, who had been nice to John about changing the tickets.

"You will know the island of Rhodes is supposed to be the island of roses," she was saying. "*Rhodos* means a rose. But it is more probably truly the flower you see here, the hibiscus." She gestured towards some beds of red hibiscus flowers.

"Let's find that hotel," he said. "Let me carry that. She said it wasn't very far away."

They set off towards the town. In front of them half a dozen cab drivers stood beside their Chevrolet taxis. The drivers began to call to them as they came nearer. Two rushed forward to carry the bags. Larsen lifted his head to the side and said no in Greek. He had to say it twice, and Amy said no thank you.

The hotel was small, new, and looked clean, but the room was small, too. There was just room enough to stand up between the bed and the window. The shutter was down because of the sun.

"Can you ask him if there's a shower?" Amy asked. The man who had shown them the room beckoned them out again and down the hall. There wasn't any shower, but there was a bath. They took the room and began to unpack. They didn't take out much, as they were only staying the two days.

"I'll go see about the car," John said.

"There must be a bus."

"But it would be nicer by car. And we'll need it tomorrow."

"It's your money," she said.

He went out of the hotel, rented a car for two days, and drove it back. Amy walked out the hotel door as he was putting the key in his pocket. She had been sitting downstairs near the door, watching out for him.

They got in, and John took out the map he had been given at the garage.

"I think I'm okay, but if you see any signs that say *Petaloudes*, sing out. That's us."

"Does *Petaloudes* mean butterflies?"

"I don't know. It might. It sounds like it ought to mean petals."

"That's because of the way they look when they fly. Like petals," she said, and made her hands do butterfly motions.

He looked at her face. She was looking happy, and was calm enough. He started the car.

Once they got clear of the town, the roads began to wind and to climb steeply. And the island was lusciously green, unlike the art book photographs of the rest of Greece, where temples which turned out later to be made of gray, orange, or honey-colored stone appeared stark white under annihilating sunlight and set in landscapes of sand and rock and cracked, impoverished earth.

"It seems to be way up in the mountains," he said.

"I wish it were the right time of year."

"So do I, but we can see the place, anyway. It's nice to see a couple of places that are just pretty without all the history."

"And maybe they'll have postcards. Oh! Oh, John! Stop the car."

He slammed on the brakes.

"What is it?"

"I forgot to mail my postcards."

"Jesus H. Christ, Amy. You could have killed us."

"I've got to mail them," she said, reaching for the door handle.

He pulled her back.

"One hour isn't going to make any difference."

"No!" she said. She started to scream, "No, no, no! I've got to!"

He shook her by the shoulders and then held her head between his hands.

"Just calm down, now. Just relax. We can buy lots of postcards in a few minutes, and then we can send them all together."

"But—"

"We can send them all together, and everything will be all right. Okay?" He kissed her on the nose three times. "Okay?"

"Okay."

He started the car again. Luckily they hadn't been on a corner when she had made him stop.

They drove around more corners and the road kept banking upwards, and then suddenly there were lots of trees very close to the road.

They did not speak. He kept his eyes on the road but was thinking, *So, we're not going to get out of it so easily.* And the right half of his body seemed to have taken on the sensitivity of a third eye; if his wife were to make another dash at the doorhandle, or perhaps towards him, trying to get at the wheel, he would know it even though he was looking ahead through the windshield.

The road leveled out, went down, and then up again. The air was cooler, the coolness seeming to come from the trees. Perhaps it really did, he thought—released oxygen or something, causing a freshness around the trees. But perhaps also part of the sensation was induced by a mental reaction to the green color. The previous spring, the university store had had a large pile of notebooks on sale, the paper of which was a peculiar green color, and inside the cover of each notebook you could read a statement to the effect that "research had shown" green to be extremely soothing to the eyes. He had bought one and found the color irritating, but there might be something in the idea after all.

All these things were connected: the eye, the mind, the body. Hip bone connected to the thigh bone. Yet even when the whole business was going right and healthy, it was fundamentally mysterious. Research showed, but you could dig into your past till you were blue in the face and it still wouldn't help you to feel confident walking into a room full of strangers if that was the sort of thing that had always made you nervous. Research could probably stop you washing your hands fifty times a day, but then you'd start something else, like picking your nose. Or worrying about postcards.

They came over a ridge and began to descend into the valley.

"This is it," he said. He guided the car up a slope and around to the right where there were three other cars parked under the trees. They could see the weathered wood railing and the steps going far up the mountainside, and the two lower ponds and the little waterfalls between. Everywhere was the sound of water.

"It's pretty," she said.

He locked up the car and took her arm. He led her past the postcard stands and made sure that he didn't seem to be trying to distract her attention. And she didn't notice.

They began to climb the stairway. The wood didn't look very solid. Down below, where there were other railings around the watercourses, the wood looked yellow, like bamboo, and the water was a vivid green, even greener than the trees. Three people, slung with cameras, came down the path and passed them. It was very narrow, and John had to pull Amy back from the edge. There were more people farther up, and it looked like a long climb.

"Do butterflies need a lot of water?" she asked.

"I don't know, Amy."

"It's a nice place for them, though. Think of having a place where you go to every year like this. They fly for miles and it's the same place they've been coming to for generations."

"Yes," he said. "It's nice."

"I wonder why people don't do those things. I mean, why don't people have places they go to? Migrating and hibernating and all that. It's very strange when you think about it. But then it's very strange if you suddenly wonder why not."

They climbed to the level of the third pool and looked down at the emerald circular ponds in their nests of yellow railings, with the sun dappling over everything through the leaves of the overhanging trees.

"It looks like some place in Africa," he said. "I wonder what makes the water so green. Maybe it's very cold."

They stood there for a while and then she looked farther up the path. He could see that she was suddenly frightened of going up to the top. She looked back down at the water again.

"It makes you dizzy to look all the way down."

"Yes," he said. "It's a long climb to the top, too. How are your loafers holding out?"

"Oh, they're okay. John, did you ever think—you know, people who say there isn't any life after death think it's because it would be so peculiar. But it's even more peculiar to be alive in the first place, isn't it? So why not?"

"Well," he said, "I don't know. I think it's one of those things you believe in or you don't. I don't believe it has much to do with thought. I mean, you're predisposed to believe one way or the other. And I don't think it has much to do with how you feel about the sacredness of life, if that's what's bothering you. Do you want to try going to the top?"

"I'm sort of tired," she said.

"As a matter of fact, I've had enough of a climb, too."

They began the descent.

"It's being on board the boat for so long," he said.

"But we walked all over Delos and Crete."

"But your legs get to feel different."

At the bottom of the path she saw the postcard stand and made a beeline for it.

"Oh!" she said, picking up one card after another. "Oh look, they've got pictures of all the butterflies." She handed him a picture of a leafy tree with a brown trunk. He didn't see any butterflies. Then he looked more closely and realized that the entire trunk of the tree was composed of hundreds of butterflies lying next to each other.

"That's amazing," he said.

"Aren't they pretty? It looks like they're just sleeping there." She kept picking up more postcards. "Just sleeping," she cooed.

The woman behind the stand had caught the spirit of the thing and began to select better and better pictures to be looked at.

"Look at this one, John," Amy said, and handed him a picture of a flight of pink butterflies taken against a background of dark leaves. If you squinted your eyes they looked exactly like flamingoes flying in formation.

The postcard seller was even shorter than Amy Larsen. The top of her head only came up to Amy's chin. She began to talk in French about the butterflies, and handed John a piece of paper which had the history of the place written on it.

"What's she saying?"

"Wait a sec. Her French is worse than mine." He interrupted her and asked why the butterflies chose that particular spot. It seemed a nonsensical thing to ask, but the woman answered him straight away: it was because of the trees, because of the resin in the leaves.

"Isn't that interesting," Amy said. Then she picked up one of the things on the tray full of keychains, paperknives, cheap unworkable ballpoint pens, and other souvenir objects.

It was a green-enameled brass frog with red glass eyes. Its head was on a hinge and the mouth opened up into a spout. When you lifted the head, the belly of the frog became an ashtray and the bottom jaw a cigarette-rest. She clicked the head up and down several times, and then bought the frog, though neither of them smoked.

They walked back to the car. A Greek soldier passed them on their way. Two other cars had pulled in to the left of theirs, and six soldiers were standing leaning against the fenders. Amy's hands were clenched on her postcards as they walked forward. John unlocked the car door, got in and leaned over to unlock the other door, and pulled the handle back.

She sat down on the seat and left the door open. She put all her postcards up on the dashboard and set the frog beside them. John got the map out of the door pocket. He left his door open, too. Now that they were away from the coolness of the water, the heat was noticeable.

"Why are they all looking at me like that?" she said.

"Soldiers always look at girls, honey."

"They're looking at me like I was some kind of a freak."

"You're just freakishly Nordic, that's all. Probably your hair."

"My hair is dark."

"Not in this country." He opened the map. "We've got time to go someplace else. We could go visit this temple. That's on the other side of town, but we'd have time."

"Okay," she said. She began to click the frog's head up and down.

"Do you like my frog?"

"Sort of."

She opened the head again and looked into the bowl of the frog's belly.

"It's built just like me. Slim as a lily down to my tiny waist and from there on in like a battleship. Like a kangaroo."

"The ideal female shape," he said, punching the map to make it fold up again. He looked to the left and saw that the soldier they had passed had returned, and three of the men were drinking out of bottles.

"Lucky I bought so many stamps," she said, and took a ballpoint pen out of her purse.

"You cleaned then out. Would you like something to drink?"

"No, thanks."

"I'm thirsty. I'm going to see if they're selling soft drinks back there."

"I'll write my postcards."

"Okay. If they've got any ice cream or something like that, would you like that instead?"

"No, thanks."

He got out and closed the car door after him, knowing that she would be crouching over her postcards, having dragged her hair over most of the left side of her face because the soldiers were looking at her. And then, of course, she really would look like a freak.

At the postcard stand the woman sold him a fizzy lemonade, opened the cap, and gave him a straw. It wasn't very cold. He walked back to the car and drank most of it there. Beside him Amy was writing away furiously. He drank through the straw and put his right hand on the back of her neck and then squeezed her shoulders.

"It isn't inherited, Amy," he said.

She went on writing. He finished the lemonade and looked at the postcards she had finished, lying beside the hideous frog. The date, still complete with year, was on each, and the lefthand side crammed with minute writing. He got out of the car and looked around for a basket or some sort of container to put the bottle in, but there wasn't one. The soldiers had stood their empties at the foot of one of the trees. He put his bottle down beside the others and went back to the car.

He waited till she had finished writing the postcard she was working on, and said, "All set?"

"I haven't finished yet."

He appropriated the remaining cards.

"How many have you done?"

"Wait. One, two, three—six."

"Well, that's quite a lot. We'll leave the rest till we get

back to the hotel. You wouldn't want to get stuck there without any and have to go out and buy some new ones."

"But if I finish these, I can send them off and get some more later."

"Nope. Right now we're going to see that temple."

He put all the written postcards into the outside pocket of her purse, leaned over her, and closed her door. She kissed him on the cheek.

He started the car and gave her a hug with his right arm.

"Better put that away," he said. "I don't want it to fall off."

"It can't break. It's brass or something."

"Supposing I had to put on the brakes suddenly? It could hit one of us in the eye."

She put the frog in her purse and he backed the car out and down the slope and onto the road. He hadn't expected the kiss and it had made up for a lot of things.

They were halfway to the town when she said, "I've got to go to the bathroom again."

"Didn't you go at the hotel?"

"Yes, but I've got to go again."

"Can you wait till we get into town?"

"No."

He looked for a field with bushes and finally found one, pulled over to the side of the road, and stopped. She bolted out the door and ran across the field, the handbag, which contained wads of Kleenex as well as everything else, clutched to her chest.

He leaned forward over the wheel and closed his eyes. A car passed on the road. He sat up again, then leaned back on the wheel, and by mistake sounded the horn. When she returned through the field, she said, "What's the rush?"

"No rush. We've got plenty of time."

"You were honking the horn."

"Oh, I leaned up against the wheel. I didn't mean it to hurry you."

They drove on, back through the town, and he decided to be smart and get her to mail half the postcards so that she wouldn't pull another stunt like the one earlier in the morning.

"How nice you are to remember. It just slipped my mind," she said, ducking out of the car to put the postcards in the slot. He had made sure that she took the ones she had written on instead of the others; they were all stamped. She had bought one hundred air mail stamps in Heraklion. That wasn't counting the stamps she had been buying for two weeks. He hadn't even known she had brought the money with her, and then she had simply said, "Oh yes, just in case of emergencies."

They drove through the town and he kept along the shore road. It wasn't so far as he had thought.

"Look," she said. "There's a temple."

He overshot, and parked the car off the road where he had stopped, and they walked back along the tar road. On either side of them grew flat fields full of wildflowers. They could see the tops of the orange-yellow temple columns, only three and a half of them left, the three entire ones with the epistyle on top. And when they moved into the field and then downhill, they could see some big trees in the distance over to the right, and ahead beyond the building, the ocean dancing with light.

"Oh, I like it," she said. "It's like the bones of a lion. Is it Apollo's?"

"I think so, but I may be wrong. I should have brought the guidebook along."

"Let's just walk around," Amy said.

They walked hand in hand, looking at the temple, the fields, the sea. A fresh, light wind blew inshore.

"That's nice, to have a breeze," she said. "It was hot in that valley once we got away from the water."

"Let's sit down."

They walked forward into the columns and sat on a broken slab of stone. The remains of the temple looked smaller and much less grand from inside, but so did every temple he had ever seen except the Parthenon. They sat looking in the direction of the ocean. He wanted to talk to her, and realized that he couldn't.

The first days in Athens had been all right. And the trip through the Peloponnese had started out all right, too. They had arrived in Corinth near lunchtime and gone through the gates. Amy had been hopping up and down with anticipation, since they could already see it: a temple islanded in a sea of yellow flowers, just like the picture on the cover of his highschool second year Latin book. They had gone in and sat down inside the temple, and after a while had had the place to themselves. It was very hot for the time of year, he had thought. The sun had come straight down. And when they had left and come to the gate, it had been padlocked and there was nobody around. "I'll climb over and hunt somebody out," he had said. And she had told him no, that she was climbing over, too. And up she had gone, over the wire fence. He had been worried that she would slip and fall, and had tried to stop her, but she had gotten angry, and had gone over like a bundle of laundry, and then had been so proud of her athletic ability and laughed with pleasure. Later in the day she had had a bad headache from the sun, and he hadn't felt so well himself, but he had thought for the first time in a long while that everything was going to be all right. They had stayed at a hotel on the beach, where they were the only couple in the whole place, and that was all right. And then in Olympia, the weather had been beautiful and there were pine trees everywhere with the wind making swooshing noises in the branches, and that had been nice. But then they had gone to Mycenae, and that was the place where he had become really worried about heatstroke. The sun kept pounding down like lead over them. She had been holding a branch of orange blossoms he had yanked off a tree from the car window. And they had walked around the ruins for about fifteen minutes, and sat down so that he could read the guidebook aloud. He had been reading for quite a while before he noticed the stupefied look on her face. "This is a terrible place," she had said. "It makes you feel that people have been murdered here. Not just one or two people. Hundreds. Thousands. It's monstrous and squat and barbaric and awful." Not seriously, in an exasperated way, he'd asked, "Well, would you like to go?" And the look had left her face and she had said, "Yes, please." Nauplia had not been a wild success, but not a disaster, either, and on the day they had gone to Epidaurus, he had felt everything take a turn for the better. They had gone to see the theatre, and she had insisted on climbing all the way up to the very last row of stone seats, where they had sat down. "Oh, what a wonderful place," she had said. "What a wonderful place. I only wish it was the right time. To see the plays here. It wouldn't even matter that we couldn't understand them." And while they were sitting there, with the enormous theatre going down, down like a huge bowl in front of them, about four busloads of Greek schoolchildren in dark blue uniforms had come running on to the stage, three teachers following along behind. They had been able to hear every separate footfall. The children had fanned out over the stage and then climbed up and seated themselves in the first five rows. And the head teacher, a man, had stood on the center stone and given them a talk in a perfectly ordinary tone of voice, and from where they had been watching, way up in the topmost row, he and she had been able to hear every syllable as clear as a bell, although they could not under-

stand the language. They had reached for each other without saying anything, and with her hand in his he had thought
that he would never forget this, he could never forget it as
long as he lived, and it would always make him feel good
just to think about it. Later in the day they had gone through
the museum and seen the reconstructions of how the columns had been arranged in a snail-like interior passage of
one of the shrines. They walked around and around, looking
at the design which changed at every point. He did not
mind reconstructions unless they pretended to be the real
thing; he found it very difficult to visualize what the ruins
would have looked like with the inner walls and a roof on
top. But these passages in the museum had the original
marble capitals set on top of the columns, and they were
carved with lily patterns, which had the strength and del-
icacy of living plants. That was what all the business of
classical things was about: if once they hit that balance, the
result was an impression of reality so strong that it was
unearthly, and as wonderful as if they had created a breathing human being. They had both been happy that day. But
then there had been the drive back to Athens and difficulty
about the hotel, where the staff had read the date the wrong
way around, or rather, the European way. Then the boat,
where their cabin was very cramped. But still he had had
the feeling that it was going to be all right.

If only it hadn't been for the postcards.

"Enough?" he said, and looked at his watch. She nodded,
and they started walking back to the car. As they came out
on the road, they saw two little girls with bunches of flowers
in their hands. When they crossed over to the car, the
children smiled at them and gave them the flowers. Amy
said thank you in Greek, and John said thank you, and then
looked suspiciously at Amy, who was awkward with children, but not knowing more than six words of the language,
seemed to feel for once that she wasn't expected to join in

any coy questions and answers, to play the "aren't we cute" game habitual to so many children because the parents enjoy it. The only children she really felt comfortable with were somehow eccentric, like his nephew, who had given her a long stare through his thick-lensed glasses, held out his hand, and said, "Hello. This is my guinea pig. His name is Winston. Would you like to see my train set?"

Still smiling, she took the flowers from him and put them together with hers. The children were friendly, but standing with their arms relaxed at their sides, so it didn't look like a bid for money, but he was upset about the whole incident. Amy got into the car, which he had forgotten to lock, and he brought out a handful of coins from his pocket and gave one of the smallest to each of the little girls. They seemed surprised and very pleased. They clutched each other and giggled, and as he turned the car and headed it back towards town, they waved. Amy waved back, but they drove to the hotel in silence.

In their room he read out parts of the guidebook to her. She had put the flowers in one of the basin glasses, and lay flat on the bed with her arm over her eyes.

"It's nearly time to join the group for lunch," he said.

"With group," she murmured. She rolled down and buttoned the sleeves of her blouse, which she had turned up on the way to the temple because only he could see her arms, and she had suddenly become self-conscious about the hair on them.

"Everybody has hair on their arms," he had told her.

"But not like mine. Mine are like a sailor's."

"Well, you could take it off if it bothers you. It doesn't bother me."

"No, that just makes it grow thicker."

She got up off the bed to go out to the bathroom again. He washed his face and hands. Before they left the room he put his arms around her.

"How do you feel?"

"All right. I just don't feel like it, that's all."

"Not at all?"

"No. I'm sorry. I don't know why you're so good to me."

"Don't keep saying that. As long as you don't get worried about anything, everything will be okay."

"I hope so," she said.

They walked to the other hotel. Three buses were parked down the street from the entrance. He looked at his watch again and they hurried through the lobby and were shown into a diningroom where only two couples were eating, and out onto a terrace with a green and white striped awning above all the tables of the group from the boat. The English-speaking guide nodded from a distance and the waiter sat them at a table where two old women were speaking French together and a German couple were eating in silence, cameras laid out at rest before them in leather cases, like a cowboy's six-shooters in their holsters. The meal consisted of a very good moussaka and some dark green vegetables that looked like tiny parachutes. John had wine and Amy drank one glass. Afterwards they ate a fruit salad with ice cream, and were served instant coffee because so many tourists wouldn't believe that the real Greek coffee was coffee at all. But since it was a very good hotel, the coffee was poured from a pot. The Frenchwomen took out cigarettes and blew the smoke in the direction of the Germans. The German took out a cigar.

"Want to walk around the hotel?"

"Sure," Amy said.

They strolled back through the diningroom and into the front lobby.

"*La plage?*" John asked.

The man behind the desk called a bellboy over and spoke to him. The boy gestured towards the Larsens and began to lead them ahead down a wide carpet with palm trees in tubs against the walls. Amy looked around at the impressive surroundings. When John caught her eye, she pulled a face at him. They went down some stairs and were gestured towards two doors, the changing rooms, one for men and one for the women.

"*Pas pour baigner, seulement pour voir,*" John said in his half-forgotten French. He only really remembered enough to understand, not much to speak.

"*Oui, ça va,*" the boy said, indicating the door for women. They both walked in, and saw through the open doors ahead, the beach and the sea. There were no guests on the beach because it was midday, but maybe also because it was out of season. Yet everything had obviously been cared for, just the right number of deck chairs set up at the back of the promenade, the right number stacked, fresh paint on everything and the green and white striped beach umbrellas in place.

"What a wonderful hotel," Amy said.

"It sure is. We've got to stay here some day. We should move out and stay here now."

"No," she said, "we can't afford it."

They went back out of the changing room and up the stairs. He thanked the boy and gave him a tip, and asked where the washrooms were.

"This time I've got to," he said.

"I will too, just in case. And before the mob gets off the terrace."

They separated and he told himself that she was still thinking about it, she would never be able to forget what he had said that time about not being able to afford it.

The three buses took them to the foot of the fortifications, and they all herded forward over a bridge below which lay a dried-up watercourse filled with red hibiscus and purple

bougainvillea and palm trees, and some pink flowering bushes
that he didn't know the name of. At the very bottom of the
decline it looked as though crops were being grown.

"I have a feeling that guide was wrong this morning," he
said. "I'm sure the flower of the island was the rose. I'm
sure it was in ancient times anyway, and probably till very
recently. Sounds like the kind of interesting misinformation
that makes a hit just because it's wrong."

"I haven't seem a rose since we got here."

"No. It wouldn't have been a modern rose, anyway. Just
the simple kind with five petals."

They passed under the great stone archway. Then they
started up the narrow street and lost the English-speaking
guide.

"I'm tired," Amy said.

They stood to one side to let the others stream past and
John looked around, but there was no place to sit down.
Up the street, guides were explaining the history of the
different places where the crusaders had had their head-
quarters.

"I'm okay," Amy said. "I just want to get out of this
place. There isn't any room, and such a crowd. I can't
breathe."

"Let's cut through everybody and go on ahead."

"Okay."

He took her by the hand and pulled her forward. The
other people were going off into the courtyards at the side
and looking at the inscriptions and carvings. He dragged
her by the hand till they came out ahead of the group.
There was still no place to sit down. They kept walking,
Amy with her head down. He saw she was in a bad mood
and he was worried. They came to postcard stands and
shops, but she didn't notice. The road broadened out into
a modern road but became ever steeper and there seemed
no end to it. He stopped walking. She stopped, too, looking

straight ahead and bad-tempered. He sighed and put his hands in his pockets, and looked back down the road and then up the slope.

"There's a camel," he said.

"Where?"

"Hanging out in front of that store. A picture of a camel."

"Don't like camels much," she said.

"He looks a little tacky, I must admit."

A few other people from the group came up behind them and walked on ahead.

"They're selling lemonade over there," he said, and began to walk forward again slowly. She followed, her head down, her whole attitude mulish.

"I can't stand that fizzy stuff they have here."

They walked on, passing brass pans, andirons, jewelry, clothes.

"There's another frog just like yours, only bigger."

"As a matter of fact, I hate it. I don't know why I bought it. Maybe because it was so ugly."

"For God's sake, honey, cheer up," he said. "Don't like this, don't like that. You're a real bundle of fun today, aren't you?"

She kept her head down, lips tight together. They moved through the street and more people kept coming up behind them. Suddenly her arm shot out and went under his elbow. He took his hands out of his pockets and felt her arm wrap around his back and her hand settle at his waist, gripping him through his clothes like a small tree-living animal.

"I like you," she muttered. "I like you all right."

"That's more like it." He put his arm around her shoulder and with his free hand tried to lift her head.

"Glad to hear it," he said. "Tell me some more. Tell me about how you like me."

She looked up. There were tears on her face. She put her other arm around his neck. "I love you," she said, as though she were drowning. "I love you. I love you so much sometimes it makes me want to throw up."

They had stopped in the middle of the road and there was still nowhere to sit, only shops and their doorways. Her body had gone heavy in his arms as though she might sink down to the ground. He half lifted her over to the side and, still held in her arms, leaned her up against a shop window. There were clothes and beads hanging from hooks, and brass objects up on tables. He had pushed aside a hanging rack of peasant blouses to find a solid place. On each side of them was a table strewn with knickknacks. Her hands around him started to knead at his back and she was breathing as though she would choke.

"Let's go back to the hotel," he said.

"I don't think I can walk that far. Oh, what's happening? It just came all over me—whoosh. I don't think I can walk at all."

He thought he knew what was happening, but it might be something else.

"Listen, Amy, are you in pain?"

"No, no. Not pain. Just feels so strange. Feels so weird. I'm burning up."

He got a good grip on her in case she fell, and smoothed her hair and kissed her on the neck and face. She turned her head from side to side.

"Whoosh, just like that?" he said.

"Oh God, John. I feel like one of those women who can't get to the hospital in time and have their babies in a cab."

She was laughing, now, with the tears still on her face, and her face red, and her breath still panting. A crowd of people pushed by them up the street, the Fischers among the group.

"Okay, kids, break it up," Mr. Fischer called over. "Just look at them, going into a clinch in the middle of the street. In the middle of the day, yet."

Mrs. Fischer made as if to come over to where they stood locked around each other, hunched against the window. She was wearing a pale-blue jersey suit, carrying the jacket over her arm, and looked hot.

"Are you all right there?" she asked.

Amy turned her head. "I'm fine," she gasped. "I'm fine. It's just that I love him so much."

Mr. Fischer smiled, took his wife by the arm and tugged her away.

"Now why don't you say nice things like that to me?" he asked her.

"You get rid of that beerbelly, Superman, and you'd be surprised what I'd say to you."

"Is that right?" he said.

John watched them going away up the street with the others, and saw Mr. Fischer make a playful lunge at his wife, and heard her voice saying, "Not my new girdle, darn it!"

"I feel so hot," Amy said. "Don't let go."

"I won't let go."

"John, something's happening to me."

"You're telling me."

"Oh Jesus, do you think I'm going crazy?"

"Not a chance. You're doing fine."

"Don't let go of me or I'll fall over."

"I won't let go of you."

"I think I'm dying," she said. He held her as tightly as he dared, and felt her back and shoulders jump. Then she was like a sack of potatoes and he was holding all her weight. A voice said, "Are you having any trouble?"

He turned his head and found himself looking into a bespectacled woman's face inches from his own. There was a battery of rhinestones at the top of the lenses.

"Just a private domestic argument," he told her.

"Oh," the woman said, and moved away.

Amy took her hand from his neck and stood straight on her feet again.

"Better?" he said.

"Yes. What happened?"

"You're kidding."

"Is everybody looking at me?"

"Just me."

"Everything's all right, isn't it?"

"It's fine. Everything's fine. Do you think you can walk?"

"Oh yes, I'm fine now."

They started to walk with the other people from the boat. He kept his arm around her and looked at her face. She looked happy.

"Is that it up there by the trees, where all those people are sitting on the wall?"

"I think that's just where we assemble. I can see the French-speaking guide."

"I passed out, didn't I?"

"Sort of."

"But I feel fine now. Maybe it's just the heat."

"I don't think so," he said. "Let's skip the museum and go back to the hotel and do it together next time.'

"Oh, it wasn't," she said. "I felt as though I was dying."

He started to laugh.

"Honestly!" she said.

They reached the wall, which went up the square like a ramp. The buses were parked below, and the entrance to the next building on the tour was across the square. She sat on the wall and he stood beside her. The people around them were speaking French.

"Everything's all right now, isn't it?" he said. "About that other business, I mean. It's like I told you, the doctor said it couldn't be inherited. Not possibly."

"Shut up about this inheriting stuff. I'll inherit you right on the nose if you don't quit talking about it."

"Okay, I just want you to know."

She looked past him and yawned. "This is a nice place," she said.

"Yes, it's nice."

"I like this place."

"Good."

"Only it's a little hot right in the sun."

"We can move over to the entrance there."

He helped her down off the wall and they started to cross the square.

"Oh, John, I've got to go to the bathroom again."

"I don't believe it."

"I mean it."

"We'll miss the group."

"That doesn't matter." She looked from one side to the other.

"Down that other street. There's a café."

"All right," he said.

She marched off quickly down the street. The café was crowded with working men sitting out at the tables. Without hesitating, she stepped through the open doorway, through the hanging plastic strips for keeping flies out, and went inside. There were a few more tables, but most of the men were standing up at the counter. They all looked at her. He felt like a man in a cartoon, his head turned away while his dog strains on the leash to get at a lamp post. She went straight up to the counter, said hello in Greek, and then asked in clear American French, *"S'il vous plait, lavatoire."* The man serving didn't understand. She repeated it. John stepped up beside her and reeled off *sotto voce* all the various cognates for toilet he knew. Finally, hoping that it wasn't an indecent gesture, he made motions of washing his hands, and that seemed to get across. The man called into the back room and a boy in an apron came out. He explained something to the boy in Greek, and Amy bustled forward and out into the back room. Then there was silence. John ordered a coffee and felt uncomfortable. Gradually people began to talk again, but not much. The coffee was very hot and sweet. He had finished it long before she came out again.

She was still looking happy, and did not seem to mind the fact that everyone was looking at her, although she was normally so self-conscious. She said thank you in Greek to the man behind the counter, which seemed to gain her the approval of everyone, and they left.

"I was beginning to wonder what had happened to you," he said. "I had visions of you waking up in Rio de Janeiro, doped to the eyeballs and forced to lead the rest of your life as a white slave."

"Ha!" she said. "It was just miles away and like a real old farm privy. I'm dying to wash my hands. They have a little garden out back there, full of flowers."

"Did it have a half moon on it?"

"No," she said, and laughed.

There was no one to be seen in the square. They went through the entranceway of the building across the square from the wall and couldn't see anyone there, either. Then they found a guard and asked where the museum was. He walked back with them and pointed up the street to what looked like another part of the fortifications.

"This must be it," John said.

"I can hear them inside."

The guard at the door tried to sell them tickets and John pointed ahead, saying, "Group" until he let them in.

It was a small museum, cool inside, with several lovely busts and funeral reliefs and a small kneeling Aphrodite, which was famous. There was also a bust of Alexander the Great as a youth, hair down to his shoulders and the nose knocked away. John looked closely at this, liking it very much, and decided that portraits of Alexander never looked ruined if they had been damaged, because somehow you had the feeling that it had happened in battle. He was still thinking about the idea and looking from a three-quarter view at the bust, when Amy from the other side of the room announced in a loud, isolated voice, "There aren't any postcards in here."

His head went around fast, and he saw her turning from side to side and glaring. People were beginning to bunch around her as he reached her side.

"Where are the postcards?" she demanded. In an even louder voice, imperious, she called again for the postcards.

He moved her away by the arm.

"They're outside, honey. This way," he said. He wanted to go through the floor.

"I don't see any at all," she said, still loudly, but not shouting.

"Right out here. I'll show you."

Behind them the Germans were making comments. They passed the man of the couple who had sat at their table for lunch. He had a pair of sunglasses folded in one hand and his cameras around his neck, and was standing up like a boiled slab of meat with his eyes turned coldly on Amy. *Oh God*, John thought, *oh God*, oh *God*. He got her out into the hallway with the desk and its racks of postcards, and the belligerence left her immediately.

"Oh good," she said, "they have lots. And pictures of the town, too."

She started to thumb through the cards, smiling.

"I don't want that one," she said, lifting out a picture of the Aphrodite.

"Why not?"

"Well, I couldn't send Mother a picture of a naked woman, could I?"

"Why not? It's a work of art."

"It's a naked woman. Look. They'd never let it go through the mail."

"Sure they would, Amy. It's a postcard."

"Well, it isn't right. And Mother wouldn't like it anyway. It isn't the kind of thing you'd want to send your mother. Specially if she's sick."

She put the card back, and chose seven others.

"That's enough, now," he said. She still looked peaceful and composed.

"Where can we sit down? I want to get them off right away."

He led her out of the room and over near the entrance to a place where the wall jutted out into a shelf. They sat down and she put the cards beside her and opened her purse. He picked up the postcards and took away two and put them in his pocket, not in the same pocket the others were in, since she might notice. She put stamps on the five he had left her and began to write.

"Do you think she can understand all the things you're writing?"

"Sure. The nurse can read them out."

That hadn't been what he had meant.

"And she can look at the pictures," Amy said. She wrote quickly, putting the cards down one by one as she finished. He picked one up and read it through. It was perfectly lucid. Then he looked at the date at the top. He picked up the other cards. On all of them it was the same day and December, 1963; the day they were married.

"Do you mind if I just add my regards?"

"Go ahead. That would be nice."

She was working on the fourth card and beneath her hair her face looked full of sweetness, and serene. He took his ballpoint pen out of his pocket and changed the dates on the cards, inking out the date she had written. He did the same for the last two, and quickly read through her messages. She had described every chink in the walls, every corner of the hotel they were staying at and the hotel where they had had lunch, and what they had eaten, and what they had seen, not to mention the historical parts.

"Well," he said. "All we need now is a mailbox." He kept the cards in his hand and she packed up her handbag and they stood up. When they came out into the sunlight the change of temperature was a shock. They walked hand in hand.

"I see one," she said. "Isn't that lucky?"

They came up to the mailbox and he said, "Do you want to put them in, or can I this time?" He didn't want her to see the dates.

"Oh, you can."

He pushed them in.

"Aren't you being nice to me today?" she said, smiling up at him brilliantly. "Mailing my postcards and everything. Aren't you nice to me."

"My pleasure, Miss Amy," he said.

She hugged him, and he smiled at her and hugged her back. *It's going to be all right*, he was thinking. *It's got to be all right. This is Amy, her face and eyes and mouth and hair and the way she looks and all the things about herself that she thinks are ugly which I love so much, and she's the only person who's ever understood me and it's just got to be all right.*

They walked down the street with their arms around each other. They passed the café where she had had to go to the bathroom. She took his other hand in her free one and squeezed it and held on to it, and they kept walking slowly, a bit like drunks tied to each other. Her hand was much smaller than his and damp, and still clung the way a tree animal clings to a branch. He began to sweat.

"It's hotter in the sun," he said, and took a handkerchief from his pocket. He hugged her shoulder to him as he took away his hand.

"But it's nice," she said. "I like this place."

He wiped his forehead and his upper lip, and put the handkerchief back in his pocket.

"So do I," he said.

They turned a corner and passed four more tourists coming up the street. They passed by a man selling honey and almond cakes, and turned in to a narrow street where there was shade, and saw a donkey carrying a load of sacks, and walked under a hanging wall of bougainvillea flowers. He began to sweat again.